RESCUED
BY THE VIKING

Meriel Fuller

MILLS & BOON

First Published in Great Britain 2019
by Mills & Boon, an imprint of HarperCollins*Publishers*
1 London Bridge Street, London, SE1 9GF

© 2019 Meriel Fuller

ISBN: 978-0-263-26890-4

MIX
Paper from
responsible sources
FSC C007454

This book is produced from independently certified FSC™ paper
to ensure responsible forest management.
For more information visit www.harpercollins.co.uk/green.

Printed and bound in Spain
by CPI, Barcelona

Chapter One

September 1069—north-east Lincolnshire

Sunshine quivered across the water. A skin of limpid light sealing in the deep blue-green depths, bright sparkles forcing Gisela to narrow her eyes as she paused in her work. Touching the brooch at her throat, making sure the long pin secured the wrap of linen around her head and neck, she stared bleakly across the water at the longships entering the mouth of the estuary. Her heart plummeted. Oh no, not them. Not the Danes.

Her hands released the bucket handles and she straightened up, rubbing her chafed hands, raw from rope burn. Blisters had formed on the undersides of her fingers: white, water-filled sacs that would soon start to hurt. The ships were coming closer, their round red shields, gold bosses gleaming, lining along the side of each vessel. The sails had been lowered, rolled up into great bundles of canvas and rope, and the men had taken to the oars to steer the narrow, lightweight crafts up the river. Strings of jewelled liquid trailed through the dusky air as the paddles lifted, then dipped again. A guttural chanting, rhythmic, echoed across the water. The sharp jabs of sound coupled oddly with the dainty twitterings of the wading birds who picked their way through the vast salt marshes that led down to the river, powerful current brown and churning. Like a burn of flesh, panic seared her veins and she chewed fretfully on her bottom lip, forcing herself to control her breathing. They would be all right, the three of them. She would make sure of it.

A cheer went up beside her. Then another. One by one the men and women who worked beside her spotted the ships, then put down their pails, the thick salty water slopping over the sides. Thrusting their fists into the air with jubilation, they turned to each other, smiling, clasping at hands and shoulders. Someone snared her sleeve. 'We are saved!' the woman cried, her bony fingers digging into Gisela's forearm. 'The Danes will help us! The Danes will send those Normans home with their tails between their legs!'

Gisela pinned a wide smile to her face, hoping to mirror the woman's excitement. These people could not guess who she truly was! She had to be so careful. Look at their joyous reaction to the Danes' arrival! They couldn't wait to be rid of the Normans. What would they do if they knew one was standing in their midst, carrying the salt pails alongside them? They would surely kill her! Her head swam suddenly and she wriggled her toes in her rough leather boots, searching for stability.

The woman said something else to her, nudging her conspiratorially. Failing to understand the quick words, Gisela's mind washed blank. Even now, even after being in England for all this time, her brain struggled to decipher the outlandish Saxon vowels. She spoke little, her voice clipped and low, hoping not to give away an accent, or any clue to her true identity. Her sister, Marie, was the same, comprehending little of what was said around her, but their father was more adept, having learned the barbaric language as a child.

'Eh?' the woman cackled, shoving her, jolting her sideways. Drying salt streaked the other woman's lined forehead. 'Don't you agree, my girl? There'll be some fun between the bed-sheets tonight, you mark my words!'

The woman referred to the Danes, of course. Their reputation for womanising was renowned, notorious, but not all of it was by mutual consent. She'd heard the tales of Saxon women being dragged to the longships by their braids, or flung across fur-covered shoulders, kicking and screaming all the way, to be taken back to the Norse countries, claimed as Viking brides. She shuddered. England was a heathen country, but the land where these Danes came from? That was infinitely worse.

'Pick up those pails and move along!' an older man, beard grey and straggling, bellowed at the workers. 'And don't think you're finishing any time early! We'll keep going as long as that sun is in the sky!' His gaze alighted on Gisela, mouth tightening in disapproval. She could tell he thought there was something odd about his latest worker, this slim young woman who had asked him for work a couple of days ago. Gisela spoke quietly, keeping her head lowered, but every time she glanced at him, she knew her brilliant blue eyes held a challenging look. She hoped he wouldn't consider that she might be a noble, someone of higher rank, and not just a poor peasant desperate for coin. She knew her slowness to respond when he talked to her and the way she fingered the scarf at her neck constantly, like a talisman, might give her away, but she couldn't help herself. Ultimately, she was a hard worker and so felt confident he wasn't about to turn her away.

'Hey, you there!' He jabbed his fist towards Gisela. 'Go out on to the flats and help the children bring the brine in from the lower pans! They must be emptied before the tide comes in.'

Turning her head, she stared over the thick oozing mudflats that sloped gently down towards the narrow, fast-flowing channel in the middle of the river. Trepidation flickered in her belly. The tidal flow was sluggish now, almost on the turn, having drained out of the estuary and into the vast North Sea beyond, exposing the slick-topped expanses of mud. Studded with clumps of bristly sedge, the wet bluish-brown surface shone in the evening light. She watched the children head out to the water's edge, to the rectangular pools filled with the precious salty brine. Why was he sending her out there? The children were half her weight, able to scamper across the wooden planks laid end to end across the mud without disappearing into the treacherous, stinking ooze.

'But…surely I will sink…?' Gisela's voice

faltered. A long wisp of pale sable hair had escaped the confines of her headscarf; dancing in the air. She shoved it impatiently back beneath the cloth.

The bearded Saxon narrowed his eyes. He was big and burly, clearly used to having his orders followed. 'Are you refusing to go out there, girl?' He folded his arms, wrinkling the supple leather of his jerkin. 'Because you'll receive no coin from me if you don't!'

Some of the other workers slowed their movements, glancing over at Gisela. Colour rose in her cheeks. The last thing she wanted to do was draw attention to herself. 'No, no, I'll do it!' she said, grabbing the rope handles of her buckets. Up until now this job had been physically hard, hefting the pails of brine to the sheds where it was boiled down to form the precious salt. The work was arduous, boring, but there had been no danger. But now? Now, in order to quash her rising fear at the thought of going out on the mudflats, she had to remember her real purpose for doing this job. To earn enough money to pay for the ferry across to the north. And to find Richard.

With a practised eye, Ragnar Svendson ran his gaze along the undulating shore of the river, searching for a safe spot where the boats could draw up. Jumping down from the prow, bracing his long legs against the gentle pitch and roll of the ship, he strode along the middle of the ship, through the men working the oars, towards his friend leaning against the gunwale.

'What do you think?' Eirik asked, glancing up as Ragnar joined him.

Ragnar turned his lean, tanned face to glance across the jumbled roofs of Bertune. 'I think it will do for tonight,' he replied. 'The men are tired; they need to rest.' He flexed his fingers over the smooth wood of the gunwale, rolling his shoulders forward. The journey had been easy and quick from Ribe, the North Sea mercifully flat for once, with light breezes speeding them across the waves to the north-east coast of England.

''Tis a pity that we cannot land on the north side, but the tide is too low.' Eirik smiled. 'Do you think this small town is ready for us?'

Ragnar stuck one hand through his hair; the vigorous strands fired to white-gold in the light of the setting sun. He laughed. 'Who knows? We've come to help them after all; they should welcome us with open arms.' He glanced back into the belly of the longship, at the coxswain beating time on a small drum to the forty men on the oars. Each man sat on a chest: wooden boxes that contained their scant possessions for the journey to England. And behind this ship, three more identical vessels followed them up the narrow channel.

'We can cross on the morrow.' Eirik smoothed his palm along the polished prow. The curved wood rose up into a figurehead: a dragon's head with prominent eyes, a tongue of wooden fire. 'My brother won't arrive with his fleet for another day or two.'

'And then you can march together to meet with Edgar Aethling in Jorvik. The city is directly north from here, across the water.' Ragnar glanced at the far side of the vast, wide river where stiff, dull-yellow reeds bisected oozing, creaking domes of mud. Seabirds wheeled in the limpid sky above, mewling and squawking: lonesome, plaintive sounds cutting the air.

Eirik nodded. As the eldest son of Sweyn, the Danish king, he had been sent to help the deposed Anglo-Saxon king in his fight against the Norman invasion. 'In that case, this place is perfect,' he said, clapping a large hand on Ragnar's shoulder, 'and you and I and the rest of the men can have some fun! I've heard these Saxon maidens can be very comely!'

Ragnar shook his head: a swift, brutal movement. 'Nay, Eirik, I've not come here for that.' His eyes pinched to emerald slits; a muscle twitched in his jaw.

'I hadn't forgotten.' Eirik's face fell. 'But you'll be with us until tomorrow, will you not? It will soon be too dark to travel. Why not have some fun this night, while you can, eh?' He pushed his knuckles against Ragnar's jaw, a teasing punch. 'Besides, what fair maiden could resist that clean-shaven face?'

'The weather's too hot for a beard,' Ragnar said. 'It's much better this way.'

'If you say so,' replied Eirik, 'but I swear your mother had something to do with it. Is she trying to turn you into a Norman?'

Ragnar grinned, his teeth white and even in his tanned face. 'Thor's hammer, Eirik, what do you take me for? Of course she's not!'

'If you say so.' Eirik chuckled, raising his black eyebrows in mock surprise. 'Well, I still think you should take advantage of this town's hospitality.'

'I might.' Ragnar threw his friend a non-committal smile, reluctance slicing through him. As the shallow-drafted longships approached the shoreline, he gazed across the jumble of thatched, earth-walled huts that made up the town of Bertune. Trickles of woodsmoke rose vertically, hazing the air; figures moved on the shoreline, people stopping and pointing as they watched the vessels approach. He had no idea how long his journey north would take. All he knew was that he had to find the man who had wrecked his sister's life. Who had turned the happy, confident figure of his sister into a listless, silent wraith. She had not spoken a word since she had been carried off the ship at Ribe.

'How will you find him anyway?'

Ragnar shrugged his massive shoulders. 'All I know is that he's a Norman lord, given lands to the north of Jorvik by the Conqueror. That's all I have at the moment.'

'How will you get close to him? These Normans guard themselves well, especially in this hostile part of the country.'

'I have no idea, Eirik. But once I do, I will find out what happened to Gyda after she was abducted.' Guilt jabbed through him. 'We've tried everything else.'

He had been the one to encourage her in the first place, told her to travel to England with the man she loved. He narrowed his eyes. *For helvede,* he had even lifted her on board the ship! He remembered his sister's delighted laugh as he swung her up and over the gunwale, up to the grinning boy who wished to marry her. Now her betrothed was a dead man and Gyda, when she eventually returned, had changed beyond all recognition.

Eirik peered at him, sensing his friend's distraction. 'Are you set on this idea, Ragnar? I hope you deal with him quickly, for I will miss you at my side if there's any fighting to be done.' He grinned, a wolfish glint in his eyes.

'Eirik, if you're involved, then there will be fighting.' Ragnar laughed, shaking off the pall of remorse that cloaked his shoulders. Now was not the time for self-recrimination or brooding. That time was done. It was time for action. He owed it to his sister to track down the man who had wrenched her from her lover's side. To find out what had happened to her.

'It's the only thing I live for,' Eirik replied, turning down the corners of his mouth in mocking sadness.

'As well as Bodil and the children,' Ragnar added. 'Don't forget them.' His firm lips quirked with humour. Although Eirik was a warrior, he was also a devoted husband and father who liked nothing better than cradling his latest son against his chest and crooning out the old Norse songs into the poor baby's ear. Ragnar often stayed with Eirik as he and his family lived nearer to the port at Ribe and so he had witnessed his friend's softer side on several occasions.

'And Bodil and the children, too.' Eirik agreed enthusiastically. 'That goes without saying.' He peered over into the water as the ship slowly altered its course towards the shore. 'Ah, good, it's not muddy here,' he said. 'I can see the bottom. We can haul the ships straight up and keep our boots clean.'

At his words, the wooden hulls scraped gently against the stones and sand; oars were drawn in through the holes cut into the wooden sides, secured for the night. Men leapt out, lithe and long-legged, bracing their cloaked shoulders against the prows, lifting the flaxen ropes to pull the boats further up the shore. Jewelled hilts, from short swords stuck in leather belts, shone out in the dying light as the men shouted, called out instructions to each other. And then the townsfolk ran down to help them, laughing and patting them on the back like old friends, happy that these tall, handsome Danish men had come to help them throw off the punishing yoke of the Norman infidels.

The narrow wooden planks wobbled beneath Gisela's feet, tipping one way, then the other, brownish water bubbling up from the mud and washing over the flimsy boards, staining her leather boots. Stepping cautiously, she made her way out to the gaggle of children dipping their buckets. Sea birds wheeled about her head, spreading huge white wings, cackling and screeching; fear snaked through her diaphragm. A child squeezed alongside her with a full, slopping bucket, then another, almost pushing her off the plank in their haste to reach the boiling house on the shore.

These salt pans were more basic than the ones nearer the town: shallow pools dug out above the low-water mark, edges shored up with lumps of stone to stop the unstable mud sides caving in. She knelt down on the stone lip, swinging her bucket into the dense salty water, setting it beside her while she repeated the action with the other bucket.

The light was dimming fast now, the sun dipping below the horizon in a riot of pink and orange hues. The Danish longships pulling up to the shore turned to dark silhouettes, the masts a cluster of black poles against the shimmering sky. Although it was only September, the evening air was chill, heralding autumn; Gisela shivered in her thin gown. Her sleeves were wet, splashed with sea water, and she pushed the coarsely woven wool up to her elbows to stop them becoming even more soaked.

For their journey north, her father had insisted that both she and her sister Marie change their fine noble garments to more lowly outfits for travelling, so they would not attract attention. The servants in their castle on the south coast, their new English home given to her father for his loyalty to William the Conqueror, had been happy to supply both girls with serviceable gowns. An underdress of fawn undyed wool, an overdress of darker brown, crudely patched at the hem. The only things Gisela retained from her previous life were her fine woollen stockings, her leather boots and her mother's silver brooch that held her scarf in place.

'Come on, mistress!' a little girl called to her from the end of the plank. 'The tide is coming in! We must go back now!' Looking around, Gisela realised that all the children had gone and were walking back to the shore. She glanced at the river; the brown water slopped and churned, the foaming tide beginning to fill the deep crevasses that scored the mudflats. The blood in her toes prickled; she had been kneeling for too long. Scrambling to her feet, pausing a moment to gain her balance on the rickety wooden plank, she reached down to heave up the buckets. Her arms ached, as if they had been stretched to twice their length already.

Not far ahead, some of children had stopped, their gaunt, undernourished frames clustering around each other. She heard a wail, then another, and increased her pace towards them, carrying the heavy pails. A child, the small girl who had called out to her, had fallen into the mud, and was now up to her knees in the thick, gelatinous ooze.

'How did she get there?' Gisela asked sternly, looking down at the wan, grime-streaked faces.

The children appeared puzzled for a moment, as if they hadn't quite understood her. She was used to this, for as much as she tried to disguise her foreign accent, sometimes the Saxon vowels evaded her. She repeated her question, more slowly this time, and a boy eventually spoke. 'It was him, mistress.' He poked another boy in the arm. 'He pushed her in, she was teasing him, you see...'

'I understand...' Gisela said sharply, seeing the girl's face whiten with fear as she struggled in the mud, slapping down futilely with her palms. Placing her buckets carefully on the board, Gisela took two long strides out from the plank on to the mudflat, intending to pull the child out.

'Oh, mistress, no…!' the boy shouted out in warning, as her feet encountered the mud. She sank, promptly, her feet disappearing, swiftly followed by her calves and knees, her body lurching forward in shock. 'Oh, God…no!' Gisela cried out in horror as she realised her mistake. The hem of her gown rose up around her and the thick cold mud hugged her knees, her thighs.

'Oh, mistress, you shouldn't have done that!' another child said. 'That mud is dangerous, it'll suck you down. That's why we use the planks. To stop us disappearing…'

Gisela let out a long, shaky breath. In her effort to reach the girl, she had forgotten. Sweat gathered beneath her linen scarf, along her neckline. She longed to rip it off and feel the cool air against her skin. Do not panic, she told herself sternly, fear bubbling treacherously in her belly. Do not. Beside her the little girl wept openly, her pinched face marred by tears and grime.

'I will get you out of here,' Gisela said confidently. Putting her hands beneath the child's bony arms, she pulled and lifted, ignoring the fact that she sunk lower in the process, until she heard a satisfying sucking noise. The mud released its grip on the child's legs; Gisela fell sideways, the child in her arms. Relief coursed through her.

'Crawl flat on your belly over to the plank,' she told the girl.

The child frowned at her, her sweet face doubtful. 'But what about you, mistress?'

'Tell someone to come for me, when you reach the shore,' Gisela told her. 'Find someone to help me!' she called to the rest of the children, watching the girl slither across the mud to join them. They nodded in unison, pointing at her, then nodded again, the bedraggled group chattering in subdued voices as they made their way back along the planks.

As the wind whipped away their high-pitched voices, a gust of vulnerability, insidious and threatening, enveloped her. In this windswept barren landscape, she was completely alone, up to her thighs in mud, unable to move. Her buckets of brine sat on the wooden plank, mocking her. How long would it take for the children to send someone out? Would they even come? The salt-pan master had no care for her, he knew there was something peculiar about her, despite her rattling out the same story that her and her father and sister had all told on this journey. They were Anglo-Saxons heading north to live with relatives as the Normans had dispossessed them of all they had owned in the south. Maybe her mangled use of the English language had finally given her away.

She tried to bend forward, lying down flat on the mud, scrabbling with her hands to try to reach a clump of reeds, to try to pull herself out. The mud seeped through her gown, cold and wet against her stomach and breasts. She tugged on the grass, slowly, gradually, hoping for the smallest movement around her feet and legs, a sign that the mud was giving up its hold on her. Nothing.

To her right, the river slopped and gurgled, an ominous sound; the water spilled over the lower walls of the salt pans, starting to fill the shallow ponds. The tide was coming in quickly now. With a sickening dread, Gisela eyed the water gushing towards her. Sinking in the mud was not her only worry. Now, drowning seemed like a more likely option. Screwing her eyes up, she sought and found the figures on the shore, pale ghosts in the twilight. The children had surely reached the adults by now and were telling them to come and fetch her. Aye, that was it. As she straightened up, the thought comforted her and she kept her eyes pinned on the bleached lines of the planks, heading back to shore, squinting in the half-light for any sign of help, watching for someone, anyone, to come out to rescue her.

But then, to her utter dismay, the cluster of people by the boiling houses walked away. Not one face turned towards her! Nay, they were heading towards the Danes, newly arrived on the shore. Arms raised in welcome towards the visitors, the shouts and calls of greeting echoed out across the mudflats. Distracted by the Danes' arrival, they had forgotten, or had not even been told about her, stuck yards out from shore in the mud. No one was coming. Panic swirled in her chest, a great flood of terror that she would die out here, her breath choked off by the incoming tide, until the air in her lungs expelled in a scream of sheer desperation. She screamed and screamed, her voice shrill and clear, waving her arms violently towards the shore, for her life depended upon it.

Chapter Two

❧

As the Danes jumped from the longships, calf-length leather boots splashing through the shallows, the Saxon townspeople crowded on to the strip of shingle, slapping the tall seafaring warriors on the back, shaking their hands. Smiling widely, the men accepted flagons of mead from the dark-eyed Saxon maidens, hefted steaming meat pies from passing wooden trays, eating with real appreciation. Ragnar ran an eye along the bows of the longships, making sure all vessels were drawn up high enough against the incoming tide. The six boats had carried more than two hundred men across the North Sea; Harald's larger fleet would bring double that number in the next few days, swelling their ranks to a sizeable army to help the Saxons throw off the Norman yoke.

'Torvald has found us an inn for the night.'

Eirik walked over to him, handing back his empty tankard to one of the Saxon maids. 'The men can sleep in the ships, but I, for one, wouldn't mind a comfortable mattress, as I'm sure you would.'

'Age getting the better of you, Eirik?' Ragnar grinned.

Eirik laughed. 'Perhaps. I have the choice so I may as well be comfortable.' His gaze fell on a nearby Saxon maid, her face blushing with attention as she moved deftly around the crowd with a tray of ale tankards. 'This town is as good as any for us to spend the night.' His mouth twisted with a rueful grin as he pushed strands of dark hair from his eyes.

'Too bad you're married,' Ragnar said. The corner of his mouth quirked upwards.

'Aye,' Eirik said wistfully. 'But you're not. Sure you won't take what's on offer?' He jabbed Ragnar in the ribs.

His short hair, thick golden strands, riffled in the sharpening breeze. 'No, Eirik.' Guilt crashed over him, black, coruscating. A flock of geese flew low over the mudflats, necks stretched out, honking wildly, and he followed their path in silence, his body gripped with regret.

'It's a shame.' Eirik folded huge leather-bound arms across his chest. He looked out across the water.

It's only what I deserve, thought Ragnar, after what had happened to Gyda. His younger sister was worsening by the day, a thin pale effigy of the maid she once had been, shrinking before his eyes, before his parents' eyes. Her silent presence haunted his days, as she brushed past him like a ghost, or perched, mute, at the end of the table. She hadn't spoken a word since she'd been brought back from this godforsaken land.

'What I could never understand, though,' Eirik continued, 'was why Gyda decided to travel to England with Magnus in the first place? On a raiding mission, of all things.'

Because I told her to do it, thought Ragnar. By Thor, I encouraged her! I could see how much in love with Magnus she was and could see how against that love our parents were. I told her to go, that I would explain everything to our parents: Gyda and Magnus would marry in England and return to Denmark as husband and wife. All would be well. But then, suddenly, it wasn't.

Raised voices nearby yanked Ragnar's attention from his memories. He was thankful. He had no wish to dwell on his sister's plight any longer than was necessary. His eyes traced the

shadows, hunting out the sound of an argument.
Beneath the overhanging thatch of a building, a
woman tugged at a man's tunic sleeve, a large
bulky man, his flabby red-flushed face slack
from alcohol. She was pointing desperately, ges-
ticulating with her fist out to the mudflats, her
voice a shrill cackle, pitched with urgency. Not
many people were around now; the crowd by the
longships had drifted away, eager to show their
Danish visitors the delights of the town, funnel-
ling eagerly up the narrow streets that led from
the shore. Only Eirik and Ragnar and a few of
their men remained on the shingle.

Lifting one meaty fist, the man clouted the
woman around the ear, shoving her backwards.
'You have no right to speak to me like this. Get
away! I told you, I'll fetch her when the tide
comes in.'

Hunching over, her hand cupping her throbbing ear, the woman replied sullenly, 'The tide
is coming in, you senseless oaf! The maid's up
to her knees in it already. You need to do something, otherwise she'll drown.'

Staggering back against the uneven cob wall
of the building, the man lifted his tankard and
took a huge gulp. The ale trickled down his chin.
'Let the girl drown, then! What do I care?'

'She rescued little May, did the children

not tell you? That's why she's in the mud. She stepped off the planks to save her.'

Anger flaring in his gullet, Ragnar covered the shingle in three long-legged strides. To see a man hit a woman like that filled his mouth with sour distaste. 'Are you all right?' he asked the woman, touching her elbow with concern. Clutching her ear, she stared up at Ragnar in astonishment, then nodded slowly.

As Eirik came up beside him, the drunk man raised his head, regarding the tall Danes with a churlish, guarded look. ''Tis our business.' He cleared his throat noisily. 'Go into town with the rest of your men.'

Sensing an ally, the woman lifted her eyes to Ragnar, plucking nervously at his tunic sleeve. 'The maid is stuck in the mud!' Her cheeks were pinched, crusted with salt. 'And the tide is coming in so fast, she will surely drown!' Guided by her pointing finger, Ragnar scanned the bluish-brown marshes, the clumps of stiff grass, his gaze snagged by the deep grooves cut into the thick brown ooze. The setting sun flashed against something, a brooch, or a ring, he knew not what, and his eyes honed in on that spot. And then he saw. The silhouette of a figure calling plaintively through the twilight. The foaming edge of tide swilled around her knees, floating out the hem of her dress. The woman was correct: time was not on her side.

'Fetch a long rope from one of the ships,' he ordered one of their men who had followed Eirik and him across the beach.

'You're not going out for her, are you?' Eirik frowned. 'Let these people rescue their own, I say. We should not involve ourselves in the business of the town.'

'Then what in Odin's name are we doing here?' Ragnar lifted brindled eyebrows, burnished arcs of copper below his flaxen hair. 'We're supposed to be helping them throw off the Norman yoke, yet we can't rescue a Saxon maid from the mud? She is going to die out there, unless we do something. Do you want that on your conscience?'

'Nay, of course not.' Eirik grimaced, his expression rueful, as if ashamed of the way his thoughts had run. Despite his superior rank to Ragnar, they were friends first and foremost, having grown up together on neighbouring estates in Ribe.

'Besides, you're not going out there.' A muscle quirked beneath Ragnar's high cheekbone and he smiled. 'The King of Denmark's son, wading through the mudflats? Your father would never let me hear the end of it.'

'Then go with Thor's blessing,' Eirik replied, as their man returned with the unwieldy coil of rope slung around his neck and torso. 'Let's hope she's alive by the time you reach her.'

Gisela's throat was dry, scraped raw by her continued shouting. Exhaustion made her head swim, her thoughts dancing about with chaotic abandon. Crossing her arms over her chest, hugging herself, she wished for the hundredth time that she had worn her cloak that day and not just her thin gowns and chemise. She was cold, shivering uncontrollably now, the icy mud gripping her legs and thighs like an iron fist. Treacherous sea water swirled around her, embracing the tops of her legs, curling lovingly around her freezing limbs. As the tide lapped higher and higher, a panicked fear took hold, silencing her screams. For what was the point of calling out? No one was coming for her now. The shore was visible in the limpid twilight, snagged by lingering sunlight, but it was empty, deserted. Everyone had gone.

Unable to settle on one spot for any length of time, her vision scurried across the silvery mud. Twinkles of light shimmered out from the huddle of cottages that formed the town. A weakness suffused her muscles, draining the last of her strength; her stomach was empty save for the small bowl of gruel she had eaten with her father and sister that morning. Her brain jumped and twitched with hunger and fatigue; the temptation to lower herself into the swirling brown water, to sink her hips into it, threatened to overwhelm her.

How would her father cope without her? Her sister? Poor Marie, she had been through so much already. Her beauty had been the bane of her life, her angelic looks catching men's interested gazes wherever they went. Tears welled in Gisela's chest, spilling hotly down her cheeks, blurring her sight. She would no longer be there to protect her. Pressing trembling palms to her face, she wept at the sheer hopelessness of her situation, the sea water creeping to her waist, soaking the coarse fabric of her gown. She had never been prone to self-pity, but at this moment in time, as the tears dripped down through her fingers, she truly believed that she was going to die.

The slim outline of the maid's wavering figure became gradually more distinct as Ragnar strode along the narrow wooden planks, the rope tied around his waist for safety playing out behind him, back to his men on the shore. Shiny tussocks of grass perched on top of the carved mudflats; seabirds wheeled around his head, flapping and croaking at his presence as he passed by. Halfway across the mudflats, the incoming tide lapped his calf-length boots, frothing around his ankles. He cursed. The leather would take an age to dry out.

Jerking his head up, he suddenly realised the maid's screaming had ceased. Had she even seen him? For if she saw him, it would give her hope. But the girl stood with her hands over her face, the brown churning current of the river at her back. A coarse linen scarf wrapped tightly around her neck and head, secured with a fearsome-looking silver brooch, the silver that had flashed in the dying sun, attracting his attention before.

'Hey!' he called out in Saxon. 'Hey! You there, I'm coming for you!' He was expecting her hands to fall away from her face, for her to look up and see him. But she remained as she was, face covered with her hands, as if she hadn't heard him. Which, of course, she might not have, given the noise that the seabirds were making. The maid's garments were shabby, ripped in places, loose threads dancing in the shimmering light. Layer upon layer of earth-coloured cloth enveloped her, garments that every low-born Saxon seemed to wear.

Ragnar sighed. Any one of their men could have come out for her. But he knew what had driven him out here: the same thing that made him ride headlong into battle, always at the front of the pack, swinging his axe with violent dexterity around his head; the cursed restlessness of his soul, the tortured guilt over what had happened to his sister. His mind and body never settled, beset with a constant, driving energy.

When he finally reached her, the water was up to his knees. Still she did not look up. Had she not heard him approach? Legs braced apart, Ragnar stood on the plank, the maid a couple of feet away, her gown floating around her, swirling in the vicious tide. 'Give me your hand!' he shouted at her.

The voice stabbed in her chest. A harsh, guttural order, in Saxon, which she struggled to understand. Her hands dropped from her cheeks, midnight-blue eyes rounding in shock. A huge man stood in front of her, his hand stretched out across the churning water. The dying sunlight caught the ends of his hair, firing them to a molten bronze. A golden halo, springing out around his head. Like an angel, she thought stu-

pidly, her mind befuddled. Had an angel come
to rescue her? The heady scent of leather and
woodsmoke rose from him, mingling with the
strong salt-laden smell of the sea. Was he an illusion, a figment of her exhausted brain dreamt
up by her desperate plight?

Gisela frowned as she peered more closely.
Nay, not an angel. The man towered over her,
spreading his long legs wide against the surging
rush of tide. Clad in a sleeveless leather tunic,
criss-crossed with leather straps, fearsomely
riveted, he looked more like a barbarian, scowling darkly at her failure to move, or to even
stretch her hand out towards him. Secured by
an ornately wrought brooch, a length of woollen cloth wrapped around his broad shoulders
served as a cloak; woollen braies encased his
powerful legs. Honed thigh muscles flexed beneath the cloth. The sun's low angle threw his
face into relief, like a carved statue, the craggy
angles of his square jaw and the shadowed hollow of his cheeks beneath sharply delineated
cheekbones.

Her heart plummeted foolishly. She was not
often given to fanciful notions, but her imagination, dulled with fatigue, had certainly excelled
on this occasion. Her fear of drowning, of near

death, had forced her mind to evoke this image of perfect masculinity. She folded her arms, mouth set in a mutinous line, challenging the vision to disappear. An apparition dreamed up by her mad, unfocused brain through fear and lack of food. The man did not exist. If she stared at him long enough, he would surely vanish. Gisela tipped her head to one side, waiting.

'What is wrong with you?' the man roared again in Saxon, his generous mouth twisting in frustration. 'Do you understand me? Give me your hand!' The water caressed the hemline of his woollen shirt, hanging beneath his shorter tunic. Frowning, she struggled to work out his identity; he wore no surcoat to denote his coat of arms like any Saxon or a Norman knight. With that mass of golden hair around his head, he appeared before her like a Norse god of old. Laughter bubbled up in her chest. What would her confused mind come up with next?

Something gripped her shoulder, shaking her violently. Then a hand pushed against her cheek, fingers calloused and warm, one thumb digging into her chin. She reared back at the contact, but the fingers held tight, pulling her forward. Bright green eyes loomed into the centre of her vision.

'Look at me,' the man said, his harsh voice clipping the Saxon vowels. 'You have to help me, otherwise you are going to drown. Do you realise that? Put your arms around my neck and I will pull you out of here.' As he reached over, his hands dug intimately beneath her armpits, gripping her flesh through the layers of clothing. Gisela flinched, a jolt of heat racing through her; his thumbs brushing against her breasts.

But this isn't happening, she told herself dully, as a small squeak of protest fell from her lips at his cursory manhandling. Bending double, the man reached out from his place of security on the plank, the white wood palely visible beneath the water, and pulled and pulled, dragging her slowly, inexorably, from the mud. 'Put your arms around my neck!' he demanded again, growling against her ear. Stung to compliance by the harsh command, Gisela lifted her slim arms, linking her fingers at the back of his neck. His skin was warm; the fronds of his hair tickled her hand. She frowned, her muddled mind trying desperately to make sense of the situation. Was he truly pulling her out of this godforsaken mud?

Air sucked around her frozen limbs as the mud released its cruel snare upon her legs. Her feet, caked in heavy mud, dangled uselessly as arms of thick-roped muscle lifted her, shoving her slender frame against a hard, masculine body, chest to chest. The man thrust one arm beneath her hips, swinging her legs up high. Her soaked gown clung to her thighs, to the soft flare of her hips.

Warmth surged through her, a delicious puddle of sensation that broke through her vague, dream-like state of semi-consciousness. His nearness was brutal, a curt slap on the jaw, buffeting her sensitive core, wrenching her body to a state of full, throbbing alertness. Breath squeezed in her lungs; it was as if his cursory touch ripped the clothes from her body and exposed her nakedness for all to see. She felt stripped bare, vulnerable, her breasts bouncing treacherously against his solid chest, her arms flailing away from his neck, not wanting to hold on to him for support.

'Put your arms back around my neck, or we shall both be in the water!' He began to carry her back to shore, jolting her light weight deliberately so that she was forced to hold on to his neck, his shoulders. Twisting her face up to the rigid features that loomed above her in the semi-darkness, she released one hand to brush her fingers across his jaw, a fleeting butterfly touch, in wonderment.

'*Êtes-vous vrai?*' she asked in French, using her mother tongue without thinking. *Are you real?*

Ragnar's step faltered in surprise; he almost lost his footing on the plank. The maid's speech was soft, musical; her lilting French accent tunnelling into him. It was not often he heard the language out loud, but he understood it, for his mother had spoken in her native tongue to him from birth, but only when they were alone, for his father did not approve. His father hated any reminder of how he had abducted his wife from France, all those years ago, despite their happy marriage now. Ragnar peered down into the pale glimmer of the maid's face. What, in Thor's name, was she doing here?

'*Je suis,*' he replied, confirming her question.

'*Dieu merci,*' she gasped out in relief. *Thank God.* Her light-boned frame sagged against him, ropes of unconsciousness binding her into oblivion.

Chapter Three

'Who is she?' Eirik demanded as Ragnar laid the maid down carefully. Her face was grey, pallid. She was so still. Kneeling beside her, his big knees grinding into the shingle, he seized her wrist, pushing up the fraying cuff, searching for a pulse. Against his fingers her blood bumped reassuringly; relief flooded over him. He rose to his feet, his eyes assessing her calmly. Her over-gown was loose, a plaited belt gathering the shabby, patched material at her waist. Dark brown in colour, stained with white streaks of drying salt, clagged with mud at the hem. No decoration around the plain circular neck, the centre slit opening. Her garments denoted her status: a peasant, living hand to mouth on whatever coin she could earn. Foolish of him to be so concerned; the maid was quite clearly a nobody, nothing to him certainly. And yet her plight plucked at his soul. She seemed so alone, and vulnerable, with no one rushing to protect or claim her.

'I've no idea.' Reaching down, Ragnar yanked the rucked hem of her longer underdress over her shapely shins, woefully caked in layers of grey, cracking mud. He was not about to reveal the traitorous words the maid had spoken to him out on the marsh; he would keep that knowledge to himself until he found out her reasons for being in Bertune. Why here, of all places? In a part of the country where Normans were truly hated. A place where the Saxons had begged the Danes for their help in overthrowing them. But this solitary maid, whey-faced and slender? Whoever she was, she was no threat to him, or to anyone else. Had she any idea of the danger she was in?

The woman who had originally alerted them to the maid's plight lurked by the cottage wall that backed on to the beach. Ragnar turned to her. 'Who is she?'

'She works out at the salt pans with us,' the woman replied, a wary look half-closing her red-streaked eyes. 'And a hard worker she is, too. But she's only been with us a day or so. Needs coin for the ferry, I think. Doesn't talk much.'

'Where does she live, then?' Eirik said, his

tone faintly peevish. 'We can't leave her lying here.'

'Eirik, why not go and join the rest of the men in the town?' Ragnar suggested, hearing the growing frustration in his friend's voice. 'I'll deal with this.'

'Are you sure?' Eirik's boots crunched heavily across the shingle as he came towards Ragnar. 'I could do with a drink.' He touched his leather-bound toe to the maid's right flank, lifting her body in a desultory manner, a sneering twist to his mouth. 'Surprising that such a little thing should cause so much trouble, don't you think?' he said disparagingly, removing his foot so abruptly that the slim body rolled back on to the beach. The maid's arm fell out to one side; her palm, delicate pink lines creasing the soft underside, scraped against the jagged stones. Ragnar's fists curled tight; he resisted the urge to shove his friend away. *Hell's teeth, treat the woman like a human being,* he thought, *not an animal!*

'Go.' Ragnar pinned a wide grin on his face that he hoped was convincing. He pushed at Eirik's shoulder, a friendly gesture. 'I can take her home.'

'After one look at you, she'll run anyway.' Eirik laughed, starting to walk up the beach.

'You're enough to scare the hell out of any woman. Don't waste too much time on her. I expect to see you in the inn before full dark!' He lifted his arm in farewell, the strengthening breeze ruffling his dark hair. Then he disappeared down an alleyway between the gable ends of two cottages, the shadowed twilight swallowing up his tall figure.

The maid was shivering now; a blue caste tinged her face. Unpinning his cloak, Ragnar dropped to his knees, the shingle poking through his braies into his muscled shins. His sword hilt jabbed upwards as the tip of the leather scabbard hit the beach; he shoved it to one side so that the weapon rested against his hip. He frowned, drawing thick coppery brows together. Was Eirik right? Despite Ragnar's vicious reputation on the battlefield, his skill with an axe and sword, he had no wish to scare any woman, let alone this delicate effigy lying on the stones. She lay so still, like one of those statues in the new church in Ribe, her cheek as smooth as marble, unblemished. Hulking over her slight figure, he felt like a cumbersome idiot, awkward and unwieldy, his body too big to tend to a woman so slight. He spread his cloak over her chest, then, sliding his hands beneath her, he raised her carefully so he could tuck the woollen cloth around her back.

The fragile knobs of her spine pushed against his fingers. As he laid her back down, the faintest smell of roses lifted from her skin; his solar plexus gripped, then released with the sensual onslaught. His senses jolted, quickening suddenly. When was the last time he had been this close to a woman? Close enough to smell her perfume? He couldn't remember. His sister's desperate situation had consumed his days and haunted his nights. Any desire had been crippled by guilt, his couplings with women rare, and, if they occurred, tended to be swift, joyless affairs in which he took little pleasure.

Impatient with his memories, Ragnar swept his gaze around the beach. He needed to rid himself of this girl and concentrate on finding the man who had bullied his sister into a ghostly shadow of her former self. But now the shingle was deserted, save for a lonesome gull, orange-beaked, stalking along the foaming edge of the incoming tide. Strange that no one wanted to help her. But then, these were troubled times—trust had to be earned. He wondered whether the townspeople had sensed the maid's difference, her foreign ways, without actually putting a name to them.

A slight moan made Ragnar look down. A whimper of returning sensibility. The girl's long eyelashes fluttered rapidly against her pallid cheeks, mouth parting fractionally. Her lips were full, plump, stained a luscious rose-pink. Inexplicably, he yearned to see the colour of her hair, fingers itching to pluck at the constricting headscarf, unfasten the silver brooch and cast the voluminous length of material aside. Sweat prickled on his palms; he rubbed his hands down his braies.

Her eyes sprung open. Huge pools of deep blue dominated her face, sparkling like sapphires. The inky depths of the ocean on a bright summer's day. In the fading light, he drank in the magnificent colour, devoured it, nerves spiralling round and round in increasing excitement, pushing his heart to a faster beat. What was happening? Inconceivable that such a dull little maid should have such an effect on him, bundled up as she was like a nun in her drab, mud-stained garments, every inch of skin hidden from view apart from the white terrified circle of her face.

Wait. Nay, not terrified. Ragnar read the flare of anger in her eyes, the lips compressed in tight rebellion. The mutinous clenching of her fists by her side. 'I'm here to help you,' he said in English, trying to keep his voice gentle. He reached out to touch her shoulder.

'Get your hands off me!' the maid squawked at him. Knocking his arm sideways, she struggled to sit up. His cloak fell forward, pillowing in her lap as she brought herself upright. She threw his garment irritably to one side, digging her palms and heels into the shingle, rocking her hips, struggling to shift her body backwards, away from him.

'Easy, maid,' Ragnar said, sitting back on his heels. 'I'm not going to hurt you.' Despite her efforts, she hadn't managed to move very far.

'I know that, you blundering lump!' The maid stopped, seemingly frustrated by her lack of movement. She touched a finger to the brooch at her neck, as if reassuring herself that the silver pin remained in place. 'Why would you bother to pull me out of the mud, if you were going to kill me?'

Ragnar bit his lip to stop himself laughing out loud. Where on earth had she learned her English? From an army camp? Her cursing was on a level with any common knave. He grinned, rapidly adjusting his original opinion of her. Out there on the mudflats, she had been a forlorn, helpless figure, her diminutive frame and finely honed, angelic face denoting a benign, docile character. How wrong he had been. She was worse than feisty, a regular termagant. He folded his arms across his wide chest, almost as if he prepared to do battle with her. Curiously, he relished the thought.

What, in heaven's name, was he smiling at? The man hulked over her, great shoulders blocking out the darkening sky, his green gaze intense, flaring over her with bold scrutiny. Her eyes ran rapidly across his leather-strapped torso, his calf-length boots stained with salt water. Was he a Saxon? Or worse…one of the men from the longships. A Viking? Despite her truculent bravado, anxiety gripped Gisela's chest; she knew she had to stand up and walk away, but at the moment, the task seemed impossible. A horrible weakness engulfed her, sapping the strength in her legs, numbing her arms and hands.

'Who are you?' Her blunt question, hard-edged, accused him.

He tilted his head to one side. 'I'm a Dane,' he replied. 'We have just landed here, on the shore.'

Oh Lord, he was a Viking, after all! They were even worse than the Saxons with their bloodthirsty reputation for merciless fighting, laying waste to whole villages without a hint of remorse. 'But you…you can't be.' A wary light entered Gisela's eyes. 'You…you're speaking English!'

He laughed. 'English is very close to our Norse language. It's easy for us to change from one to the other.'

Her thoughts tumbled, fuzzy and confused. What was happening to her? She felt caught, trapped in some nightmare for which she couldn't find a way out, despite the way her mind twisted and turned. She had no memory of how she had arrived back at the beach. 'Did you carry me?' Her tone was brittle, sharp.

He lifted one shoulder, then let it drop, unconcerned. 'Yes. You fainted. I'm not surprised. You probably thought you were going to die out there.'

Gisela stared rigidly at the shingle, the slick of green algae across white stone, remembering the slosh of water around her thighs. Her throat was raw from shouting. Yes, she had truly thought she would die. But why had he come out to rescue her, this man, this stranger, of all people? Beneath the intense scrutiny of his emerald-green eyes, she shuffled her hips uncomfortably, glowering at his hands, loose fists curled against his brawny thighs. Hands that had moved over her insensible body, hoisting her high. How could she not remember his touch? Her cheeks flushed suddenly, a livid stain dusting her high cheekbones. Lord, he could have done anything! She would have been at his mercy, him, a Dane! Her eyes flashed blue fire. She crossed her arms over her bosom, jutting her chin forward. 'What did you do to me?'

Ragnar drew his dark-blond brows together in a deep frown. What on earth was the woman talking about? Her expression was stony, openly challenging him, as she waited for his answer. What was she expecting him to say? His eyes traced the curving top line of her lip, the fierce, determined set of her mouth. Tipping his head to one side, he recalled the soft weight against his chest, the sensual roll of her breast as she folded against him.

'Er... I carried you from the mud to the beach. That's it.' His speech was a low burr, rumbling up from his ribcage.

'What else?' she fired back at him. Her hands dropped to her sides, balling into fists against the pebbles.

He followed their movement, wanting to laugh. What was she about to do? Clout him around the jaw? Beat him senseless? It was as if... His mouth parted slightly as the line of her questioning became clear. Of course, he was a Dane and she would judge him as such. 'Nothing else, maid. What were you expecting? That I would rape you midway between the river and the beach? How low your judgement is of me.'

An angry flush tore across her pale cheeks. 'It wouldn't have surprised me. Your reputation is notorious.'

'Not to the Saxons,' he replied curtly. 'We've come here to help, after all. The town is welcoming us with open arms.'

The maid's head knocked back as if he had hit her; she bit her lip as if she had made a mistake. 'Yes, of course, I forgot myself.'

He wondered whether she had forgotten speaking to him in French. He would keep her secret; it made no difference to him whether she was Norman or Saxon. She had been a maid who needed help and that was the end to it. Her agitated fingers played with the ragged filaments of her scarf fringe in her lap. The damp fabric of her gown moulded to her thighs, revealing their curving, slender contours. 'Can I take you home?' he offered.

She threw the fringe of her scarf aside, raised her huge blue eyes to his. 'No. But...thank you for coming out to me,' she said. 'You can leave me now. Please, go.'

He nodded, acknowledging her grudging thanks, hearing the dismissal in her voice. She wanted to be rid of him, that much was obvious. He thought of Eirik, and the rest of the men, slugging ale down their throats in the nearest inn. The lusty singing would have started by now. He was reluctant to join them. 'And what are you going to do?' he asked. 'Sit here on the beach all night?'

Her magnificent eyes gleamed up at him. 'It's no concern of yours,' she said tightly, sliding her knees up to her chest, hugging them. 'I told you to go.' Her voice held a hard edge, disdainful.

She was ordering him about as if he were some common foot soldier! He raised his eyebrows at her rudeness, hips rocking back on his heels. Pins and needles started to prick the soles of his feet. 'And I'm telling you that you should mind your manners. I've just saved your skin.' A warning lilt entered his voice. 'A little humility wouldn't go amiss. You would have died if I hadn't come along.'

She flinched at the sudden harshness in his tone. 'Someone would have come eventually.'

'No,' Ragnar said. 'No one was going to help you. Your master was prepared to leave you out there to drown. Care to tell me why?'

'I've no idea what you're talking about.' Plac-

ing her palms flat on the stones, she levered herself upwards. As she rose, she tottered forward
unsteadily. Rising with her, Ragnar grabbed her
upper arm, fingers pincering her flesh, preventing her from falling.

'*C'est possible parce-que tu est Normande?*
Maybe because you're a Norman,' he murmured
close to her ear.

She lurched away from him in shock, but he
held her fast. 'I don't understand you,' she replied in English. 'What are you saying to me?'
She rolled her arm forward in a circular motion, tugging downwards, trying to release his
fearsome grip.

But Ragnar had seen the terror strike her
gaze. He tugged at her sharply, forcing her to
stagger closer, the startled oval of her face mere
inches from his own. Her skin was like pouring cream, a polished lustre of silk. 'You do
understand me,' he continued in English. Her
delicious rose scent curled around him. 'You
understand me very well. What are you doing
here, a Norman maid, living in the middle of all
these Saxons? Don't you realise they would kill
you if they had any idea?'

God in Heaven, what had she done out there
on the mudflats? What had she said? She wanted

to weep with the thought of her own stupidity. How had she managed to give herself away so easily, to this man of all people? This tall broad-shouldered Dane, with his flare of bright gold hair and eyes of green who had come to help the Saxons. Was he going to kill her now?

'Let me go!' Gisela cried, struggling in his grip. 'Otherwise I'll…' Her voice faded away as she realised the futility of what she had been about to say. Her fiery anger leached away, her spirits exhausted.

'What…otherwise you'll scream?' His tone was sarcastic, grating. 'And that will do a lot of good, won't it? For we both know that no one will come. And we both know why.'

Her shoulders caved forward, as if his words had delivered a physical blow. She stopped fighting his grip, her slight body drooping. 'Let me go, will you, please?' Gisela said quietly, the breeze whipping away the end of her sentence. His glittering gaze moved over her, stripping away her courage, leaving her exposed, as if her inner thoughts were stretched out on the ground for all to see. 'I'm none of your concern.'

She was right. She was none of his concern… and yet, Christ, she intrigued him. He knew that if she had been anyone else, he would have walked away and left her on the beach. But some small part of him urged him to linger at her side. 'I will take you back to where you live,' he offered. 'The town's not safe.'

'You said it,' she said, her tone faintly mocking. 'But do you really think anyone would bother with the likes of me?

'I only have to go down that alley over there,' she explained, pointing to a shadowed gap in the distance. 'And my family will be waiting for me.'

Relinquishing his grip on the soft muscle of her upper arm, the Dane gave her a little push, sending her staggering off across the shingle. 'Go then,' he said bluntly. 'Have it your way.'

Chapter Four

Gisela walked quickly along the alley, away from the beach, away from *him*, eager to reach the safety of her lodgings. The shadowed light made her step disjointed, uncertain; a couple of times she stumbled and her hands flew out to check her fall, scraping against rough exterior walls. Her hem, weighed down with thick, drying mud, clagged unhelpfully around her ankles, hampering her gait. Tears wobbled in her chest. She had only needed a few more days of working on the salt pans to earn enough money for them all to cross the river and be out of this place. Why, oh, why had she agreed to go out on to the mudflats with those children?

Desolation rolled over her, the air catching in her lungs. She had had no choice. The master had told her to go out there. If she hadn't followed his orders, then she would have had no work at all. But, because of what had happened out on the salt marsh, they would have to leave this place as soon as possible. Tonight, at least. A pair of sparkling green eyes punctured her vision. The Dane. Because of that man, they would have to leave. It wouldn't take him long to tell others of his suspicions about her. She whipped her head around, checking that no one followed her, disquiet threading her nerves, making her increase her pace.

The foul smell of the town's midden, stinking and sour, washed over her as she approached the tiny cottage that served as their lodgings. Wrinkling her nose, she pushed against the wooden door, stepping down on to the earth-packed floor. Thick smoke hazed the chamber. She coughed, waving her hand in front of her, trying to clear the smoke so she could see. A fire burned feebly, smoke coiling up to the hole in the rafters, a chimney of sorts. Marie, her older sister, sat on a low stool, poking a stick fretfully into the damp, smouldering wood. Her golden braids, long plaits falling to her waist-belt, shone out in the gloom. She stared miserably across to Gisela, her face streaked with tears.

'Where is he?' Gisela's heart filled with trepidation. A swift glance around the chamber told her that her father was not there. 'Where's he gone, Marie? Tell me!' A rising fear laced her voice.

'Oh, Gisela, he wanted to do something! Something to help you. He hated the way you were working so hard to make coin, while we sat around all day!'

'But he can't work…' Gisela spluttered. 'His leg…'

'He felt so useless. Surely you can see that?' Marie's voice pleaded with her. 'As I do, Sister. This is all because of me! I feel so guilty, I should have… I should have married…' Her eyes, a stunning turquoise colour, wavered with tears as her sentence trailed away to a desperate silence.

'No! Don't say it!' Gisela responded angrily. 'Don't ever say such things again! We did the right thing, Marie, even if our brother was taken.' She crouched down, taking her sister's hands into her own. 'None of this is your fault, do you hear me? That man…that man is a monster, the way he treated you…'

Marie's hand reached out, touching the brooch that secured Gisela's linen headscarf around her neck. The intricately wrought silver glittered as her fingers grazed the metal. 'And the way he treated you, Sister. For that I am truly sorry.'

'It was a small price to pay.' Gisela's eyelashes fluttered down with the memory of that horrific day: the swift retort of the sword, the slice of blade against her neck, the blood. But she had held on to Marie, held on to her sister as if her life depended on it, dragging her away from that awful man, dragging her to safety.

Marie's hand fell back to her lap. 'Not that small,' she responded sadly. 'Does the scar pain you?' Dropping the stick, she hugged her knees, rocking slightly on the stool like a child. Despite being three years older than Gisela, her delicate beauty, her frailty, made Marie appear younger. Her ethereal looks attracted attention wherever she went, however much they tried to hide it, making her vulnerable. It was for this reason, as well as the fact that she was physically stronger, that Gisela had sought work in the town. Her plain features and short muscular body drew few glances, an attribute she was glad of while living among these Saxons; she could slip unnoticed through a crowd. Up to now. A shudder gripped her as a male voice barged through her thoughts, speaking in French. *Is it because you are a Norman?*

Gisela shoved the unwanted memory away, pinning a bright smile on her face. 'It's fine.' Her response was clipped. She had no wish to talk about her injury, or to go over the details of that day, the regrets and recriminations. She had no wish to worry Marie any more than was necessary. At this moment, the only thing she wanted to do was find their father.

Marie was peering at her, suddenly noticing the mud caking her sister's clothes, her wan, drained features. 'Gisela? Did something happen to you today? You're much later than usual.'

'No, nothing. We had to work later, that was all. Further out in the mudflats.' Easing herself up from her crouching position, she rolled her shoulders forward, trying to relieve the ache along the back of her neck. Although she was used to using her body physically, the days at the salt pans were long and hard, and the buckets of brine were heavy to lift. Her upper arm pained her, a sore bruised spot where the Dane had gripped her; she chewed on her bottom lip, resentful, annoyed at him, at the way he had unwittingly managed to spoil their plans.

She sighed. 'Tell me where Father is.'

'He's gone to the inn. The one in the market square.'

Her heart sank, fluttered wildly. 'But why, Marie? What could he possibly hope to achieve by going there?'

Marie hung her head, a listless, defeated gesture.

Gisela folded her arms, mouth compacting

into a stern, forbidding line. 'He's gambling again, isn't he?' Darting to the corner of the cottage, she opened one of the three travelling satchels that were stacked against the wall, pulling out the few personal items that lay at the top and flinging them on the floor. Two cloth sacks full of gold coins nestled at the bottom of her father's satchel.

One sack was missing. 'He took a third of the ransom money, Marie! A third! Why didn't you stop him?' Distraught, she turned back to her sister. 'You know how long it's taken us to save up that amount!'

'I tried, Gisela. I'm so sorry.' Marie hunched her shoulders, winding her arms across her chest. 'But he was adamant; you know how he is.'

Gisela knocked her fist against her head, straightened up. 'Hell's teeth, Marie! What does he think he's going to do? The town's awash with a Danish fleet that's just come in! They'll take it from him in an instant!'

'He's good at dice.' Marie's voice quavered with doubt. 'He knows how to win.'

'Maybe against these dim-witted townspeople,' Gisela replied harshly. 'But against the Danes?' She stared fiercely at the floor, toed the packed earth angrily with her boot. 'We were so close, we almost had all the money. We almost had our brother back. Why did he decide to risk this now?'

Marie's fingers fretted with the end of one of her blonde plaits. 'He wanted to help, Gisela. He thought he was doing the right thing.'

Gisela drew a length of coarse red wool out of her own travelling bag, wrapping it around her shoulders, a makeshift shawl. 'I'll have to go and find him.'

Rising from the stool, Marie nodded. Reaching out, she snared Gisela's hands with her soft fingers. 'I'm so sorry I couldn't stop him.'

Gisela gave her sister's hands a quick little squeeze, a gesture of reassurance. 'You know we can't let him lose that money. I must track him down before it's too late.'

A frustrated anger at her father's behaviour drove her on, driving out her fatigue. Stepping out into the alley, Gisela held her heavy, mud-clagged skirts high above her ankles, her stride rapid and light through the maze of narrow streets. In the gap between the thatched roofs, the sky had darkened to a midnight blue, pinpointed with stars, a waxing moon. The cold, ethereal light picked out the street for Gisela as she hurried along, the constant roar of men's voices drawing her towards the town's main square.

Something brushed against her ear; her headscarf had worked loose, slipping back over her silky hair. Ducking into a shadowed doorway, she un-pinned the brooch at her throat, quickly adjusting the material. As her fingers fumbled with the silver pin, she heard masculine voices, loud and strident, coming down the street, moving closer to *her*. Panic flared in her chest. Her nervous fingers dropped the brooch and it clattered down on to the muddy cobbles, the filigreed silver sparkling in the moonlight. As she dipped down to reach for it, a meaty hand scooped the brooch up before she had time to curl her fingers around it.

'Give that back to me!' Gisela demanded, straightening up.

A flush-faced Saxon man peered closely at her. 'Who do we have here, eh lads?' He grinned at his friends, swaying in various stages of drunkenness around him. Before Gisela had time to stop him, the man snatched the scarf away from her hair and pushed his hand around her chin, forcing her head up so he could see her face more clearly. 'A beauty, methinks, and no mistake! What are you doing out on your own, maid? Touting for business in this busy town?'

They thought she was a whore! Her mouth was dry and she licked her lips, trying to find her voice, the blood hurtling through her veins in terror. 'Get your filthy hands off me,' she spat out fiercely.

'William…' a young man stepped forward, his mouth coiling with disgust. 'Are you out of your mind? Look at her! Look at her neck! Someone's dealt with her, good and proper. Why would you want to bed that?'

The man's gaze slid to the scar on her neck, the line of puckered skin that stretched from behind her ear to a point just shy of her windpipe. 'Sweet Jesu,' he muttered. His hand dropped away, the scarf and brooch dropping from his shocked fingers to the ground. 'No wonder you're out on your own, girl. No one will touch you, marked as you are.' Turning away, he spat on the ground, ushering his friends away. 'Keep moving, lads, before she gives us the evil eye.' The men moved off down the lane, sniggering, jostling each other.

She listened to the sound of their laughter, their whispering and tittering as they staggered off. Tears pooled in her eyes as the familiar shroud of humiliation descended; her skin hummed with shame as she bent her knees to retrieve the brooch and scarf. Why was she so surprised? What had happened then was precisely the reason she kept her scarf wrapped securely around her neck. She had experienced similar expressions of disgust aimed at her in the past, masculine declarations of snide revulsion; why should she subject herself to any more derision than was necessary? She knew she was ugly, that she would never marry or have children because of what had happened to her.

Emerging into the open area from the narrow street, Gisela lifted her gaze across the cobbled square, across the smiling faces of Danes and Saxons, the tethered horses, the dogs trotting to and fro, sniffing the ground, eager for scraps. Even in the freshening breeze, the air was thick with the smell of ale and mead, roasting meat. Fires burned beneath iron skillets; glowing sparks flew up, reflecting against chainmail hauberks, jewelled sword helms. The small Saxon town had gone to a great effort to welcome these Danish warriors.

Her feet teetered on the cobbles. She took a deep shaky breath, her flesh still trembling from her encounter with the Saxon men. Where was her courage? She needed it now, yet those men had driven it from her with their disparaging glances, their ugly words. Forget it, she told herself firmly, forget *them*. Your father needs you now. And yet, as she stared across the square to the inn, the sign of a gilded angel swinging above the entrance, her heart sank. Was she really going to have to fight her way across this crowded space to the inn and pull her father out? Suddenly all she wanted to do was to turn around and fly back to Marie. There was a possibility that her father might win more coin, after all, and return home unscathed.

She pressed her lips together, hugging her arms about her middle, staring at the heaving mass before her. It was a remote possibility, at the very least. If she failed to retrieve the ransom money before her father lost it all, then her brother's life would be in jeopardy. And it would be her fault. *Come on, Gisela*, she chided herself, *you are made of sterner stuff than that*; as a family, they had come too far and gone through too much to give up now.

Snapping her shawl across her body, she ducked her head, plunging into the fray, squeezing and sliding her way through the crowds, her eyes pinned firmly to the ground. Nobody spared her a second glance, the huge blond Danes intent on slugging back their tankards of ale and singing their songs. Some had their arms firmly fastened around dark-haired Saxon maidens, claiming them already for the night ahead. Edging her way around the horses tied to the wooden rail at the front of the inn, Gisela stopped for a moment, gathering her breath and her resolve.

Over to the left, a group of Danes were gathered around what looked like a bundle of clothes on the ground. One man dropped to his haunches, reaching his arm out, shaking something, then another man crouched by his side. Nay, she realised, not clothes; it was a man, stretched out on the cobbles. She twisted her mouth into a sneer: these Danes were renowned for drinking themselves into a stupor. Twitching her gaze away, she stared back at the inn, light flickering out through the cracks in the wooden shutters. How was she going to go in there, a woman, without everyone turning to look at her as she came through the door? Sweat prickled her armpits, a cold sliding sensation coiling in her belly.

Then something made her turn back to the man on the ground. There were more men around him now, voices raised in consternation, the thick Norse vowels floating across to her. They had managed to shift him into a sitting position, his grizzled head cradled in his hands as he slumped against the wall. Between the calf-length boots of the Danes, she could see the man's scuffed short boots, green woollen braies. Not a soldier, by the looks of him. Her heartbeat increased by a notch, then began to pound, her knuckles whitening around the wooden rail. She knew who the man was.

'Father!' she yelled, careful to use the Saxon language. These Norse barbarians would understand her. She raised her fists, thumping against the broad phalanx of Danish backs, criss-crossed with leather straps over shining mail-coats. 'Let me through!' As the men turned in surprise, Gisela pushed forward, squeezing through the jumble of thickset bodies. One man placed his arm in front of her, barring her way. 'Nay, mistress, 'tis not for you to see.'

But she had already seen. The hunched body of her father, crumpled against the wall, head cupped in his open palms. The grey grizzled hair and beard, matted with blood. His face, deathly white, scored by familiar creases. Blood trickled down over his large bony wrists, dripping to the ground.

'What have they done to you?' Her voice was a long, low moan. Sliding to her knees beside him, she untied her shawl, wrapping it around her father's shaking shoulders. 'What happened?'

Her father's dull stare lifted to her face, his eyelashes flicking up in recognition. He cleared his throat, licking his parched lips. 'I won, Gisela, I won a lot. And they took it all.'

Fury seized her, a white-hot blinding anger at the unfairness of the situation, at her father's stupidity to attempt such a foolhardy deed. Her eyes dropped to her father's sword, the hilt gleaming from his belt. With no thought other than to exert revenge on those that had stolen from her father, Gisela grabbed at the hilt, wresting the shining blade from the leather scabbard. Springing up like a cat, she jumped to her feet, turning on the watchful circle of Danes.

'Which one of you took his money?' she cried out, slicing the air with the knife. The blade gleamed ominously, catching the light of the fires from the market square. 'Who did this?'

'Nay, not us, mistress,' one of the men replied. 'You are mistaken.' His blond hair straggled down over chainmail clad shoulders. 'We found him like this, unconscious and bleeding. It was us that helped to sit him up.'

'I don't believe you!' Gisela planted her feet firmly apart, as if bracing herself for a physical fight. Her fear of these warriors slipped away at her father's plight; she had to retrieve the money, one way or another: their situation was desperate. 'We all know what you Danes are capable of. Why not attack an old man and take his money? He's easy prey, after all.' She swung the sword around in a half-circle, the movement haphazard, jerky. 'Give it back to me, now! I'm warning you, I know how to use this!'

'But we don't have it, maid,' another man explained, holding his hands out, trying to placate her. 'We...'

'What is going on here?' From the back of the group, a voice rang out, deep and commanding. Immediately the men bowed their heads, forming a gap to let another man step forward. Half a head taller than his companions, with seal-dark hair and eyes of molten brown. A young man, who carried himself with the arrogant swagger of authority, his head cocked to one side as he listened to a rapid explanation from one of the men. He swept a cursory glance down at her father. Keeping his distance from her blade, surrounded by the burly Danes, he stared at Gisela, narrow lips curling with disdain.

Sweat prickled from her fingers against the leather hilt, but she held her ground, her expression mutinous, fierce, the blade tipped up in front of her.

'What is all this nonsense, maid?'

'Are you the leader of these men?'

'Aye, I am Eirik Sweynsson.' He wound his

arms across his leather-bound chest. 'Tell me, what goes on here?'

'Your men, your godforsaken men, have taken all my father's money, and his winnings!' Her challenging blue gaze swept over the men, fully expecting one of them to step forward and admit his guilt. 'They attacked him!'

Eirik smiled slowly. 'But I think you are mistaken, maid, for they tell me that they did not. On the contrary, they helped him.'

'And you believe them?' Aghast, Gisela's speech juddered out. 'You need to search them, at the very least!'

'Why should I believe you over my own men?' Eirik lifted his chin, regarding her with contempt. 'A lowly Saxon maid, dressed in rags.' He cast a disparaging eye across her patched gown, the drab linen scarf around her head and neck. 'For all I know, it probably isn't your money anyway. You probably stole it from someone else.'

His goading words ripped through her; her temper flared. 'How *dare* you?' she cried out. Forgetting the sword in her hand, she lunged forward, wanting to hit out, wanting to wipe the smug, supercilious smile off his handsome, self-satisfied face.

Whipcord arms snared her waist, a punishing, bruising grip, jolting her roughly away from her intended target. She was lifted, feet dangling as if on strings, then crushed back against an iron-hard body. Fingers twisted into her wrist, pinioning the flesh, until the sword slipped from her hand and clattered to the ground. Swinging her legs, she kicked her heels furiously against the shins of her unseen opponent, pushing down angrily on the muscular forearm clamped around her waist.

'Cease, maid, if you know what's good for you.' A voice, horribly familiar, drilled into her ear. Her belly plummeted in recognition., No, not him, not the Dane from the beach! Gisela began to struggle more, desperate to extract herself from his tight, unforgiving hold.

Watching her futile efforts, Eirik laughed, a mocking sound. 'I wish I could applaud your efforts, maid. But it'll take more than a short sword to do away with the likes of me.' He raised his gaze above her head, catching the eyes of the man who held her. 'I owe you one, Ragnar—' he grinned '—although I'm not sure my life was in any danger.' His eyes dropped to the blade glinting on the ground, the smile vanishing from his face. 'Make sure she's punished for what she's done.' He turned away, clapping his arm around the man next to him. 'Come, we're

missing valuable drinking time here! Ragnar
will sort out the girl.'

Ragnar. So that was the name of the man
who held her. The same man who had pulled her
from the mud. Not a gentle name, but one that
suited his flashing eyes and the craggy angles
of his face, the tall muscular body that spoke
of the open sea, of lands unexplored: a restless
soul. As she watched the Danes walk away, his
chest pressed into her spine. The dusky scent
of leather and salt, a fresh vitality, poured from
him, enveloping her.

She closed her eyes, a flush rising across her
cheeks; her breath caught, then emerged in staggered gasps at the intimacy of her situation. His
honed thighs riding against her hips, nay, cradling them! His thick arm grazing the underside
of her breasts. Sweet Jesu, she had never been
this close to a man! And after what had happened to her and her sister, she had vowed to
keep away from them for ever. But now? Now
heat flickered, deep in her belly, spiralling upwards: a slow sensual climb. Her heart lurched
in despair.

'Let me go,' she croaked. Her mind danced
chaotically as she tried to think what she should
do next, but the thoughts flicked away from her,
flighty, ephemeral.

Around her waist, the burly forearm released fractionally, allowing her feet to slip to the ground. Hands planted heavily on her shoulders, spinning her around. His chin was on a level with the top of her head, clean-shaven, shallow grooves on each side of his generous mouth defining his jaw.

Gisela tipped her head up, catching his emerald gaze. 'Those men have my father's money.' Fatigue swept over her and she swayed a little beneath his firm grip. 'I must go after them. I must get it back.' The tiredness leached through her voice, draining it of conviction.

'There's no need,' Ragnar said calmly. 'They don't have it.'

She rolled her shoulder irritably beneath the weighty impact of his hand. If only he would go and leave her alone, for then she would at least be able to think in a logical manner. His direct green gaze muddled her, turning her brain into useless pulp. 'What are you doing here anyway?' she said grumpily. 'Shouldn't you be off drinking with the rest of them?' She was so close to him that her knee nudged against his thigh; she wrenched her leg away in annoyance, jolting against him as she did so.

Ragnar laughed. For such a little thing, the maid showed astonishing courage. Either that or

complete stupidity, he hadn't decided yet. As he
and Eirik had approached earlier, she had been
completely surrounded by his fellow men, those
big lumps of masculinity who towered above
her. And yet she had seemed completely in control, swishing that small blade around as if she
would tackle each and every one of them in
hand-to-hand combat.

Was she even afraid of him? Of what he
might do? Eirik had asked him to punish her.
Not a trace of fear showed in her face. Her skin
glowed, fine marble in shadowy light; a delicate
rose colour flushed her cheeks. The sapphire
sparkle of her magnificent eyes dominated her
face, flashing with defiance. Her whole frame
bristled with undisguised hostility; he should
have been annoyed, but strangely, he found himself drawn to her shrewish, belligerent manner.
He liked it. The majority of women he met, and
that was not many, to be fair, seemed pathetic
and feeble, pale ghosts compared to this fire-
brand.

He brought his hand up, deliberately cupping
her cheek, knowing such a gesture would rile
her. 'Did we spoil your little game, maid?' His
thumb rubbed across the satin pelt of her skin, a
cursory touch; she flinched at the contact, jerking her head away.

'Game?' she flared at him, jerking her head

at her father's defeated posture. Her red shawl looked incongruous around his shoulders, the one bright spot of his drab attire. 'That is my father sitting there! Attacked and left for dead, his money stolen…by them…' She jabbed a finger in the direction that Eirik had taken his men. 'I wanted them to give it back.'

'So you thought that pushing a knife into the King of Denmark's son would be the solution?' Ragnar stuck his hand through his hair, no doubt leaving the vigorous blond strands sticking upwards, haphazard. His gaze narrowed. 'What on earth possessed you to do such a thing?'

'You mean that dark-haired oaf is a prince?' she replied scathingly.

'Aye, maid,' he confirmed, his mouth twitching with amusement, 'that dark-haired oaf, as you like to call him, is the heir to the whole of Denmark. So you had better watch your step.'

'But the money—'

'Hell's teeth, woman, are you completely stupid? Leave it alone. Go home and shut the door and try not to go around threatening to stick knives into people. Do you understand? No wonder your poor father has his head in his hands, with a daughter like you! First the mud and now this!'

Gisela glared at him, her mouth compressed into a wilful line.

Ragnar shook his head at her, a boyish grin pinned to his face. 'And don't you look at me like that, maid. You can hate me as much as you like, but you know I speak the truth. Go home. You might be foolhardy, but you're certainly not stupid.' He brought the harsh contours of his face closer to hers. 'And your use of the Saxon language seems to have improved since I saw you last.'

Shock flooded through her, a chill shudder of foreboding. How could she have forgotten? Somehow she had given herself away out on the salt marsh. Ragnar had spoken to her in French, but she hadn't responded. He hadn't guessed her true identity, had he? For, as far as she could remember, she hadn't uttered a word of her mother tongue in his presence.

Down on the ground, her father was trying to scrabble to his feet. To her surprise, the Dane leaned down, grabbing his upper arm to help him up. Gisela leapt to his other side, and together they brought the older man on to his feet.

'Which way?' Ragnar said companionably as he laced her father's arm around the back of his neck.

Gisela, her arm supporting her father's waist on the other side, peered around to Ragnar in astonishment. Suddenly, her father's fragility was all too apparent, his gaunt frame hanging off the Dane's broad shoulder. A wave of vulnerability washed through her. 'We don't need you,' she replied resentfully. 'Don't you think you and your lot have done enough for this evening?'

A look of disdain crossed his lean features. 'As you wish.' He pulled away roughly so that her father's full weight fell heavily against her. She staggered backwards, heels striking the wall as she fought to hold him upright. Her slight frame buckled beneath her father's bulk and she wondered whether she was even capable of taking one step forward. She hated the fact that the Dane watched her, saw her weakness with his knowing eyes.

'I can do it!' she whispered fiercely as he came towards her.

Scooping the man's arm around his neck, Ragnar regarded her coolly. 'No, maid, you cannot. Even I am not so heartless as to leave you here, at the mercy of a town full of drunken Danes.'

Chapter Five

As the odd trio made their way across the crowded square, Ragnar curtailed his long stride to take account of the maid's shorter legs and her father's staggering gait. He led the way, shoving his tall, solid bulk through the jostling hoards of people, forging a path. Her father's head lolled against his shoulder, sour waves of alcohol rolling off his breath; Ragnar suspected the girl had little idea of how much he had drunk. He had no wish to tell her, to burst her bubble of self-delusion. He glanced with grudging admiration at her mud-smeared features, the exhausted lines of her face. She wilted beneath her father's considerable weight, her slim frame hunched forward, chin jutting out with fierce determination. The maid had endured enough today. Let her believe that her father's stumbling gait was caused simply by the blow to his head.

'Shall we rest for a moment?' Ragnar suggested, as they reached the other side of the square. Between them, her father moaned, shaking his head slowly from side to side. Blood, trickling from the gash on his forehead, flecked her bodice, pinpoints of red.

'No,' the girl managed to gasp out. The muscles along her spine ached with tension. Her father's arm pressed heavily against her neck, dragging against her linen scarf. 'I must take him back. His wound—'

'The wound is not serious,' Ragnar replied mildly. 'And I doubt we will make it anywhere unless you rest now...'

'Nay, I can manage,' she protested, clearly annoyed by his judgement. 'I'm stronger than I look!'

His emerald gaze flicked over her wan face, the purple patches of fatigue beneath her huge, limpid eyes. She was dressed like a nun, garments drab and muted. Her ill-fitting dress billowed out around her, blurring any outline of her figure. But he remembered what lay beneath. The slender curves that had jostled against him when he carried her from the mud and again when he had pulled her back from Eirik. The curve of her hip, a smooth sensual line. The rounded touch of her breast against his forearm.

Delight stung him, a quick dart of sensual pleasure. His loins burned.

Surprised and irritated by the way his mind travelled, Ragnar twisted his mouth into a tight line. This woman had barrelled into his life with all the finesse of a spitting cat, yet, at the slightest contact, jolted his broad frame into shudders of desire. It made no sense. The girl had a temper; even now, the fierce rigidity of her expression appraised him with disdain. Despite her diminutive figure, her spine was straight, stiff and unyielding. Ready to do battle at any moment, like a Norse goddess of old.

'Let your father rest then,' Ragnar insisted, his voice gruff. 'Even if you want to carry on, I think he needs to sit for a moment.' Bending from the waist, he lowered the older man to a sitting position on a stone step outside a cottage. Forced to follow his movements, the woman allowed her father's arm to slip from her shoulder. His head rolled back against the door, the sagging skin on his face a pallid grey colour. The deep lined pouches beneath his eyes were sunken.

Ragnar straightened up, looping his arms around in big, lazy circles, stretching his shoulder muscles, eyeing the girl with curiosity. 'Most women would accept my help without question.'

His eyes drilled into her, green gimlets, flashing fire. 'Why do you persist in arguing with me?'

Because you take away my strength, Gisela thought. She laced her arms across her chest, a guarded gesture. *Around you, I feel vulnerable.* She had always been able to fend for herself and her family. With her father and her sister, she had always been in charge, the one to make decisions, the person that they both leaned on and turned to in times of trouble.

'Why?' he prompted.

'Oh, I don't know!' she replied testily. His glimmering gaze caught her, held her captive. 'It could be any number of things: the way you keep hauling me about, your insufferable arrogance, or the fact that you're a Dane!' She planted her hands firmly on her hips, glaring at him, as if squaring up for a fight.

A wry grin lit up his face at her rudeness. 'Or maybe,' Ragnar said slowly, 'it's because I know your secret?' He lifted his coppery eyebrows, thick and unruly. A question, left dangling in the air.

His low voice knocked into her, the slicing blade of a knife; she struggled to keep her features in a set, neutral position and not react to his words. What had happened, out there on the marshes, to give herself away? If only she could peel back the layers of fog that had engulfed her as the water swirled around her hips. She remembered being lifted high against his chest, carried, but nothing else. Tossing her head back, she fixed him with a wide-eyed sapphire stare. 'I don't know what you're talking about.'

'Who are you then?' Ragnar rapped out. He took a step forward, his leather-covered toes nudging hers beneath her mud-encrusted hem, his broad shoulders hulking over her, deliberately intimidating. 'What is your name?' He was being a bully, using his height and bulk to unnerve her.

Rearing back from him, Gisela felt her heels strike the cob wall behind her. 'Why do you want to know so much?' Her breath emerged in shallow truncated gasps. 'Who I am should not matter to you!'

Aye, the maid was right. Whoever she was, and whatever she and her father were doing, was none of his concern. But ever since he had plucked her from the rising tide, he had felt a growing need to protect her, a duty of care in the face of her obvious vulnerability, despite her protests to the contrary. She seemed so alone, an outsider in this Saxon town, a foreigner speak-

ing her oddly accented English, bereft of support
or protection. Her bristling feistiness sparked
his curiosity; her twilight eyes, breathtaking,
kept him standing over her, rooting his feet to
the spot. In a moment, he told himself, he would
walk away, rejoin Eirik and his men. He should
not be wasting his time on her, especially when
he needed to concentrate on the other, more serious, matter of finding his sister's abductor.

'What matters,' he said sternly, honing in on a
plausible reason to stay for a little bit longer, 'is
that you attacked my commander and he will be
asking questions about you. So you need to tell
me something, maid, otherwise he is very likely
to come after you in person. And he would not
be as lenient as me.' This was an outright lie,
for Eirik would be well into his cups by now,
having completely forgotten about the encounter with the maid and her father.

'Why can't you leave us alone?' Lunging forward, the woman placed her palms flat against
his chest, trying to shove him away in a futile
effort to gain some space between them. Her
delicate touch seared into him; his muscles quivered. The pit of his belly contracted, sending a
ripple of delight down to a place that had lain
dormant, barren, since his sister's ordeal. Guilt
had stifled his desire on that fateful day, choked

the air out of all feeling. But this woman, with her quiet, understated beauty, ignited a devil within him, a devil that whispered in his ear, nudged at him and drove him on. The cool, logical part of his brain clamoured at him to stop, to hold himself in check. He ignored the warning. Self-restraint fled, chased away by the limpid blue of her huge eyes, the promise of her slim, curving body against his.

Ragnar leaned in, closing the gap between them, deliberately pressing his heavy thighs and chest against her. Her chin jerked up at the shocking contact: his taut, honed muscles against her slim thighs. Inches from his mouth, her lips shimmered, like the velvet petals of a rose, luscious and enticing. A sweet, plush curve that he longed to trace with his finger. And his mouth.

'What are you doing?' Her fingers clawed frantically at his tunic, digging into the fine red wool, trapped by the bulk of his body.

'There are other ways to gain information.' Ragnar trailed one lean forefinger across her cheek, savouring the satin of her skin. Awareness smouldered, a slow kindling fire engulfing his heart, his belly.

'Nay! Not like this!' she cried out. What did he intend to do? Throw her down on the cobbles and flick up her skirts, in full view of her father? 'Go away!' she said. But her voice was weak, lacked conviction.

Ragnar heard the faint surrender in her voice, the spark of compliance. His mind fell across it, seizing it like a wild animal. Wanting to take, consume, without thought or consideration. He dipped his head; a brindled lock of hair fell across his brow. Lust stirred his loins, a deep, visceral yearning. He gripped her shoulders like a starving man, lifting her up to him. A simple kiss, he told himself. Nothing more. Such a little thing to take, after all this time in the wilderness. His mouth slipped over hers, brushing her bottom lip. The softest touch. Blood pounded along his veins, gathering speed; his heart bumped faster, erratically. Her cheek brushed against his, the rose fragrance lifting from her skin, filling his nostrils. Beneath his questing lips, her mouth parted. Her fingers relaxed against him.

'Gisela...?' A wavering voice called up from the step. An old man's voice. Her father.

Ragnar's mouth broke from hers in a moment, a swift, brutal ending. His head rocked back in shock, strips of colour searing his high cheekbones. His hands fell from her shoulders, dropped to his sides, chastened. His strong sinewy fingers curled into tight fists. By Odin, what on earth had possessed him?

Bereft of his grip, Gisela staggered back on useless legs, knocking back against the cottage wall. A flake of loose plaster dislodged itself, scattering small white pieces across her dress. Dazed, she brought her hand to her quivering mouth, almost in wonderment. Her fingers trembled, shaking with reaction. Why was she not shouting at him, berating him for what he had done? Slapping him across the face? Instead she sank back, knees barely supporting her, belly wound tight in a coil of longing, a craving for... what?

She had a tentative idea of the carnal ways of men and most of what she knew was bad, cobbled together from servants' dire stories, her mother, God rest her soul, and her sister's terrifying ordeal. So how could she explain this, this crazy senseless fluttering through her veins? How could she explain the way her body had folded into his, when the only thing she should have been doing was pushing him away? Staring at the ground, she hung her head in shame, cheeks burning with embarrassment. Darting her gaze towards her father, she hoped he hadn't seen. But, although he was stirring, his eyes were still closed. She almost wept aloud with relief.

'Don't worry,' Ragnar said mildly, following her glance. 'He saw nothing.'

'You're despicable,' she spat at him bitterly, incensed by the lack of concern in his words. Lunging towards him, she raised her hand to slap him hard across the cheek. 'You took advantage of me!'

He caught her wrist, mid-air, snaring the delicate bones with long fingers.

'You had no right!' Her voice was shrill.

'Perhaps not.' Ragnar shrugged his shoulders. 'But we both enjoyed it.' His eyes traced the outline of her mouth, her lips no doubt reddened by his kiss.

'Nay, I did not!' Gisela replied vehemently. 'You men are all the same, be you Saxon, Norman, or Dane! Savages the lot of you, riding roughshod over women, pillaging and raping...'

'I did not rape you.' A small line appeared between his raised eyebrows, creasing his tanned, sea-roughened skin.

'You were going to.' A half-sob hitched her voice, tart, accusing.

Ragnar sighed, a long exhalation of breath emptying his lungs. A muscle twitched in the shadow of his cheek.

'Nay, you're mistaken, maid. Believe me, if I wanted to sleep with a woman, I would have chosen someone other than you.' He swept his eyes from the top of her head, over her drab, stained clothes to the scuffed boots poking out from her hem: a look of utter scorn.

His cruel tongue lashed her, as if he had hit her, violently, across the jaw. Her mouth whitened with the cold slosh of comprehension. What had she been thinking, to accuse him of such a thing, to go as far as to consider herself as an item of desire? The idea was laughable. Normally, she was under no illusion about her lack of attractiveness towards the opposite sex, content as she was to live in the shadow of her older sister's beauty. But from the moment she had met him, this tall, blond Dane, this day had been anything but normal.

Gisela shrank from him, touching the brooch at her throat like a talisman. This man made her act like a fool, turning her into a different version of her normal persona: a more beautiful, seductive version. How he must be laughing at her inside. She had not the slightest doubt that he would return to his men and regale them all with tales of the short ugly Saxon maid who truly believed she was about to lose her innocence.

And yet, even now, in the flickering aftermath of their brief kiss, her heart still pounded, thumped with the hurtling pace of her blood. She was lying to herself, deluded. With him, she was not safe at all.

The door of the cottage creaked inwards at Gisela's knock. Marie's pale, anxious face peered out. Gisela placed a quick finger to her lips, a warning to her sister to speak in Saxon and not their customary French that they spoke when they were alone. Marie's eyes widened at the sight of her father, at the man supporting his other side, then nodded swiftly. She understood.

'I was worried,' she said. 'What happened to—?'

'We'll take him inside first, then I will explain,' Gisela said briskly, cutting off her sister's question. She resented the Dane at her side, hating the way she had had to rely on him to help bring her father home. The latter part of the journey had been conducted in complete silence, Gisela quietly determined to build up her reserves of self-reliance after her wretched humiliation. The Dane's disdainful words had undermined her, stripping her briefly of her fighting confidence. She needed to regain her inner strength and courage. Pushing the sweet memory of his lips swiftly to one side, she had managed to gather her scattered wits, marshalling her defences, ready to do battle once more.

'Of course.' Marie darted about, spreading her father's padded bed-roll next to the smouldering fire. 'Put him here, so he can warm up.' Her eyes fell on her father's forehead, the seeping blood. 'Oh, his head!'

'He was attacked,' Gisela explained, her voice hollow. 'And the money has been stolen.'

Ducking beneath the lintel, Ragnar helped Gisela to manoeuvre the older man through the doorway and down the steps. He lowered the man's large frame on to the sleeping mat. The man groaned, slumping to one side as Marie crouched down beside him, tending to him. A bucket full of water stood at the edge of the room; she scooped up some of the liquid into a small bowl and brought it over to their father. Dipping in a clean cloth, she proceeded to dab at the ragged gash on the older man's forehead.

Ragnar straightened up. His unruly hair brushed the ceiling rafters as he sought the maid's bright face in the smoky gloom. There she was, eyes blazing, her mouth compressed in a tight, hostile line, her arms folded decisively across her chest: a fighting stance. For some reason, he was glad to see that spark of combat return after his brutal dismissal, even though he knew he would be the only one on the receiving end of that anger. It made him feel alive again.

'Gisela,' he said, repeating the name spoken by the older man. 'So that is your name.'

She nodded stiffly.

It suited her somehow, the quick delicacy of the vowels mirroring her swift step, the liquid beauty of her eyes. Like a fawn in the forest, alert to every footstep, nimble and quick. But also strong. In mind and in body. He was in no doubt about that—beneath her voluminous clothes, her limbs were honed, as if she were accustomed to physical exercise, and the way she tussled verbally with him was evidence of a sharp intelligence.

'I am her sister.' The other maid glanced up from her ministrations. 'Marie.'

The two young women were very much alike, he realised, although Marie must have been older. Small lines fanned out from the edge of her eyes; her angelic beauty holding a haunted, chastened look. Next to her, Gisela blazed with vitality, her cheeks flushed pink, magnificent eyes dancing with a vivid blue, brimming with thwarted anger towards him.

'Where are you from?' Ragnar asked, a hint

of steel entering his voice. 'What are you doing here in this place?'

'We have a castle down in the south,' Gisela replied vaguely, clearly hoping it would be enough. She lifted her chin, jutting it forward with stern determination. 'I must thank you once again for your help, but you can return to your men now. I'm afraid we have no money to pay you for your service.' Her voice was cold, bitter, holding the hard edge of dismissal. She glared pointedly at the door, the clearest indication that she wanted him to leave.

Ragnar ignored her, tilting his head to one side. 'Why not pay me with the truth, maid,' he said, his low voice rumbling conspiratorially. 'I know you're Norman, so why keep denying it? I'll do nothing with the information, I swear.'

'You're wrong!' Gisela blurted out, panic flaring through her. 'And anyway, why would I trust you, a Dane?' She took a step forward towards him, then faltered, as if thinking the better of it. Her eyes dropped to his mouth; she flushed, wrapping her arms about her belly.

Ragnar tracked the path of her eyes and knew she was thinking of their kiss. An unexpected warmth curled about his heart. 'When I carried you in from the mudflats, you spoke to me in French and I knew then what you were. Anyone else would have delivered you straight to the Saxon sheriff of the town, but I did not.'

Gisela glanced at him sadly. 'What did I say?'

'You asked me if I was real,' he replied slowly, remembering. Her delicate weight against his chest. The sift of rose perfume in his nostrils. 'And when I confirmed it, you said, "Thank God."'

'I thought no one would come.' Her voice dropped to a whisper. In the flickering firelight her skin adopted a limpid sheen, like rich pouring cream. 'I thought I was going to die out there.' The words fell from her mouth unbidden and she clapped her hand across her lips, as if ashamed of the fear revealed by her speech. Twisting away, fretful, she dipped her slight frame to pick up a bunch of sticks from a pile near the door and threw them on to the fire.

'But I did come.' He watched the revelation chase across her finely honed features, the disappointment at giving herself away. 'And I didn't take you straight to the Saxons. So you know that you can trust me.'

The silver rivets on his leather surcoat danced before her eyes. A haven for her troubled mind. What would it be like, to lean against that generous expanse of muscle for one sweet moment and draw comfort from that hard masculine body? To breathe in his heady, musky scent? Her lungs constricted, held within an iron cage. Eyes springing upwards, she caught his sparkling gaze, teetering on the edge of confession. His words made sense and she clung to them, momentarily, like a lifeline.

A moan from her father made her glance down at Marie, as if she could find the answer in the neat folds of her sister's headscarf. She remembered how they had trusted a man before and how he had destroyed his sister's life. She couldn't tell this Dane, this stranger, anything. Like danger in human form, he unnerved her, volatile and intimidating. Shedding energy and power in rich, seductive waves. Filling the small chamber with his muscled bulk, pushing her off balance.

'I owe you nothing,' she said finally, her speech wobbling slightly, rough-edged. She fingered the silver brooch that fastened the scarf around her neck. 'Least of all a confession.'

'You owe me your life.' His reply was swift. 'I would have thought that counted for a great deal.'

'I didn't ask you to save me,' she responded grumpily.

'Then next time I'll leave you there!' Ragnar

stared into her eyes, as if willing her to confide in him.

'Thank you for helping with our father.' Standing up, the wet cloth dripping between her fingers, Marie lifted her chin towards Ragnar. He nodded curtly, acknowledging her gratitude. Then he dipped his head beneath the low-slung lintel, the buckled wood flaking with age. Looking back, his gaze swept what must have appeared a stiff tableau: the old man lying beside the fire, his injured head in a makeshift bandage, and the two women standing shoulder to shoulder, Marie's expression one of benign lenience, Gisela's face set in lines of truculent relief. He stepped out into the twilight chill, a strange pang knifing Gisela's heart at the thought of him leaving for good.

Chapter Six

For a long moment, Gisela maintained a stony glare at the shut door, making completely sure that Ragnar had gone. Then she darted across the room, lowering the wooden bar to span the half-rotted planks, a barrier against any more unwanted visitors. Despair creased her face as she turned to her sister. 'Oh, Marie, what a mess! A complete mess!'

'Who was that?' her sister asked. Curiosity rippled through her voice. 'He looked like...well, he wasn't a Saxon, was he?'

'Nay, he was not,' Gisela replied bitterly. 'He's a horrible, stinking Dane!' Her eyes shuttered briefly. A Dane who made free with his hands and his mouth, she thought. She jabbed her teeth down into her bottom lip, trying to erase the lingering burn of his kiss.

'Why did you bring him back here, then?' Marie said. She wrinkled her pert nose critically.

'It wasn't my choice,' Gisela replied. 'He insisted on helping me back with Father. I…' Her voice trailed away as she remembered the moment as she lunged for the Danish prince, the powerful arms dragging her away, hard sinewy fingers gripping her hand, forcing her to release her father's sword. She had no wish to cause her sister any further anxiety by telling her about what had happened in the town. 'When he rescued me from the mudflat… I spoke in French, not English. By mistake. I was so afraid, thinking I would die out there. For a moment, I must have lost my head.'

'Do you think he is suspicious of us…?' Marie threw a nervous look towards the door.

Gisela nodded. 'He understood me. He spoke to me in French; he knows the language. How, I don't know.' A dry exhausted feeling pulled at her eyelids; she rubbed savagely at her eyes. She needed to sleep, yet her body coursed with ripples of pent-up energy. 'We must leave this town, Marie, and we have to leave it now. That Dane…he knows too much; it won't be long before he's back, possibly with others.'

'But…the ransom money?' Marie twisted the wet cloth that she had used to clean their father's wound between her hands. Droplets of water fell on to the earthen floor. 'Is there no hope of trying to find it?'

'I don't dare.' Pushing away from the door, Gisela moved over to her father. He was asleep now, a gentle rattling snore emerging from his grey, chapped lips. Red lines of cracked skin, sore and peeling, radiated out from the corners of his mouth. Kneeling beside him, Gisela glanced up at her sister. 'I'm too worried about being caught. If the Saxon townspeople find out who we really are, then…' She stopped midsentence, her stomach churning. 'Our only option is to leave this place and I will try to earn the coin in another town. It's not safe here any more.'

Marie dropped to her knees beside her, touched her elbow gently. Her woollen skirts puddled around her. 'This is not like you, Gisela. I've never known you to run away from anything. You've always been the one to protect me, when it should have been the other way around.' Her eyes fell to Gisela's headscarf, wrapped tightly around her neck. 'Why, even with Ralph de Pagenal, when you dragged me away from him…' Marie's voice wavered, dropping to a whisper. 'Even on that awful day, you never gave up.' She touched the brooch jabbed severely into the linen cloth at Gisela's neck, the intricately wrought silver winking in the stuttering firelight. 'And you paid the price for it, for which I am truly sorry.'

Gisela shook her head, a swift negative movement. 'It's nothing, Marie. Don't make more of it than it really is. I was never going to let that man force you into a marriage like that. A barbarian such as him.'

'And yet you stood up to him.'

'Yes, I did.' A small crease appeared between her fine arched brows as she pondered the crumpled figure of her father. Was Marie right? If she had lost her nerve, then she knew the reason why. A pair of glittering green eyes swept across her vision.

'The Dane has made me afraid,' she whispered. It wasn't the Saxon townspeople that scared her; it was the thought of meeting him again. Her stomach flipped in agitation. The thought of what he could do to her. The rough tussle of his firm lips against hers. Her loins gripped with a sudden, intense longing; a nervous anticipation, thrilling along her veins. She flushed, guiltily.

'Is he any worse than Ralph de Pagenal?'

Nay, he could not have been more different. Instinct had told her, from the very moment she had encountered him, out there on the mudflats,

that he was not a cruel man, despite the stories
they had been fed since childhood of the notorious Danish ways. She hung her head, massaging
the skin that pained her beneath her scarf. 'He's
nothing like him.'

'Well, then,' Marie said sensibly, 'surely it's
worth the risk to try to find the money? It will
take you months to earn back the same amount
if we leave now. We don't even have the coin to
pay the ferryman!'

Gisela's heart curled with despair. Her sister
spoke the truth. For a moment, she longed to
squeeze her eyes tight shut and let the big, fat
tears of failure dribble down her cheeks. Allow
her slight frame to shudder with bleak anguish.
But, no, she would not give in to such weak af-
fections; she was made of stronger stuff than
that. It was the Dane who had nibbled at her
courage, the Dane who she must erase from her
mind in order to regain her confidence and go
out looking for the money.

She picked at a loose piece of skin on her
thumb. 'You're right, Marie. I know you are. But
he's not the only Dane in town and you know
their reputation. It does make me think twice
about venturing out again.'

'But you are clever, Gisela. They're all idiots,

block-headed; you can outwit men like that, just as you've always done.'

'Maybe.' But the slender thread of her voice lacked conviction. There was nothing idiotic about Ragnar; his whole demeanour conveyed a quick-witted intelligence. Those iridescent eyes missed nothing. She sincerely hoped she would never see them again, for she could not shake the feeling that she had met her match with the tall, broad-shouldered Dane.

'Ragnar! Over here!' Spotting his friend appearing through the inn doorway, Eirik raised his tankard in greeting, yelling over to him, 'By Odin, man, where have you been?' A suggestive leer tugged at the side of his mouth. 'I didn't think it would take you this long to tup the maid! I hope she was worth it.'

Ragnar walked towards Eirik, his fellow Danes stepping back with respect for the tall warrior so he could pass through the crowds. The inn was large, the cavernous height topped by an impressive ceiling of thick vaulted arches. The whole company of Danes crowded into the space, as well as many of their Saxon supporters, including women. Heavy acrid smoke belched out from the fire, filling the air and stinging the eyes, coupled with the stench of stale beer and horse dung trodden in from the street. Tallow candles, set in iron holders along the roughly-plastered walls, cast a feeble light on to the ground, creating shadowy corners, dark spots.

Irritation rose in his chest at Eirik's words; of course, his friend would expect him to have bedded the maid, against her will, as justified punishment for what she had done. His loins stirred, mind darkening. The thought of those soft, pliable limbs against his own sent renewed flickers of desire coursing through his veins. He had wanted her. But not like that, not clamped against the wall of some darkened alley. And definitely not against her will. Despite her rudeness, her wayward behaviour, the annoying maid was worth more than that.

'Sit down and tell me everything!' Eirik slurred. His burly arm tightened around the girl on his lap. 'Nay, don't go, sweet, you're fine where you are.' Ragnar threw himself into the empty chair next to his friend, his long legs stretching out across the greasy, ale-stained flagstones.

'Nothing to tell,' he replied brusquely. He was reluctant to share the details of the maid with Eirik, even if the man was his closest friend. It felt like a betrayal, somehow. She was in such a dangerous, exposed position in this town; the last thing he wished to do was to make that position worse. Gisela. Her name whispered around his brain, a gentle torment, distracting him.

'What was she like, eh?' Eirik nudged him roughly in the arm. 'Did she fight back? I bet she did, little wildcat, she looked just the type. Why, I thought she was going to kill me, with that knife in her hand and that look on her face!'

Nausea rose in Ragnar's gullet, a vast tide of revulsion. He wasn't that sort of man, never had been, and Eirik knew that. Normally. It was only because he was so drunk that he was saying such things. He wanted to steer his friend away from the subject of the maid and fast. Someone handed him a tankard of ale and he stared moodily at the pieces of straw floating on the scummy surface.

Eirik studied Ragnar's grim silent profile, his clenched jaw. 'I expect you did what needed to be done to prevent her doing anything like that again. Crazy wench! What on earth possessed her to attack me?'

Sheer desperation, Ragnar thought. Sheer desperation had made her lunge at Eirik, with no thought to her own safety. The maid had been furious that their money had been stolen and a great deal of money by the sound of it. He wondered why they were carrying it, the reason why it was needed. 'I'm not sure.' Picking out a floating piece of straw from his ale, he threw it on the floor.

'This place is a hell-hole,' Eirik said, following the disgruntled flick of Ragnar's fingers. 'You'll be pleased to know that Guthrun, the local Saxon lord, has offered us board and lodging for the night. Good news, eh?'

Ragnar nodded, meeting his friend's eyes, relieved that the subject had been changed from the Norman maid. The less she was spoken about, the better. That way, he could push her from his mind and concentrate on the reason he was here in England. She had been an entrancing distraction, nothing more. He wondered what she was doing now. Were they packing up and moving on, the maid anxious at her unwanted disclosure in front of him? Disquiet lodged in his chest, a heavy sense of foreboding, and, aye, responsibility. The maid was none of his concern and yet he felt responsible.

Eirik stood up, so abruptly that the woman slid from his lap, landing with an outraged squeal on the straw-covered flagstones. 'Let's go then,' he said, ignoring the girl's grumbling threats as she scrambled to her feet, brushing down the front of her gown. 'Guthrun has offered us food and I, for one, am starving.'

'Just us?' Ragnar rose from his seat.

'Some of the men have gone to sleep on the ships.' Eirik reached for his cloak, drawing the heavy felted wool around his shoulders. 'Most of them have walked up to the castle already. Guthrun has a large hay barn that they can bed down in. It's only this rabble left to accompany us.' He stuck his brooch pin through the thick wool to secure the two sides of his cloak, his fingers fumbling with the catch.

Realising their leaders were about to leave, the Danish warriors drained their pewter mugs and wiped their mouths with their sleeves, prepared to follow. Sensing an immediate loss of coin, the innkeeper remonstrated with them, his tone wheedling, imploring them to stay. They ignored his pleas. Tankards set aside, sword belts were hitched up and adjusted, and any willing Saxon maidens were scooped up for the night ahead.

'This way,' said Eirik, as he and Ragnar emerged from the smoky haze on to the cobbled street. A couple of the Danes had taken burning torches from the inn, holding them aloft to light the way. The wavering flame shed sparks through the darkness, along a street lined with cottages. Shutters were latched firmly over the window openings; the townspeople would be huddled around their fires by now.

Eirik caught his foot in an open drain and swore loudly, staggering against Ragnar. 'Nay, nay, I'm fine,' he said, as Ragnar reached for his arm. 'Thor's teeth, that Saxon ale is strong!' Regaining his balance, he led their men with a lurching, disjointed gait towards the castle, visible in the moon-soaked night on a wooded hillock to the south of the town, away from the river.

At the far end, beneath the overhanging gable of a house, a huddle of Saxons appeared, heading towards them, two men holding up what looked like a bundle of clothes, a stretch of dangling rags between them. As they came nearer, Ragnar realised it was a young boy, his feet swinging uselessly above the cobbles, each shoulder gripped in a Saxon's meaty fist. The boy's head hung down, features obscured by a large floppy hat.

'What's going on?' Eirik stepped to one side, his men ranked around him, allowing the Saxons to pass.

'Caught this varmint stealing!' The man nearest them uttered a curse, then spat on the ground. His rotten teeth glowed, stained a brownish yellow in the light of the Danes' torch.

Drunk, uninterested, Eirik threw them no more than a cursory glance, then walked on. Moving out from the shadow of the gabled house, Ragnar made to follow, when a hint of rose perfume caught his nostril, a smell so faint he thought he might have imagined it. But, no, there it was again, a whisper against his brain, tickling his senses. Memory shoved through him, a shard of recognition driving through his mind like a blade of steel. His heart knocked against his ribcage. It was her smell. Gisela.

Ragnar peered at the figure suspended between the two men. Was it her? Or was his conscience playing tricks on him? His eyes raked the coarsely woven tunic, the long baggy braies tied at the ankles and the enormous hat. Delicate hands, fragile wrists, hung down against the nondescript clothing. She might have fooled these slow-witted Saxons, dressed as a lad, but he knew exactly who this was. The clue was in those hands. The urge to reach out and pluck her from the men's cruel grip surged through him; he bunched his fists by his side, to prevent himself from seizing her. Take it slowly, he told himself.

'What are you going to do with...him?' Ragnar's voice was hoarse, tangled in his throat.

'Why, lashes, of course. That's what all the thieves get in this town.'

Ice coagulated in his veins, chilling his thoughts. These men would strip that tunic from her back and see. See that she was a woman and, instead of whipping that perfect skin, they would surely punish her in other ways.

'Surely you should take any wrongdoers to your lord, for him to mete out justice,' Ragnar found himself saying. His speech was oddly truncated, constricted, as if emerging from a narrow gully. He cleared his throat; his palms were sweating. He could not let this happen to her! She might be reckless and naive, but she had no one in this town to stand up for her, no one at all. Apart from him.

Eirik was looking back at him oddly. 'What of it, Ragnar?' he slurred, bracing his shoulder against a lumpy cob wall. 'Don't get involved. Let these townsfolk deal with the lad as they see fit. It's none of our concern.'

It is, he thought. She is. She is my concern. I want her to be my concern. I can't let this happen to her.

Eirik had closed his eyes, his body slumping suddenly against the wall. The skin on his face was ashen, greasy in the flickering torchlight. 'I don't feel well,' he mumbled.

'Take Jarl Eirik up to the castle,' Ragnar rapped out the order to their men. 'And you...' He jabbed a finger at the nearest Saxon. 'Give that lad to me. I will take him up to Lord Guthrun.'

'The thing is, sire...'

'Are you refusing to give me the lad?' Ragnar's voice contained the hint of a threat. Between the two men, Gisela's head had begun to sway; she uttered a faint groan. He had to get her away and soon. Eirik had moved off, men supporting him on either side.

The biggest of the Saxon men eyed Ragnar up, his scowling gaze assessing across the Dane's massive shoulders, the heft of his sword, then sank back, obviously thinking the better of challenging him. Ragnar's superior height and obvious fighting strength was intimidating, oppressive. 'Here, you can have the little thief then, if you insist!' The Saxon shoved the pathetic figure towards Ragnar. 'At least we have our coin back!' He held up a bulging leather bag, swinging it tauntingly, before they all strode off, grumbling to each other.

Ragnar caught Gisela before she slid to the ground, the soft felt hat crumpling against his tunic as her head bumped forward against him. Hitching her up, he braced her against his hip, tipping up the brim of her hat. A purpling bruise marred her cheek; a patch of redness, like a graze, scuffed her forehead, above her right eye.

Shock coursed through him, a jolt of anger, at the damage to her face. He wanted to hit, punch out at the man who had done this to her. 'In Odin's name, you foolish woman, what has happened to you?' he murmured, hauling her against his muscled flank.

Dazed, her mind scrabbling frantically for lucidity, Gisela rolled her head up to the man who held her. She caught a distinctive fragrance: of woodsmoke and the sea. The Dane. Ragnar. Of course it would be him, ready to mock her for her stupidity. Her brain refused to help, re-fused to form any words of protest as he started to march forward purposefully, clamping her to his side. She stumbled alongside him, her body stripped of any ability to fight him. Her legs wobbled, weak and uncoordinated; a threaten-ing nausea rose in her gullet. There was no way she could walk unaided. Shameful as it was, she would have to rely on him if she were to reach the cottage safely.

The street opened out on to a grassy area, sloping up to the lip of a moat that circled Guth-run's castle. In the moonlight, the grass took on a silver sheen, waving in the slight breeze, like long silken hair. Gisela frowned. They had taken a wrong turning, surely. This was not the way back to the cottage.

'I must stop…please,' Gisela gasped, clutching the brawny arm that roped her waist.

Ragnar halted his stride beneath a cluster of oak trees. The castle turrets rose up before them, grimly forbidding against the milky-grey night sky, the shifting cloud. Chinks of light blazed out from some of the arrow slits; raised voices echoed out into the night air as the guards passed each other on the curtain wall. Unlooping his arm from her waist, Ragnar kept one hand on Gisela's shoulder, steadying her.

'What is this place?' she asked, eyeing the high castle walls warily. 'I thought you were taking me back to my father!'

'So you can do the same thing again?' Raising his fingers, Ragnar skimmed the vicious bruise on her cheek. 'I might not be there the next time. You were fortunate that I recognised you when I did.'

'It's not your place to make decisions for me,' she replied grumpily. 'Why, I barely know you. I would have found a way to get free of them.'

Ragnar raised one brindled eyebrow, clearly disagreeing with her. 'How did they catch you?'

She lifted her free shoulder, debating whether to tell him. 'My father could remember the man who had taken the money, a man who he had played cards with before. He knew where he lived.' Speaking the unfamiliar Saxon language, her speech was halting, hesitant, as she struggled to find the right words. 'I went to the cottage; no one was there. The bag with the money was sitting on the table, in plain sight through the window. The door wasn't bolted. I ran in and grabbed it, but as I turned, he…the man walked in. I was unlucky.' She swayed before him, expression mutinous and closed, tipping her chin up in a defiant gesture.

'And that was when he hit you?' Ragnar asked tersely.

She bit her lip. 'Yes. I don't remember much after that.'

'At least your hat stayed on.' He flicked her hat brim with one long forefinger, a disparaging gesture. 'Otherwise they would have seen you were a woman.' He narrowed his eyes, diamond slits in the twilight. 'It might have been a great deal worse for you.'

'The hat's tied underneath my chin with laces,' Gisela protested, throwing him a crooked smile. The bruise on her face throbbed fiercely.

'It was not going to fall off. And my father's clothes cover me adequately.'

Despite his annoyance with her utter foolishness, he chuckled at the fierce determination in her voice. 'You take too many risks.' Her father's clothes were far too big for her, he thought, any idiot could see that. The tunic hemline skirted her knees, the collar gaping dangerously below her scarf that she had tied around her head and neck beneath the hat. The braies had been bunched up and tied around her leather boots to stop her tripping over their longer length.

'Maybe,' she replied smartly, 'but at least I have the money now. That's all that matters. If you give me the bag, I'll be on my way.' She frowned at his empty hand dangling by his side, traced the diagonal leather sling of his sword belt, the sparkling hilt of his sword. 'Where is it?' Her eyes glittered from beneath the shadows of her hat, dark sapphire pools. 'You did take my money back from them, didn't you?' Behind her, a sharp breeze skiffed the waters of the moat, rustling the leaves in the tree canopy above.

How could he tell Gisela that he had cared more about her, about extricating her from the grip of those Saxon oafs, than any bag of money? That would display a concern for her that defied explanation. 'They believed the money belonged to them. Do you think they were just going to hand it over to me on my demand?' The stark moonlight washed against the chiselled planes of his jaw, highlighting the vigorous abandon of his hair. 'No, Gisela, I'm sorry, but they would not have done that.'

She shook her head. 'It was mine...ours!' she spat out on a half-sob, winding her arms around her chest.

'Come with me to Lord Guthrun and tell him what has happened. He will be able to get the money back, rather than you taking the law into your own hands.' Beneath his fingers, the bones in her shoulder were fragile, delicate. This woman chanced with her life as if she were a soldier in battle, rather than the sweet bundle of femininity that stood before him. Did she have any idea how beautiful she was, even dressed as she was now, like a lad? How desirable?

She wrenched from his hold, chewing on the dewy fullness of her bottom lip. 'I can't do that.' Her voice was subdued. 'I cannot go to Lord Gurthrun.'

'Because...'

She stared at him helplessly. 'Because it would draw too much attention to the three of us.' Lifting her head, she jerked it to one side, almost in challenge, almost as if she were daring him to run to the Saxons and tell them about her.

He laughed softly. 'With your antics this evening, I think you have drawn enough attention to yourself already.'

Gisela stiffened, picking fretfully at the skin around the base of her thumb. Her nails shone out like luminous shells. The urge to grab her hand, to enfold those nervous fingers in his own, swept over him. 'I have to go and get it. Where did those men go? Do you know where they were headed?' A sudden gust of wind pressed the loose fabric of her braies against her legs, revealing the slim curve of her hips and thighs.

Swallowing at the dryness in his throat, Ragnar peered at her. 'Are you out of your mind? Those men will kill you. What was your father thinking? Letting you go out again, into the night, after what happened today on the marshes!'

'The blow to my father's head has made him ill. He has no idea I went out again this evening and I have no wish to worry him; he has suffered enough.'

Anger coursed through him, a volatile flame. He stepped forward, gathering up the front of her tunic in his fist, hauling her against him, forcing her to look up at him. 'And what about you, Gisela? Don't you think you have suffered enough?' He was furious with her, furious at her foolhardiness, her misplaced bravery. 'You need to know when to stop fighting, Gisela.'

'No,' she murmured. The taut fabric of her tunic pulled against her spine; his knuckles grazed the smooth curve of her chin. 'I will never stop fighting. You've no idea what's at stake.'

Above Ragnar's head, a faint breath of air ruffled the leaves, a skittering sound, like water rippling. 'Then tell me,' he said. His voice softened, lowered to a muted burr. 'Tell me what you risk everything for.'

Chapter Seven

Her eyes raked his jawline, square cut below the generous curve of his mouth. Grooves ran down from each cheekbone to his chin, etched deep, as if drawn by a formidable hand. In the moonlit shadows, his expression was difficult to read. Could she trust him? The man was a stranger to her, a Dane who had come to this country to help the Saxons. She barely knew him and yet, on this day, they had been flung together, a wild unexpected pairing that had pushed her normally sound judgement off course. How on earth could she tell him all that had happened? How her family had ended up in this Saxon town with only two bags of coin to their name?

But before she could even make a decision, Ragnar jerked his chin up, listening intently. He raised a finger to his lips: a warning. Voices carried towards them. Two men appeared, following the track from the castle, carrying torches to light their way. They grinned at Ragnar. Eirik's men.

'Eirik thought you might need some help with this one.'

Releasing his grip on her tunic, Ragnar tugged the brim of Gisela's hat down firmly, making sure her face was well hidden. He turned to the men, shielding her with the bulk of his body. 'I can manage,' he replied curtly.

'We'll take him for you, sire,' the younger Dane offered. The torchlight gleamed against the copper rivets set at intervals along his leather chest straps. 'The town court sits tomorrow in the castle. Lord Guthrun intends to deal with him then.'

Gisela stood quietly behind Ragnar, struggling with the tongue-twisting Norse sentences, but managing to decipher the gist of their conversation. Tracing the powerful line of Ragnar's spine, the breadth of his shoulders, she waited for him to dismiss the men. Fronds of his bright hair brushed his tunic collar, silky, like gold embroidery thread. Once they had disappeared, she could tell him why her family needed the money and he would have to let her go. There would be no reason for him to keep her with him any more.

'We'll go up together.' Ragnar half-turned towards her, fingers circling her arm, a sinewy bracelet pulling her slight figure against his muscled flank.

Gisela glowered at him, giving her head the smallest shake. Surely Ragnar held superiority over these men? Why had he not fobbed them off with some story, then given her a little push in the small of her back and told her to get lost? The Saxons had her money. She had gained nothing by this whole night's escapade. But he forced her to walk beside him. As she tugged moodily against his grip, his strong fingers dug into the soft muscle of her upper arm, an uncompromising answer. Her heart plummeted with anxiety. Had she misread the tone of his voice when he had asked her to confide in him earlier? Doubt coiled in her gut, churning incessantly.

As Ragnar talked to the men, she stumbled miserably over the tussocky grass towards the gatehouse. The four turrets created forbidding, angular shapes against the soft blue twilight, looming up into the velvety sky, studded with twinkling stars. Her heart pounded with fear—what did he intend to do with her? An overwhelming sense of betrayal lumped on her shoulders, weighing her down, yet, if she thought about it, the only thing that had betrayed her was her own good sense. Duped by his interest in her, the low velvet rumble of his questions, she had started to think that she would tell him everything. It had been a long time since such a man had paid her such attention and, like a misguided fool, she had fallen for that attention. The touch of his lips. She shuddered, remembering. His mouth had been a taste of heaven, the promise of another world that she could only dream about. A world to which no man would ever take her. Of that, she was certain.

As they crossed the wooden drawbridge that led to the gatehouse, the Danish soldiers drew ahead to speak to the castle guards. Tugging on Ragnar's sleeve, Gisela tipped her eyes up to his face. 'Why didn't you let me go?' A plaintive note entered her speech. 'You could have fed your men some story about me!'

'Keep your voice down.' Ragnar shortened his step, walking more slowly across the planked drawbridge. He eyed his fellow Danes, already up ahead at the gatehouse. From the shadows beneath the raised iron grille of the portcullis, they beckoned to him. 'And trust me,' he added.

Trust him? How could she trust him? She couldn't even trust herself when he was with

her. This man who smelled of brine, the salt of
the sea, who carried the wind and waves in the
strong set of his shoulders, in his long, athletic
stride. He had barrelled into this difficult, unstable time of her life with such powerful vitality that she was unable to think straight in his
presence. The last thing she needed was this
man muddling her mind, pushing her off course.
But at this precise moment, she had little choice
in the matter.

A grizzled Saxon guard stepped from the
stone arch of the gatehouse, peering closely at
Gisela from beneath his helmet. 'Down there,'
he said gruffly to Ragnar, indicating a door
cut into the gatehouse wall. He handed Ragnar a large black key and Ragnar pushed her
into the dark doorway. Flickers of panic laced
her heart. Keeping one hand on the wall for
balance, Gisela worked her way down the tiny
spiral staircase, her feet sliding carefully down
each uneven step. She had no wish to fall. As she
reached the bottom, she realised that Ragnar's
hand had been on her shoulder the whole time.

Faced with an iron gate, a dank chamber
beyond, the swirling fear in her chest reared
upwards, consuming her, squeezing the air cruelly in her lungs. He was going to lock her up!
Lurching around in terror, she raised her fists to

Ragnar's chest. 'No! You cannot do this to me!'
In her panic, she reverted to speaking French,
the harried speech tumbling out of her mouth,
garbled, unrestricted. 'Ragnar, please! You cannot think…!' Her knee bumped inadvertently
against his and she stepped back clumsily, her
hips bumping into the gate. The bars pressed
coldly against her rump, preventing any further
movement backwards.

'It's the only way to keep you safe, from my
own men and from the Saxons. It won't be for
long,' he said quietly, replying in French. His
voice smoothed over her, a honeyed lilt. 'Trust
me. I will come back for you.'

'But how…?'

His hand reached over her head, pushing open
the gate. The iron bars creaked inwards on rusty
hinges. Twisting around, Gisela stared into the
chamber in despair. The walls, cut from huge
stone blocks, were slick with moisture; ferns, a
bright, iridescent green, frothed out of the gaps
between the stones. There was no straw to sit
on, no furniture. A huge puddle lay in one corner, the surface glimmering ominously. Placing
his hands on her shoulders, Ragnar levelled his
eyes with hers. His breath fanned her cheek.
'You have to trust me, Gisela,' he whispered.
'Stay here for the moment.' Turning her, he gave

her a little push and she staggered forward into the darkness, as he locked the gate behind her.

Damn him! She wanted to cry out to him to stay, to sit in this awful place with her, but already she heard his swift stride take him to the top of the steps, heard him laugh with his fellow men. Was that it? Would he leave her here, at the mercy of the Saxon Lord Guthrun? How dare he do such a thing! Her hands screwed into fierce little fists, wanting to kill him, wanting him to come back. *Trust me*, he had said. And he had said it in French, speaking the language as if he had been born in the country itself. She clung to his words like a lifeline, standing in the middle of the cellar, humiliated, cold and alone.

A stern voice budged through her brain, speaking French. Then again, driving through the thick layers of sluggish unconsciousness. 'Gisela! Wake up!' A hand on her shoulder, shaking her roughly.

She had tried to sleep. Avoiding the damp walls, she had curled up from where she had stood, bringing her knees up to her chest, wrapping her arms tightly around her calves, trying to keep any warmth in the middle of her body. And she had partly succeeded, falling into a troubled, fitful sleep, a sleep beset by dream fragments, some bewildering, some benign. She woke with a start, jerking awake as if someone had kicked her in the spine. For a moment, she lay there, her befuddled mind sweeping across the stone walls, the bare floor, failing to comprehend where she was and how she had reached this place.

'Gisela!' the voice said again.

She rolled over, rocking straight into the roped thighs of the man who knelt beside her. Ragnar. His fresh, invigorating scent, the smell of wind-whipped water, cut through the damp musty odours of her prison. Embarrassed by the physical contact, she shuffled back, sitting up abruptly, scrubbing at her face with one fist. The bruise beneath her eye smarted painfully. Her hat had fallen off and she groped across the chill stone floor, trying to find it.

'Here,' Ragnar said, handing it to her. He had removed his leather surcoat and woollen tunic, and wore only a linen shirt and braies. His long boots were laced up to his knees. The muscled hollow of his throat cast a shadow beneath the slashed neckline of his shirt. His pulse beat strongly beneath tanned skin. What would it be like, to place her finger to that spot on his neck, to feel the heat of his blood vibrating beneath her fingers?

'What are you doing here?' she gasped, replying in her native language, slipping back easily into the lilting vowels. There was no point in pretending any longer. He knew she was a Norman. Ragnar's accent was perfect, with no trace of a foreign lilt; she wondered where he had learned her language.

'I told you I would come back.'

'I didn't believe you.' Doubt clogged her tone. She jammed the hat back down over her headscarf. In her lap, her hands fiddled with the leather binding that secured the end of her plait.

'You thought I would leave you here?' His eyes narrowed on her, faint white lines crinkling out from the outer corners.

'Yes,' she replied. Her voice was small, forlorn.

His fingers shot out, curled around her chin. A fleeting gesture, intended as reassurance. 'I would never have done that.' His hand dropped away, to rest on his massive thighs.

'But I don't know you well enough to know that.' Gisela fought the urge to close her eyes, to savour the memory of that warm caress against her skin. 'I don't know you at all.'

'True,' he said. Ragnar stood up, a swift, powerful movement. 'Come with me now,' he said, offering her his hand to help her up. 'The guard may wake up at any time.'

She seized his fingers, scrambling easily to her feet. 'Then how do you have the key to let me out? Surely you had to ask him?'

Ragnar grinned. 'I never gave it back, after I left you.' His eyes blazed with devilish light. 'And they never asked me for it.' He paused in the doorway, his brilliant eyes searching for her in the dim shadows. 'We must stop speaking in French now, Gisela, so that others do not hear.'

She followed him up the spiral staircase, past the sleeping guard and across a cobbled bailey. So grateful was she to be free of that horrible prison, she failed to question Ragnar's direction. The place was deserted, quiet. Dogs slept in a pack in one corner, their silky pelts leaning up against each other for warmth. One dog raised his head, ears pulled back, sniffing the air, watching them as they passed. Ducking his bright head, Ragnar pushed open a low wooden door and started to climb another staircase.

Gisela stopped at the bottom of the steps, one hand resting on the rope that served as a handrail. Exhaustion dragged on the bottom of her eyelids. She wanted to sleep and sleep for days. Her muscles ached from lying on the cold floor of the prison. 'Where are you taking me?' Her voice held a weak protest, echoing dully up the stairwell. 'Aren't you going to let me go now?'

Ragnar swivelled his leather boots on the angled step, the dipped centre worn away by the hundreds of feet that had gone up and down over the years. Gisela swayed below him, huge blue eyes shining up like luminous discs in the shadowy light.

'It's too dangerous to try to take you out at the moment,' he lied. 'The gatehouse is heavily guarded.'

'You said there was only one soldier,' she protested. 'Surely it wouldn't be that difficult?'

He hoped that, in the darkness, she failed to see the flush he felt cross his face.

'I think we have to be careful.' His mind searched frantically for a coherent reason to keep her with him.

'But the guards would accept any story you told them,' she persisted. 'I don't understand why you are keeping me here. The Saxons have our money and my father and sister will be frantic.'

'In Thor's name, woman, you need to keep your mouth shut!' he growled at her, exasperated by her constant questioning. He seized her hand to pull her up the stairs. 'Save it until we reach my chamber.'

'Your chamber?' She reared against his hold, teetering backwards. 'I'm not going there!'

Ragnar cursed loudly, losing patience. Bending down, he grabbed her beneath her knees, one hand against her back, deliberately knocking her off balance to sweep her up against his chest. 'Yes, you are!' he said, striding up the staircase. Clearly furious with him, her feet flailing on a level with her head, Gisela dug her fingers into his shirt, bunching the linen fabric as if to stop herself bumping against him.

'Dieu! Vous êtes le Diable!' she cursed beneath her breath in French. *God, you are the Devil!*

His mouth twitched in amusement as he set one booted foot against his chamber door and kicked it open. It did him good to hear his mother's language, even if it was only to be cursed. He strode in, dumping Gisela down on the bed furs. Placing his hands on the carved posts holding up the linen canopy, he leaned the bulk of his body forward over her sprawling figure. His knees bumped against the wooden footboard of the bed. 'I told you, don't speak your language unless we are totally alone. It's not safe.'

After the chill in the stairwell, the dank stone

walls heavy with claggy moisture, the warmth in his chamber engulfed them like a balm. Coals glowed in a charcoal brazier, throwing out radiant waves of heat; candle flame winked from niches hollowed into the stone walls. A hazy, ambient light shuddered through the space. Gisela sat up moodily, pushing her scarf away from her face. 'How can you speak French anyway? You, a Dane,' she burst out belligerently, still clearly annoyed at his manhandling.

'My mother is French,' he explained. 'I speak it, at home, with her.' And my sister, he thought suddenly, a pang scything through him. Although he couldn't remember the last time his sister had spoken anything, Norse or French, her pale, silent figure wandering around their castle in Ribe, trailed by the arthritic figure of their old nurse.

'Your mother…is French,' she repeated his words, incredulous. 'She married a Dane.' Outrage seared her voice. 'How *could* she?'

He laughed at her astonishment, flexing his fingers against the carved wood. 'Very easily, as it happens. She loves him.'

'But to betray her own country?' The question spilled out of Gisela's mouth before she had time to consider the implication.

Ragnar's eyes darkened. 'Be careful, Gisela,

you are talking of things of which you have no knowledge.'

Shame crossed her face; her knuckles digging into the pelt beneath her hips. 'I'm sorry, Ragnar. You're right, I shouldn't have said that.' Searching his stern features for some element of forgiveness for her harsh words, she threw him a tentative smile.

'You speak before you think,' he replied. 'You can't keep quiet and you won't do as you're told.' Despite his admonishment, his eyes twinkled. He turned away, shutting the door, then settling the wooden bar across to secure it.

She smoothed her hands slowly over her thighs, letting them drift to the side of her hips. Her slim legs stuck out across the coverlet in front of her, boots sticking up incongruously. The leather toes were scuffed, dulled with a layer of dried mud. 'If I had always done what I had been told to do, then my life would be very different from now.'

'Yes,' Ragnar agreed, moving back to the bed. 'Your life would be better.'

'Nay,' she replied quietly, her voice hitching with emotion. She twisted the curling end of one plait with agitated fingers. 'It would be far worse.'

Shadows deepened the blue of her eyes, her

expression stricken. Ragnar folded his arms, right flank propped against the bedpost. Beneath the gauzy whiteness of his shirt, the flat plane of his torso was visible, etched ridges of honed muscle. 'Then tell me,' he said. 'Tell me what happened to you. Tell me why you need that money.'

'Will you let me go if I tell you?'

No. The single word barged through his brain: a certainty. No, he would not let her go. Not just yet, anyway. 'Maybe,' he replied vaguely.

She grimaced, her mouth twisting down at the corners. 'I suppose I have no choice.' Reluctance traced her voice.

'You do not,' Ragnar replied firmly.

'We are travelling north to pay a ransom,' she began, her tone hesitant. 'My brother, Richard, is a prisoner at Ralph de Pagenal's castle and the money is needed to set him free. Half of that money was stolen from my father tonight. He had gone out this evening, in the hope of… winning at dice to make up the deficit. We didn't have quite enough, you see.' The words stalled in her mouth; she picked at a ragged patch on her braies, then at a thread of dried blood on the scratch on her wrist.

'So you were working at the salt pans to make some more money.'

She nodded. 'The ferry across the river is expensive.'

'And when do you have to deliver this ransom?'

'By Michaelmas. If we don't deliver by then he… Ralph de Pagenal will kill Richard…my brother.' Her voice wobbled dangerously. She touched her neck through her scarf, her fingers hesitant.

'Ralph de Pagenal.' Ragnar recognised the name. 'One of King Williams's barons. I've heard of him. But why does he hold your brother? There must be a reason.'

'He wanted to marry my sister, Marie.' Her voice slowed, reluctant to share more details.

'And…?' he prompted.

Gisela sighed. 'The man is notorious for his cruelty. Marie refused him, but he wasn't happy with that. People don't refuse Ralph de Pagenal. One night, he and his men came to our home, our new home, in England.' Her voice faltered, shadows of memory flickering across her face. 'He set fire to the turret to drive us from our beds. And as we ran out…' She bit her lip, her hand clasping her throat. 'He grabbed Marie. He tried to take her by force.'

'But he didn't succeed,' Ragnar concluded,

shoving one hand through his unruly hair. 'Did your father's guards stop him?'

'Something like that,' Gisela responded vaguely, unwilling to speak the truth, to detail the horrifying details of that night. 'De Pagenal then went to King William to plead his case. He hoped the King would force Marie to marry him. But William decided that we should pay our way out of the marriage and our brother was sent to live with Ralph de Pagenal to make sure we kept our word.'

Ragnar let out a long, low whistle. 'And you say the Danes are barbarians,' he said. Her eyes shimmered with unspent tears; instinctively, he reached over, catching one shining pearl of liquid on his thumb before it trailed down her cheek. The skin over her bruise was threaded with blood, purplish, sore-looking.

She shivered at his glancing touch, biting her lip as his hand fell away, then pulled her shoulders straight beneath her baggy tunic. 'Marie has suffered terribly. She feels she has pulled this whole sorry mess on to our family. She speaks constantly of relenting and marrying de Pagenal.'

'But you will not let her.'

'No. The man is a monster.' Clumping her hands into small fists, Gisela scrubbed furiously at her wet eyes. As if suddenly making a decision, she shuffled clumsily to the edge of the bed, dropping her feet to the floor. Fatigue daubed blue patches beneath her eyes as she stood up; her movements were slow, hampered by tiredness. 'So now you know the whole story.' She tipped her chin up to him, eyes flashing with defiance. 'You have no reason to keep me here any longer. Let me go.'

The maid was dead on her feet, Ragnar thought. His arms itched to take her close, to clasp her against his chest and tell her everything would be all right, that it would work out. But the devil in his ear told him that was not the only thing he wanted to do. How easy it would be to push her back on those soft furs, to strip off those voluminous braies and tunic and savour the sweet taste of her flesh against his own. He took a deep breath; his diaphragm shuddered with longing, forcing his wayward brain to concentrate on what she had said.

'If I let you go, what will you do?' he asked. The flame of a stubby wax candle, burning low in a niche beside the bed, guttered and wavered, casting flickering shadows across the room. Somewhere, buried in the recesses of his mind, a plan formulated.

She lifted her shoulders, a forlorn, despairing gesture. 'We have no hope of raising that amount of coin before Michaelmas. So I must go to Ralph de Pagenal with nothing and plead for my brother's life.' Hope drained from her voice. 'Whatever that might entail,' she added dully.

Odin's teeth, no! What was the maid saying? That she would offer herself to save her brother? Denial ripped through him. The ghastly thought of a Norman lord, slack flesh rolling across her soft limbs, with no grace or gentleness, punctured his vision. A sickening coil of nausea rose in his belly. He thumped the bedpost with his fist. 'Nay, Gisela, you cannot do that!'

She jerked back at his reaction, frowning deeply. 'There is no other way,' she replied. 'What else can I do?'

He cleared his throat, attempting to moderate his behaviour. His plan gathered strength. 'I have a suggestion,' he said slowly. 'You're not going to like it, but it certainly would be better than losing your virginity for the sake of your brother.'

Her head shot up at his blunt assumption of her innocence. 'Do you have to talk about me like that?' she replied testily.

Ragnar squeezed his fists together, one thumb kneading his knuckles. 'It's true, isn't it?'

A heightened flush crossed her cheeks. She

glared at him mutinously before changing the subject. 'What are you proposing?'

'Eirik and I will cross the river tomorrow and head north to Jorvik. Ralph de Pagenal's castle lies on the route to the city. Come with me and I can take you to him. You can't go on your own.'

'My father will come with me.'

'He's not fit to travel, or provide any sort of protection. Your sister will have to stay and care for him. You would be travelling on your own, not a good idea for any woman in these troubled times, but especially not for a Norman woman such as you.'

'But I can't come with you! It's…unseemly!'

Ragnar laughed, the sound dry, uncompromising. 'I think we passed that point long ago. In the last few hours, you've spent more time in my company, alone, than with your own father. You must put social conventions aside. Think of your brother.'

She bowed her head, her gaze tracing a rough knot in the floorboards, a scuff on the top of her leather boot. The string holding her braies tight to her ankles was starting to unravel. Cloudy with fatigue, her brain struggled to cope with Ragnar's words. A seed of hope, drifting in her gut, sprang slowly into life. Might this be a solution? To have this man, this tall broad-shouldered warrior, by her side when she faced Ralph de Pagenal was simply astonishing, un-believable. She struggled to understand why he would even offer, why he was prepared to do such a thing, for her, a complete stranger.

But there was one problem that he hadn't foreseen. She sighed. 'But...how can you help me? You're a Dane and the Normans hate the Danes. De Pagenal would realise what you are and probably kill you.'

'I don't think so,' he replied swiftly, quashing her speech. 'The Normans consider the Danes and the Saxons to be the same, as an irritant in their path for the conquest of this country. I doubt very much that de Pagenal would be able to tell the difference.'

She considered him doubtfully: the way he held himself in front of her, legs braced apart, crackling energy, every limb, every muscle honed to a point of fighting perfection. He stood out, head and shoulders above other men, his bronze-coloured hair like a flag, drawing all eyes towards him. Unmissable. Devastating.

He crouched down beside her, lifting her hands from her lap. 'It will work out, Gisela. I will take you to the Norman and we will fetch your brother back.'

Raising her head listlessly, Gisela fixed him with her huge blue eyes. The skin on his hands was rough, warm against her own, as he enfolded her chill fingers. 'I... I'm not sure...' she uttered, pulling her hands from his to press her fingers against her eyes. 'God, I... I'm so tired. I can't decide what to do. My mind...' Her voice trailed off in despair, too exhausted to formulate any more words.

Ragnar saw the wilting of her shoulders, her spine sagging. 'You need to sleep, Gisela,' he said, refusing to acknowledge the sense of victory swirling in his heart. This was the only option open to her, but he would give her time to come to that conclusion by herself. 'Decide on the morrow.' Stepping carefully, as if any sudden movement would startle her, he led her around to the side of the bed. Half-asleep already, she sat down abruptly, then lay back on to the coverlet. Ragnar lifted her feet up carefully on to the bed, untying the strings around her ankles so he could pull off her boots. He chucked them on the floor. Leaving her scarf wrapped around her head, he removed her hat. Her eyes were already closed.

Chapter Eight

Gisela opened her eyes. Beneath the thick swathe of her linen scarf, sweat trickled uncomfortably down her neck. Emerging from the foggy wreathes of sleep, she struggled to comprehend her whereabouts. Weak moonlight from the uncovered windows lit the chamber with a shadowy darkness. The candles had burned down to waxy stumps, extinguished; a faint glow wavered in the depths of the charcoal brazier. Her eyes moved hazily up to a gathered canopy of linen above the bed; fur pelts and a pillow filled with goose down lay beneath her. Over by the door, a large man sprawled on a pallet bed. Her heart lurched, whiskers of sensation flicking along her veins, jabbing at her memory. Her jumbled brain slotted details quickly into place. The Dane. Ragnar.

He lay on his left flank, facing her, the chiselled angles of his face emerging through the gloom. His massive arms, thick ropes of honed muscle, crossed over his chest, wrinkling the gauzy fabric of his shirt; his legs were so long that his bare feet dangled over the end of the bed. Ridged, sinewy ligaments splayed out from his ankles to his toes. Big thigh muscles traced an obvious curve beneath his tight-fitting braies. His leather boots, along with his belt and sword, had been thrown in a messy heap on the polished floorboards.

Her eyes roamed over him, guiltily, greedily, absorbing the beautiful details of his impressive frame, savouring his honed physique like a gift. Had she ever seen a man like him before? Nay, of course not. He was incomparable, larger than life, his vitality and physique able to fill a chamber, a great hall. Eyes were drawn to him, attentions snared, even, as now, when he was asleep. At her home in France, when her mother had been alive, there had been household knights and a succession of visiting nobles: potential suitors for her and Marie. Not one had affected her as strongly as this one, this wild Norseman with his unruly bronze hair and quick easy smile.

Rolling her head on the pillow, Gisela sighed. How could she have fallen asleep like that, in front of him? She only had the vaguest recollection of stretching out on the bed, of Ragnar lifting her feet. He must have removed her boots; she wiggled her toes in their stockings, blushing in the darkness at the imagined intimacy. His hands moving deftly over her feet, her shins. She cursed herself for even thinking about this in such a way, attributing such meaning, such promise, to Ragnar's simple actions. He thought she was a fool and would think nothing of it; she would do well to think the same. Drawing her brows together, she frowned. So why, in heaven's name, had he offered to travel north with her? He had made it perfectly obvious that she was nothing but an encumbrance. It simply made no sense.

Twisting her neck from one side to the other, she stretched the tense muscles at the top of her spine. Perspiration clogged her scalp. She longed to wash, to splash fresh water across her face. Over by the window, an earthenware jug sat on an oak coffer, with a bowl alongside. Chewing hesitantly on the inside of her cheek, she turned back to Ragnar's prone form, watching the breath rise and fall in his chest, a deep, regular sound. He was sound asleep and the thought of the cool water against her skin was irresistible. Very, very slowly she eased herself into a seated position on the mattress, sliding her hips sideways to inch her way off the bed.

She tiptoed towards the oak coffer, stocking-covered feet whispering across the floorboards. The large braies borrowed from her father flapped around her slim legs, the extra length hooking around her toes, threatening to trip her up. She reached out for the jug; the vessel was heavy, but she managed to lift it with both hands, pouring the water carefully into the bowl. Darting one further glance at Ragnar, she removed the tight bindings of her headscarf from around her head and neck, almost crying with relief as she placed the rumpled linen on a low stool by the coffer.

A cloth hung over the side of the bowl. Submerging the lightweight material into the water, Gisela wrung it out, smoothing the cool, damp fabric over her face. Her eyelashes fluttered downwards at the sweet sensation, the chill water trickling down, soaking the gaping collar of her father's tunic. Confident that Ragnar continued to sleep soundly, she untied the leather bindings at the bottom of her plaits, combing her fingers through the silky strands to release her hair. Turning sideways, she bent over from the waist, sweeping her hair forward from the nape of her neck to fall like a shimmering curtain before her. Pushing damp fingers through her hair, she worked from her scalp outwards, shaking dust and dirt from the glossy tendrils. Her hair brushed against the floorboards: a light tickling sound, like a mouse's pattering feet.

'Gisela.' The guttural voice echoed beside her, driving deep into her solar plexus.

Gasping, she straightened up in panic, hair tumbling around her shoulders in a silky mass. The long curling ropes, the colour of pale sand, swept the length of her spine, touching her hips, spilled forward over her shoulders. Her long hair would cover her scar, but she patted the silky tresses into place beneath her ear, over her exposed neck, just to make certain. Droplets of water pooled into the hollow of her throat, glistening in the brazier's diminished light. 'What are you doing?' she asked jerkily, plucking her scarf up from the stool.

'I...' It was as if Ragnar struggled to comprehend her question. A croak obscured his voice, as he seemed to force himself to focus his thoughts. 'You woke me up, Gisela.' Sleep had pulled the neckline of his shirt awry. The gauzy linen was rumpled and creased; red-gold hairs sprinkled his chest, below the tanned dip of his throat.

Wadding the scarf between her trembling

hands, Gisela wrenched her eyes away from the exposed skin at his throat, the tantalising definition of honed muscle beneath his shirt. 'I couldn't sleep,' she explained. 'I was too hot. So when I saw the water jug...' She shrugged her shoulders. 'I'm sorry if I disturbed you.'

She could feel a single bead of water trickling over her cheek, tracking across the satin patina of her skin, the vague patch of bruising. His hand reached out, cupping her jaw: a gesture of reassurance. 'Nay, you didn't disturb me. I was awake already.'

'What?' Her fingers flicked up to snare his wrist, to pull his hand away from her face. Blood pumped through corded sinew, pulsing against her grip. His loose shirt sleeve had fallen back, revealing the sculptured muscle of his forearm, the fine red-gold hairs. 'Were you watching me, all this time?' To her irritation, her breath hitched fractionally, her question losing all power.

'I was,' Ragnar admitted. His heated glance punched into her.

Warmth swelled through her, unbidden, at his simple admission: a strange wobbling feeling that surged upwards from the very depths of her belly. Strength leached from her knees. She should have been outraged, angry, that this man had been observing her without her knowledge. In desperation, she tried to summon up the appropriate response, the tongue-lashing that he deserved, but only succeeded in tracing the carved features of his handsome face, staring like a dumbstruck idiot. As if her short sleep had erased all the feistiness from her body, leaving her soft and malleable. *Vulnerable.*

'You should have turned to face the wall and given me some privacy,' she pronounced finally. Her protest sounded weak, ineffectual. 'But then, I suppose I should expect nothing less from a Dane, who has no idea of chivalry.'

His hand fell from her jaw and he laughed, a long low rumble emanating from his chest. 'You cannot resist, can you?' He raised his eyebrows. 'Taking the slightest opportunity to dig the knife in, I mean. That barbed tongue of yours could flay a man alive!'

'It has been known to do so,' Gisela snapped in response. Her memory tacked back in an instant. In France, with her father away campaigning, she had taken on the management of their estates with the help of a bailiff. She had worked hard, too, buying in stock, planning the crops and hiring the extra hands needed at harvest time. Sadness trickled through her: how far the family had fallen since those prosperous days.

With an unconscious toss of her head, Gisela lifted her arms, sweeping her heavy hair into a bundle on one side of her head, intending to braid the long tresses into a single plait.

Her movement revealed the silvery line stretching across her skin.

Ragnar stiffened. 'What is that?' His voice jabbed out. 'Did you hurt yourself?' He leaned close to her, staring hard at the scar.

'It's nothing,' she mumbled, clamping her hand across her neck. How could she have forgotten? She, Gisela, who was always so careful? But it was him, damn him, and his stupid confounding presence that made her forget, made common sense drop away! Fumbling with her scarf, she tried to wrap it around her head, but the fabric seemed unusually unwieldy, uncooperative.

Plucking the scarf from her hands, Ragnar held it away from her. 'That looks like more than nothing to me,' he said grimly.

Hot, salty tears filled her eyes. 'Give me my scarf back, please,' she said. 'It's an old wound that I scarce think about.'

His gaze glittered over her, incisive, missing nothing. 'You think about it all the time,' Ragnar said softly. 'What happened to you?'

She glared at him, chewing viciously on her

bottom lip. Why was she even trying to hide the scar from him? He meant nothing to her and she, as he had made perfectly clear, was a mere irritant. The air left her lungs slowly: a shuddering exhalation. 'I told you what de Pagenal did…'

'The fire beneath your chamber.'

She nodded. 'Yes, but when we ran out, when he tried to take Marie…' Her voice slowed and she wrapped her slim arms about her body, hugging herself, as if for comfort. 'He reached down from the saddle and grabbed her. But I grabbed her back, hanging on to her clothes, her hair, anything to prevent her from being taken. She was screaming. Then some of our household knights came running, to see them off. But not before…' Her voice trailed away and she stared at him numbly, bereft of speech.

'What did he do, Gisela?' It was as if he wanted to understand, to comprehend what compelled her to take such risks in her life, what drove her to jeopardise her safety.

'De Pagenal pulled his sword and slashed down, trying to force me to release my hold on Marie. The sword point caught my neck. But then his horse reared up and we both fell back and managed to crawl away.' She blinked, remembering. Her hand clamped to her neck, blood dripping through her fingers, a household knight half-carrying her back to the safety of their castle. Ralph de Pagenal cursing, shouting threats, as he wheeled his horse around, he and his men riding away.

Ragnar cursed, his eyes metallic bright, honing in on her wan features. 'He could have killed you.' His hands were shaking, sweat pooling in his palms; he tucked them behind his back. A sudden fear gripped him: the thought of Gisela losing her life at the hands of that oaf. How had he come to care for her so much?

'It wouldn't have come to that.'

'That man knew what he was doing. He's a trained knight! To cut at that point on the neck, if the blade had gone any deeper, you would have bled to death.'

Her face turned a stark white; she swayed. 'No, no, it wasn't that bad. It wasn't like that.'

He had frightened her. Stupidly, he had voiced his own fears, with no thought to how terrifying they would sound to her. She had no knowledge of the battlefield, of the ferocious brutality of knights when called to war. For her, to realise the full horrific extent of the situation would be to acknowledge the fact that she had nearly died. 'Yes, you're probably right,' he conceded, making an effort to lighten his tone. 'After all, you were there and I was not.'

'You were not,' she confirmed. Her eyelashes dipped fractionally. How different the situation would have been, if Ragnar had been there, if she had met him before this whole nightmare had started. He would have protected her, of that she was certain, like he was protecting her now. From the truth of the situation. 'It was worth it,' Gisela said, her voice gaining a modicum of strength. 'For we saved Marie from the most awful marriage.'

'*You* saved her. You did it by yourself.' Admiration juddered through him. As the first dull fingers of early morning light filtered through the window, he trailed his fingertip along the scar, the faint silvery line stitching across her skin. The pulse behind her ear bumped steadily, quickening beneath his fingers. Desire slanted through him, a whip of sensation.

Breath, wadded tight in her chest, hushed out of her at his touch. The heat in the chamber thickened, pressing on her in warm, downy layers. Blood skipped along her veins, gathering pace. His fingers tickled lightly, feathers across her skin. She flinched, but didn't draw away. As if she didn't want to.

'The scar isn't pretty, but it's a small price to pay for my sister's safety,' her voice stuttered out. 'I don't want your pity.'

'This isn't pity,' he growled. His fingers dug into her hair, the glorious strands lacing through his fingers as he drew her mouth up to his. His lips grazed over hers, fleeting, then pressing harder, deepening the contact.

'I…' she managed to gasp out. Was she about to protest? She wasn't sure. Her mind seemed bereft of thought or function.

'You talk too much.' Ragnar's mouth claimed hers, a fiery brand against her tender skin. His arm snared her spine, winching her close; she fell against him, breasts knocking tight against his hard chest. Her knees bumped against his, her soft thighs pressing into the solid muscle of his legs. The faint cry of reason clamoured in her head, begging her to stop, but she chased it away. *If I died now*, she thought suddenly, *then I wouldn't care, for I would have the memory of this man's lips upon mine to take me to my grave, and be with me for ever.*

Heart drumming dangerously, her neglected soul cried out for his touch, stuttering with delight as his hand trailed downwards, fingers sprawling over her breasts, savouring the softness. Her arms flailed out, seeking purchase, then settled on his wide shoulders, clinging desperately, hanging on to him, a raft on a storm-tossed sea. No man had ever touched her thus, no man had ever held her with such desire, as if he wanted to lie with her. As he bent over her, her slim supple figure curving under his, they staggered back together, her legs banging violently against the oak coffer.

The water jug wobbled precariously, then tipped sideways. The vessel fell to the floor with a tremendous crash, littering the polished wood with shards of earthenware. Water spread out, a dark stain creeping slowly outwards.

Wrenching her mouth from his, she lowered her head defiantly, avoiding his lips. Her heart banged wildly against her ribs. Her eyelashes fluttered downwards, shudders coursing through her from the impact of his lips upon hers. What had she been thinking? Was she mad? Ragnar didn't care for her. He had told her as much when he had helped her with her father. *If I had wanted to, I would have taken you. Don't flatter yourself.* His past words scoured her self-esteem, trampling her confidence. She hadn't resisted, had thrown herself across him like a wanton. Peeking up at him, she witnessed a look of dazed astonishment cross his face, his eyes pooled black with unrequited desire.

'Ragnar!' A voice, in guttural Norse, battered through the door. 'Open the door!'

* * *

His breath emerged in truncated gusts, forcing upwards from his chest. He shoved a hand through his hair, fighting for control. What had just happened? Gisela stood before him, her expression defensive and wary, hair flowing loosely around her shoulders. Like a fairy from an enchanted dell: ethereal, magical. A woodland sprite. And yet he saw the way her chest heaved, the air fast and quick in her windpipe, the bloom on her cheeks. The graze on her chin from where his bristles had scraped against her soft flesh. Shame splintered through him. Earlier she had chided him for his lack of chivalry, his incapability to behave decently; he had vehemently denied it. What had he done? Shunned good sense to take a slice of her beauty, trampling roughshod over her to claim her mouth, to savour that delicious softness melting into his hard contours. To assuage a thirst.

'Ragnar, open the door!'

He jerked away from her, scowling at his own lack of restraint, striding across the room. Cracking the door open an inch or two, he spoke to the man outside, a quick exchange in his own language. Pushing the door closed, he settled the horizontal bar in place, securing the chamber. His hand pressed flat against the boards; he stared at the knots in the vertical panels, wondering if he could trust himself to go through with his plan of accompanying Gisela to meet with Ralph de Pagenal. He had offered to take her because she had no one else, because for her to go alone was too risky, too dangerous without protection. He told himself it was because she reminded him of his sister, with her innocence and flashing eyes, but as his eyes ranged over the panels, he knew that was not the truth. The truth was that he wanted her. He wanted Gisela.

Chapter Nine

Gisela watched him. Her eyes traced the powerful cord of his spine disappearing beneath the curved collar of his white shirt, the bright feathery strands of his hair. His palm splayed against the door: strong, ridged sinews, eminently capable. She sagged back against the oak coffer, the shards of broken jug scattered at her feet, not trusting herself to speak, yet she knew she must in order to take control of the situation.

She cleared her throat. 'Ragnar?'

He turned, his eyes an iridescent shimmer, the translucent green of a shaded forest. The sun was rising; light tipped over the stone sill, tracing a dust-spangled shaft to the floor. Birds twittered outside the window. A shout rose up from the bailey, echoing around the high curtain walls; another voice returned the greeting, rough, guttural.

'That should not have happened.' Ragnar traced her mouth, the curve of her cheek.

Had he kissed her out of pity, after all? Had he lied to her? 'No, it should not have.' She pinned him with what she hoped was a self-assured look, yet inwardly her confidence shrank, shrivelled away like burnt wisps of parchment, caught in a flame. Her lips smarted, flickers of desire lingering from his kiss. Bunching her hand, she scrubbed vigorously at her mouth. For the sake of pride, she must act as if the kiss meant nothing; show him that what he had done was inconsequential.

Sweeping the glistening rope of her hair forward, she proceeded to braid the long, silky length into a thick single plait, securing the pale brown strands with the leather lace she had left on the coffer. Then, folding her arms across her chest, bracing herself for a fight, she glared at him archly. 'I must travel north today, to Ralph de Pagenal.'

'I must presume that means…with or without me.' Ragnar arched one bronze-coloured eyebrow.

'You cannot come with me if you continue with that sort of behaviour.' Relief coursed through her at his words, a relief that she hated to acknowledge. Thank God. He was still considering accompanying her.

Her pompous, formal tone twisted his stern expression to a reluctant grin. He laughed, breaking the tension in the chamber. 'It won't happen again,' Ragnar said to reassure her. 'I promise you,' he added.

Gisela nodded jerkily. 'Make sure it doesn't.' Her heart screwed up with a peculiar sense of loss. 'Anyway, you might have changed your mind about coming with me. I don't want you to feel obligated...'

'Gisela, stop,' he said, holding up his hand. 'Enough of this, I've said I will take you and I will. Let me find you some clothes to wear. The men are almost ready to leave; we must cross the river at high tide.'

'But I have clothes,' Gisela said, surprised, flipping her scarf around her neck, tucking in the ends securely. Her eyes sought, then found, her large floppy hat lying on the floorboards by the bed.

'Women's clothes,' Ragnar clarified. His sleeved woollen tunic lay by the pallet bed; he picked it up, yanking it over his head. A muscle tensed in his jaw. 'You cannot travel dressed as a boy.'

'Why not?' she challenged him, drawing her fine sable brows together. 'It's safer.'

He pulled his leather surcoat on, hooking his sword belt over one shoulder, a sling that crossed his chest diagonally. 'My men will question the presence of a boy. If you travel as a woman, you will draw less attention...' He cleared his throat. 'Especially when they realise to whom you belong.'

'Belong...' Gisela repeated stupidly. Her mind grasped hazily at his intended meaning. 'You mean...' Her voice trailed away, a red flush banding her cheeks, dulling the freckles sprinkling her fair skin.

'I'm sorry, but it's the only way you'll travel in safety,' he said. 'If you travel...as my woman. Under my protection.'

Breath seized in her lungs, derived her of speech. She glared at him furiously. 'I'll do no such thing!' she cried, striding around the bed to scoop up her hat from the polished floorboards. 'You may as well forget the whole thing.' She clamped her hat on her head, tugging down the sides, approaching him with decisive strides. 'There's no way I'm going to go with you...like that! I'm not going to...to lie with you...and that is final!' Shadowed by the hat's wide brim, she willed her eyes to spark blue fire, vivid, intense.

'Kissing me was bad enough, taking advantage of me…but to ask me to do that!' A dry sob hitched her breath. 'Let me out of here, please. If I'd known what you would ask of me, I never would have agreed to this. I'm nobody's whore!'

Ragnar stood with his back to the door, great arms crossed over his chest, watching her tirade with what appeared to be amusement. 'I'm not asking you to be my whore,' he replied quietly. 'You don't have to sleep with me, Gisela. I would never ask you to do that. We only have to pretend.'

'Oh!' His words punctured her spirit, made her stumble back. Understanding swept over her, an icy wind slicing through the heat of her anger. A sense of unfulfilment wrenched at her gut, a wretched desolation sweeping through her. She clapped her palms to her cheeks, embarrassed by her outburst, the unguarded torrent of speech. Had she *wanted* him to insist that she pay the price of his protection by sleeping with him? By demanding the rights to her body in return? God in heaven!

'So it's not going to be quite as bad as you obviously envisaged,' Ragnar added, as the fury drained from her face.

'It's bad enough.' She wrinkled her nose, hoping he couldn't read the disappointment in her eyes. 'Don't pretend this will be easy.'

'I wouldn't dare,' he responded lightly. He leaned across, his fingers grazing her wrist. Sensation shivered along the delicate hairs on her forearm. 'Bolt the door behind me while I fetch some clothes for you. Let no one in but me.'

'Ragnar...' She stalled him with her words; the door was ajar and he paused with one foot in the corridor. His fingers, tanned and sinewy, rested on the iron latch. 'I must go to my father and sister...tell them what is happening.'

'There isn't time,' he said. 'The tide will not wait for us and neither will the longships. Eirik means to cross the river today, to meet with the Saxon king in Jorvik.' He thought for a moment. 'I will send a message to your lodgings,' he said. 'They can meet us on the beach.'

'How...?'

But Ragnar had gone, his swift exit snuffing her speech. The door swung shut, the latch rattling into place. Her eyes traced the uneven planks, the knots and whorls in the wood, anxiety flaring in her heart. Her mind struggled to comprehend the speed at which her world had changed in the space of a day, to understand her inexplicable reaction to a man who had thrust into her life like a lightning strike from the heavens, tumultuous and devastating.

The gowns were too tight. Walking beside Ragnar down the steep incline from the castle, Gisela plucked miserably at the constrictive fabric, as if her continual tugging would somehow make the garments larger. She hadn't even bothered to tie the side lacings on the light green overdress, but it made no difference. The material hugged her bosom, emphasising the roundness of her breasts, her neat waist, falling to mid-calf. The underdress beneath was of blue wool, the hem whispering against her ankles. According to Ragnar, the garments had belonged to a serving maid at the castle and were freshly laundered.

She skipped along, matching Ragnar's quick, long-legged pace. He held her elbow, guiding her through the crowded streets. They reached the market square, stall holders filling the air with the cries of their wares, keen to make extra coin from the people flocking into town to bid farewell to the Danes. Up ahead, through the narrow chink of an alleyway, the vast width of the river gleamed, a churning silver ribbon. Gisela's heart flipped queasily; the river looked so benign, so inviting, and yet after last night, she knew the power contained in those frothing rivulets, the treacherous mudflats beneath that twinkling surface.

'It's so busy.' She chewed on her bottom lip, agitation riffling through her. She had given no thought to how she would leave this place and now the full enormity of what she was undertaking gusted through her slender figure like a whirlwind. Had she truly thought she could slink away unnoticed? What had she been thinking? It seemed that every person in the town had turned out to witness the departure of the Danes. And there she would be, a harlot for all to see, being loaded on to a longship in front of judging Saxon eyes. As her eyes moved in dismay over the jostling figures in the square, her step faltered; she stopped.

'This is so humiliating,' she said, tugging at her snug bodice. 'Dressed like this, everyone will think that I'm your...' She pursed her lips together, unwilling to say the word. Her cheeks flushed with annoyance. 'Why could you have not let me wear my other clothes?'

His brilliant gaze swept the alabaster bloom of her skin. Like the petal of a rose, plush, velvety. A rosy tint stained her cheeks, the mark of her hurried pace through the streets. The borrowed cloak was merely a length of wool wound around her shoulders, fastened with a cheap metal pin across her chest. Below the cloak's bunching gathers, the gown traced the luscious curves of her bosom and waist, skirts flaring out seductively over her slim hips. Awareness sliced through him, squeezing the base of his belly.

A hush encompassed them: a thick wadded quilt, muffling the shrieks and shouts of the market. Self-conscious beneath his quiet scrutiny, her eyelashes fluttered down, hiding the striking blue of her eyes. 'I told you the gowns are too tight,' she whispered, misinterpreting his close scrutiny. She tugged irritably at the rucked-up fabric around her waist. 'I can't believe that the serving girl was really the same size as me.'

A dog trotted past them, scrawny and underfed; Ragnar followed the animal's rangy gait, the horizontal lines of ribcage jutting out from mangy fur. He wanted to tell her that she was beautiful in those gowns, the clinging lines setting off her slender figure to perfection. But he was on tenuous ground; after that kiss in the bedchamber, how could he compliment her without her thinking the worst of him? Thinking that he wanted to bed her and nothing more? His groin tightened; he gritted his teeth, clamping down on the sweet thought. She would be right to think it. For it was true.

'I did try.' His tongue moved awkwardly in his mouth; he swallowed, trying to alleviate the dryness.

'Do I look awful?' she asked, throwing him a worried look. Another dog loped along behind her, sniffing in doorways, claws clicking on the cobbles.

Ragnar laughed. 'You sound just like my—' He bit down hard on his tongue. *My sister*, he had been about to say. Gyda would say the same thing, but in a different context. She had always sought compliments, dramatically sweeping the curtains of the great hall aside, parading through the trestle tables towards Ragnar and his parents at the top table. A new velvet gown, a different cloak: they would be shown to all. His father would roll his eyes and continue to chew on his food; his mother would half-rise from her chair so that she could see her daughter properly, showering her with compliments and suggestions. How they all wished for that girl to be back with them again.

Gisela glanced up, clearly startled by the abrupt stop to his speech. 'I sound just like your...' She repeated his words, giving him the opportunity to continue.

He ignored her question and crooked his arm out, indicating that she should take it. 'Come, we must make haste. The longships will not wait for us. And your father and sister should be waiting for us on the beach.'

But it was only her sister. Marie's tall figure hunched against the wall of the last cottage on the street, before the cobbled surface gave way to shingle. Her scarf was pulled forward across her face, shadowing her features. As always she had no wish to draw attention to herself.

'I'll come back for you in a moment,' Ragnar said, his large boots crunching across the shingle towards the men gathered around the longships. Seagulls wheeled in the air, screeching their hoarse, strident cries, orange-rimmed eyes searching for scraps on the ground. The river water lapped against the dry stones, rising slowly, endeavouring to reach the ragged line of seaweed that marked the last high tide.

'Where is he?' Gisela reached out to grasp her sister's hands. 'Where is Father?'

Marie tracked Ragnar's loping stride across the beach. 'Is that the same man...?'

'Aye, it's him,' Gisela confirmed, a resigned note entering her voice. She gave her sister's fingers a little shake. 'Marie, where's Father?'

'He's too ill to walk.' Marie's eyes caught her own. 'That blow to the head last night; it seems to have robbed him of all energy. He told me to bring you this.' She handed Gisela a soft leather bag, lowering her voice. 'The rest of the money is inside.'

Her heart plummeted; so there really was no hope of her father travelling with her. She would have to make do with that insufferable Dane after all. But as much as she tried to stifle the feeling, anticipation threaded through her: a heady tangled mix of danger coupled with excitement.

'What happened to your face?' Marie traced the purpling bruise below Gisela's eye. 'Did they do that?' She nodded fearfully over to the men by the longships, her features pale and washed out in the stark morning light. The tall Danish warriors, blond hair tufting skywards in the sharp breeze, crowded on to the loose shingle, round colourful shields and swords winking fiercely. The air filled with their rough, outlandish speech and the hard, guttural curses as they climbed over the gunwales, adjusting the position of the wooden boxes that they sat on to row.

'No,' Gisela replied. 'It was the Saxons, when I tried to retrieve the money that Father lost.' She sought her sister's cold fingers, gripped them.

'What happened? We were so worried when you didn't come back last night. Then we received the message this morning to meet you here.'

'Ragnar rescued me from the Saxons, then refused to let me go until I told him why we needed the money so much.' Gisela glanced across the shingle, squinting. The strong sun bleached the round pebbles to a harsh scouring whiteness. Her eyes found Ragnar's commanding figure with ease, his blond hair riffling in the light air, gilt-edged. Dismay clouded her expression. 'I didn't find the money. This is all we have now.' She patted the satchel resting on her hips, the leather strap cutting diagonally between her breasts.

'What is happening between the two of you?' Marie asked quietly.

Startled, Gisela's heart gave a quick leap; she frowned deeply, a small crease appearing in the smooth skin between her finely arched eyebrows. What had made her sister say such a thing? Had her behaviour betrayed her? 'Nothing. He's agreed to help me, that's all. I have no one to go with me further north. Richard's life is at stake, Marie.'

'I know all that. It's the way he looks at you... that's all.'

A deep visceral longing tugged at her chest. *If only. If only he looked at me like someone he loved.* Tossing her head up, Gisela laughed, swiftly dismissing the sentimental path on which her thoughts trod. 'Nay, you're wrong, Marie. I'm nothing more than an annoyance to him. If you've noticed anything at all, then it's because he's playing a part, so his men believe that I belong to him; it's the only way I can travel safely.' Memory snagged her mind: the firm, warm press of Ragnar's mouth against hers. Delight whispered through her chest, a languorous coil of seductive heat.

'But why would he offer to do this in the first place, Gisela? Have you asked yourself that? It doesn't make sense; there's nothing in it for him!'

Her sister voiced her own disquiet, the questions that had tumbled through her mind since Ragnar had offered to help her. But if she succumbed to fear and refused to undertake this journey, then what hope would there be for Richard? 'We have no other choice, Marie, surely you can see that? This is our only hope of getting our brother back, alive.'

'Then make sure you guard your innocence around the Dane, Sister, for that is surely what he is...oh!' Marie's head jerked up, as Ragnar suddenly appeared next to Gisela. His upper arm nudged her shoulders. A dull red colour suffused Marie's cheeks and she dropped her chin in embarrassment, staring awkwardly at the ground.

'Are you ready?' Ragnar inclined his head towards Gisela. Amusement tugged at the firm line of his upper lip.

Flashing him a brief, hesitant smile, she prayed he hadn't heard her sister's warning. 'Aye, I'm ready.' She patted the bag at her hip. 'Marie has brought me a few things. As well as the money we have left.' Stepping forward, she hugged her sister, pulling her tight. 'Take care of Father, Marie. I'll be back soon, with Richard.'

Holding her skirts high, she picked her way across the unstable shingle, following Ragnar to the waiting longships. Her heart flipped in panic; the Danes were ready to row. In a few moments, the ships would be afloat on the flooding tide. Even now, the water lapped against the shallow sides of the vessels.

She stopped at the river's edge, where curling wavelets flowed across a patch of mud and stone, a significant stretch of water, about a foot deep, lying between her and the first longship. 'How am I supposed to reach the boat…?' She glared at Ragnar in consternation, as if it was his fault that the water had risen so much.

'There is only one way,' he replied, 'if you want to keep dry.' He swept one hand beneath her knees to hoist her light weight against him. 'There is no ladder.' In the brilliant, unflinching sunlight, the bristles on his chin fired gold as he sloshed through the water. Instinctively, she clung to the back of his neck, her hip bumping treacherously against his muscle-bound chest.

'Throw her up to me, man!' a voice shouted down from the gunwale. 'We're about to leave!'

Shifting his grip, Ragnar propelled her through the air, her feet and arms flailing at the abrupt, undignified movement. Her bag hung down, a heavy lump swinging precariously. Hands reached out to grab her: large, masculine hands that roamed invasively across her curves as she was hauled upwards and held on to her for longer than was necessary, once she was on her feet again.

'Go away!' She lashed out at the grinning men circling her, bringing up her hands to ward them off. Tears prickled beneath her lids. They were handling her like cargo, an unwieldy sack of grain, a commodity. Something to be bought and sold, not a woman in her own right. A woman who, only a short year ago, had full control of her family's vast estates in France. She jutted her chin forward, narrowing her eyes in anger as if daring them to come any closer, watching as Ragnar climbed into the ship.

He jumped down on to the deck beside her, one arm drawing her close against his hard flank. Possessive. Unyielding. 'Hands off, if you know what's good for you.' His voice held a veiled warning. 'This one belongs to me.'

Chapter Ten

❦

This one belongs to me. His speech scorched her brain. Imprinted like a brand, searing, possessive. Heat surged in her belly, her chest, a swelling blanket of sensation. Stupid! Her reaction was unnerving, fluttering through her like a frightened bird. As if her physical body defied common sense, staggering haphazardly away from considered, practical thought towards a delicious wildness, a sense of abandonment, of danger, cleaving to this broad-shouldered Viking like a woman possessed. Out of control. And yet, as the sensible, rational part of her brain continued to chant at her, Ragnar was only playing the part, the role of a possessive lover, in order to protect her among his men.

He led her to the bow. A wooden seat spanned the narrowest point where the ship's curving sides met; he pushed her gently down on to the single plank, one hand on her shoulder, guiding her. The mast had been lowered, the vast square sail wrapped neatly around its length. The strength of the men at the oars would be enough to take the vessel across the river. Drawing her knees together beneath the hated gown, Gisela perched primly on the seat, unable to relax. Her shoulder blades ached from the strain of holding herself in a constant state of alertness. Gritting her teeth, she pulled the leather bag across her lap like a barricade, her neat figure shadowed by the high clinker-built sides of the ship. How on earth was she going to undertake this journey and yet remain immune to Ragnar?

The polished metal of his eyes roamed over her, the hunched, tense figure. He knew she was worried, daunted by this journey into the unknown, away from the security of her family. Her eyes were haunted, skittish, as she watched the oars lower into the glistening water on a shouted order. In the limpid morning light, her skin held the quality of pouring cream, luminous, translucent, like a pearl. In the midst of these enormous fighting men, with their lined leathery faces and rough-whiskered chins, she shone like an angel. Doubt niggled at him.

Would he find the self-restraint to keep his hands to himself?

To cover his own disquiet, Ragnar squeezed her shoulder. Bending down, he whispered in her ear, 'Try to smile, Gisela. All eyes are upon you. I know this is difficult for you to understand, but it is something of an honour to become a Viking woman.'

'That is a lie!' she hissed back at him, under her breath, her jaw rigid.

'Yes, it is,' Ragnar admitted, laughing.

The air shifted. His gentle teasing eased the strain along her back, breaking the bubble of tension that held her muscles in thrall; she released her grip fractionally on the bag strap, knuckles rigid and sore. The pent-up air exhaled from her lungs by slow degrees, heavy pressure softening behind her ribs. From the stern, an older man, his gnarled hand on the wooden tiller, gave the order to row; grizzled hair crinkled out from his head, sparse and wiry. The men dipped their oars, moving together with a combined, practised power, tunics pulling taut against their spines as they hauled back. Stones crunched faintly beneath the hull; the longship started to move.

Gisela cleared her throat. 'When do we reach the other side?'

'It shouldn't take too long.' Ragnar squinted across the smooth ribbon of still water, assessing the distance. 'The current is strong, but there's no wind to blow us from our course.' His bright eyes moved over her.

His belt buckle, a simple design of dulled silver, gleamed in the sunshine; the sword hilt that crossed his lower torso was strapped up with a long narrow piece of leather. No trappings, no extraneous decoration. How unlike the swords of her fellow Normans, she thought, with their lightweight blades of finely honed steel, the hilts studded with precious gemstones to indicate their status. 'And then we must head north. My father told me the way; it's not above ten miles from Hoesella. I presume that is where these ships are headed?'

'Aye, it's the only safe harbour on that side, big enough to take all these vessels,' he confirmed, resting his lower back against the raked planks of the ship's side. 'And then our journey should be easy if we follow the road to Jorvik.'

As the ship drew away from the shore, Gisela twisted her head, her gaze snagging on Marie's pale figure, standing in the lee of the cottage on the shore. A sense of dislocation seized her, as if her feet balanced on precarious quicksand, a tee-tering raft. She was leaving her family, the two people, other than her brother, who represented home and security, a haven where she could van-ish from the world outside. The only person she could rely on now was herself. Flicking a quick glance at Ragnar, she wondered whether, alone, she would be strong enough to withstand what-ever was to come.

'Your sister shouldn't be waiting on the beach like that,' Ragnar said, following her glance to-wards Marie. 'It's dangerous for her to loiter outside.'

Gisela hitched her shoulders forward, scrub-bing distractedly at a small grease spot on the skirts. 'She's worried about me, about what I'm going to do.' The sparkling midnight blue of her eyes hooked his piercing gaze and she flushed. 'Marie doesn't trust you. She can't understand why you are helping us. It's rare that people do such things for nothing.' Her voice was hesitant, laced with the faintest ripple of doubt.

Ragnar leaned back against the gunwale. He folded his arms, his tunic sleeves falling back from his powerful wrists.

He cleared his throat, raising his voice against the sound of the waves slapping against the keel, the chant of the men as they kept time on the oars. 'Your sister is right.'

Gisela jumped up from her seat, hands clutching the bag strap, staggering slightly as the boat pitched to the right. He caught her arm, steadying her, bringing her alongside him to shield her from the rest of the men. Trapped between his big body and the shadow of the prow, her hands wrapped around the gunwale, knuckles white, her expression rigid. 'I knew it!' she pronounced bitterly. 'I knew there would be something more to this!' Her voice lowered. 'But as I told you before, I will not be your whore.'

'What a low opinion you have of me,' he replied mildly. 'Your continual assumption that I should want to sleep with you.'

A rosy flush suffused her cheeks; she jerked her gaze away, scanning the wide expanse of river. Small wavelets scuffed the sparkling surface of the water, white curling ribbons of froth. The water running alongside the flanks of the ship made a hollow sound, cavernous. Humiliation flooded through her—why could she not guard her tongue? That was the second time she had said such a thing to him; the second time he had denied it.

'Although I will if you want me to,' he added, his mouth twitching on the edge of a smile.

Her brain acknowledged the husky edge of desire in his voice, the spoken promise. Her body jolted, alive with his proposition. What was he saying? Would it truly be that simple? That she only had to ask, to tell him that she wanted him, that she desired him?

'You don't know what you're saying!' she thrust back at him. 'Stop teasing me!'

How could he tell her that his jest was actually the truth? The thought of touching her, of holding her velvet skin against his own, savouring her, had tormented him since the moment he had met her. He cleared his throat. 'Then start trusting me, Gisela. And be assured that I am not about to hurt you in any way. I will protect you. But I do need you to help me.'

'What is it? How...?' Her speech faltered as Eirik's commanding figure approached, his straight hair glossy as a blackbird's wing. He moved across the deck with the air and swagger of one used to being in charge. A huge circular brooch holding his cloak together denoted his royal status: the heavy gold was finely wrought, the work depicting a coiling dragon, its single, enormous eye studded with a sapphire.

'Wonders will never cease!' Eirik clapped Ragnar on the shoulder, his eyes moving with predatory grace over Gisela, frowning at the bluish bruise marring her cheekbone. 'Where did you find this one, eh? A real beauty and no mistake. Are you going to have much time to enjoy her, if you are hunting down your sister's abductor?'

Gisela stared resolutely downwards, yanking her scarf forward to shield her face. Ragnar knew she probably couldn't understand a word of their convoluted speech. Angling her head away, she turned towards the prow, shifting uncomfortably in the tight dress. Would Eirik realise that she was the same woman from the previous night? When she had hauled her father's sword from his belt and threatened him?

But no hint of recognition sounded in Eirik's tone or crossed his face; his speech remained jocular, benign. 'How much did you have to pay her to sleep with you?' He jabbed Ragnar's side with his elbow, his chainmail tunic rippling in the sunlight. 'I might have a go myself!'

'She's not here for that.' Ragnar's reply was sharp, constrained. A strange possessiveness rose within him—a need to protect Gisela from Eirik's harsh assumptions, his bawdy circumspection.

'Oh, really.' Eirik's voice was light, faintly sarcastic. 'Ragnar, I don't blame you; in fact, I think it's marvellous. Why, it's been months since you've had a woman, ever since...' His eyes darkened as his speech trailed off. A ruddy colour seeped beneath the tan of his cheeks.

'Ever since my sister came home,' Ragnar supplied for him. 'You can talk about it, Eirik. It's why I'm here, after all.'

'What are you going to do with her—' Eirik shot a look at Gisela's bowed head '—while you are searching for the Norman? You can leave her with us, if you like.'

Ragnar hitched his left shoulder, turning his body so that Gisela was more effectively hidden from Eirik's prying eyes. 'Nay, she's coming with me.'

His friend brought his thick dark brows together, his large brown eyes shining with curiosity. 'I'm not sure I understand... You tell me that Gyda's abductor is a Norman lord, Ragnar. A tenant-in-chief to the Conqueror himself! As a Dane you'll be instantly recognisable; you'll be dead before you even reach the gatehouse. How is this woman going to be of any use?'

'She can speak the language,' Ragnar explained softly. 'For she is a Norman, too.'

'W-what?' Eirik said, incredulous. 'Is that the truth?' He tried to peer over his friend's shoulder, but Ragnar gripped his forearm, stalling him. His strong fingers dug into Eirik's leather-bound arms. 'What is she doing here? This far north?'

'It's a long story,' said Ragnar. 'Suffice to say that the maid found herself in trouble in Bertune; I helped her out.'

As Eirik stepped back, his puzzled expression cleared. 'Of course, you speak French, don't you? Your mother's native tongue. No one would suspect a husband and wife, travelling alone, to be asking for anything other than board and lodging for the night. Especially a Norman couple, travelling through hostile country.'

'You have it,' Ragnar confirmed. 'But say nothing. I will not have her drawing undue attention from the men.'

'You have my silence, friend. If she is here to help you, then it doesn't matter where she comes from.' He stared at the back of Gisela's head. 'How did you persuade her to come with you?'

'She had no choice,' Ragnar said. He bit his lip. 'The situation is complicated, but I think it can work.'

The ship's look-out gave a shout. Gisela bounced from her seat, eyes wide, her muscles constricting with fear. The smooth glide of the ship across the river, the rhythmic slop and wash of water against the keel had lulled her brain into a mildly soporific state; at some point she must have leaned her head against the ship's side and closed her eyes. The hull ground and crunched on the stones of the opposite shore. Oars rasped back into the boat; some of the men already stood, stretching their arms up to ease out the muscles.

Across the busy deck, across the jumble of men rising, gathering their scant possessions, her eyes searched for Ragnar, for the bright tumble of his hair. He was standing by the furled sail, laughing as he chatted in a group of men. Self-pity jagged her chest, a sense of isolation washing through her.

Then Ragnar turned, as if he sensed her eyes upon him, snaring her gaze. Across the hub-bub of men rising from their rowing positions, tightening sword straps and looping their shields across their shoulders, the power from his eyes leaped through her: a jolt of energy. He smiled. Strength poured into her, filling her with a new confidence.

'Are you ready to go?' he asked, striding towards her.

'When are you going to tell me what it is you want from me?' Her speech juddered out of her.

'Later,' he said, holding out his hand. 'And

don't look at me like that, Gisela, it really isn't that bad. A favour for a favour.'

Her heart deflated, shrinking inwards on itself. *Oh, come on, Gisela*, she chided herself scathingly. *What did you expect?* That was all this was: a simple business transaction.

Her leather bag bumped heavily against her hip as she rose, a little unsteadily. The boats had drawn up in a wide bay, sheltered from the easterly winds; already the men were jumping down and beginning to haul the longships up the beach. The land beyond stretched flat, for miles and miles, a largely featureless expanse of marshland studded with the occasional moated homestead. A stone gatehouse in the distance, signifying a larger property. An area so flat that only a vast grid of ditches and man-made earth banks kept the land from being permanently flooded by the tidal estuary.

'Come,' Ragnar said, 'I'll lift you down.'

Her chest was on a level with the polished top of the gunwale. Impossible for her to scramble over of her own accord. And there was no way she was even going to attempt such a thing, with all these men around. She inclined her head, the smallest gesture of assent.

Alerting the men on the shingle below, his large hands spanning her neat waist, Ragnar threw her up and over the side of the boat. Her skirts flapped about her, rippling around her slender ankles as the men below caught her, lowering her to the beach. Ragnar landed on the shingle next to her, his big body thumping down, leather boots sliding on the stones.

'Ragnar.' She clutched at his elbow, stalling him as he prepared to walk up the beach. 'Tell me. Please.' Her eyes pleaded with him. 'Tell me what you want of me.'

It was the first time she had used his name. His body trembled; sweet awareness tightened his chest. His name sounded different coming from her lips, more rounded, softer somehow. She had a right to know what he planned for her, but he wasn't sure of her reaction. Would she run from him when he told her what he wanted her to do?

Up ahead, where the beach flattened off at the top, some of the men had gathered driftwood to start a fire. Stacking the bone-white sticks high, a flint had been struck into a piece of dry moss. Smoke rose hazily in the limpid dawn light. The men would set up camp here, on the beach, while they waited for Eirik's brother to arrive with his ships, more men. As the flames licked up greedily around the dry wood, an iron tripod, with a pan suspended on a chain, was positioned over the fire.

'Come and sit,' Ragnar said. 'I can tell you as we eat.'

Accepting his hand to help her up the slippery stones, she sank down on to an enormous fur spread alongside the fire. One of the men handed her a wooden bowl brimming with cooked oats; dried berries had been scattered across the steaming mix. Holding a spoon, Gisela eyed the glossy black fruits with suspicion.

Ragnar laughed. 'Lingonberries,' he explained in French. 'They're a good source of nutrients when we're on our travels. They won't poison you.'

Mouth slack with astonishment, the man who had handed the bowl to Gisela stood staring at Ragnar, large serving spoon wavering in mid-air. Drops of porridge fell from the spoon into the fire, hissing noisily. 'Close your mouth, Rurik,' Ragnar chided him in Norse. 'And serve the other men. You've heard me speak French before, it should come as no surprise.' The man flushed heavily, mumbled an apology and turned away.

The porridge was cooling rapidly in her bowl, but Gisela's mouth was dry. Eating at this precise moment was out of the question. Her stomach roiled with nerves. 'Tell me what you want of me, Ragnar,' she whispered. 'You've come to fight alongside the Saxons, haven't you? I don't see how I can help with that.'

'I'm not here to fight.' His eyes pierced her, chips of emerald. 'Yes, I have come here with Eirik and his men who intend to do that, but I have come here for a different reason.' He took a deep breath. 'I have come here…to find someone. But he is a Norman lord, living in an almost impenetrable fortress. And as a Dane, I have no hope of getting close to him.'

Gisela stirred her porridge thoughtfully, the blue-black juice of the strange berries bleeding into the creamy oats, thin trails of colour. The rising steam warmed her chill fingers. 'But I still don't see how…?'

'You are a Norman. And I speak French like a native. Posing as man and wife, we would gain access to his castle as travellers, looking for board and lodging for the night. That's all I need.'

Her belly swooped, then plummeted. Of course, he had the perfect right to ask for this. He'd obviously been thinking about this ever since he'd offered to help her with her brother. Why had he not told her earlier? Did he think she would refuse? 'But why do you need to find this man, to track him down?'

The light leached suddenly from his eyes, a muscle stretching in his jaw. 'I will tell you later,' he said, looking around at his fellow Danes, chattering and laughing, as if providing himself with an excuse not to tell her. Would he ever be able to find the words to tell her about his past?

'And what if I say "no"?' she asked.

He lifted his shoulders in a silent shrug.

'This is blackmail.'

'Hardly,' Ragnar replied. 'Without me, you would have no hope of reclaiming your brother…unless you prostitute yourself with Ralph de Pagenal. And I doubt very much that a man with such a notorious reputation would hand your brother over, even after you had done such a thing.'

'But I'm going to have to do it anyway,' she replied softly. 'With you.' A sudden breathlessness seized her chest at the boldness of her own words.

'We would pose as man and wife, Gisela,' he replied. 'I would never force you to do anything against your will.' His green gaze blazed over her, suddenly hot. The implication was clear.

Her belly melted stupidly, looping with giddy

emotion. Her grip weakened, the heavy bowl tipping fractionally, and she made a conscious effort to set it straight, to avoid pouring the hot oats into her lap. But what if she wished such a thing? she thought suddenly. It was similar to his words on the boat. *I will if you want me to.* Would he stop her? And would she be able to stop herself?

Chapter Eleven

'Come back here when you are done,' Eirik said, as Ragnar slung his satchel strap over his head, positioning the narrow, worn leather across his broad chest, settling the bulky bag on his hip. 'I will leave some men with the ships. I hope it won't take you long to give the bastard the punishment he deserves.' He lifted his black eyebrows with an exaggerated significance, wrinkling the skin at the outer corners of his dark-brown eyes.

'I have to find him first.' Ragnar grimaced.

'And don't tarry otherwise we'll go back to Denmark without you,' Eirik said. 'The autumn storms are approaching; I have no wish to be trapped here all winter.' Stepping forward, he wound his arms around Ragnar, clasping him in a hug. 'Look after yourself, friend.' He cast a quick glance at Gisela, standing silently at the big man's side. 'Make sure this beauty doesn't lead you astray.'

Ragnar grinned, teeth flashing white in his tanned skin, then he turned away, cupping Gisela's elbow to bring her alongside him. Walking up the beach, he raised his other arm in farewell to the men. His stride was long, quick; Gisela was forced to skip every second step to keep up with him, first along the shingle and then through the stiff rushes that bordered the beach before stretching inland. Her fist gripped the gathered bulk of her skirts, lifting the heavy folds clear of the stones.

As they gained the level ground beyond the beach, the path narrowing to a single, muddy track, Ragnar released his hold on her and she dropped behind, following him. He had thrown on a short cloak for the journey, a simple semi-circle of woollen cloth, fastened at his throat with a jewelled brooch. His fast pace made the hem of the cloak flare out, revealing the snug cut of his leather tunic over his slim hips. Excitement flashed through her, wilting her knees. She dropped her gaze, mouth set in a tight, fierce line. How was it that this man, this Dane, had the power to affect her so? Why could he not be ugly and squat, with a face like a pig's bottom? It would certainly make this trip a great deal easier.

Up ahead the market town of Hoesella shimmered on the horizon: a low mound of clustered roofs, a church spire peeking above the flat expanse of reeds and marsh. To their right, a continuation of the inlet upon which the Danes' ships had moored, a muddy creek leading up to the town itself, navigable only by smaller boats. Thick mud, creaking oozily in the sunlight, formed smooth rounded pillows along the edges; seabirds stalked the sticky expanse, trailing delicate claw marks. Low stretches of puffy white cloud studded the vivid blue sky, tacking eastwards on a swift breeze.

'Is this the right way?' Gisela asked, puffing slightly. Beneath her headscarf, sweat trickled down behind her ear. 'My father said I should head north to reach Ralph de Pagenal's castle.'

Ragnar paused, mouth twitching with amusement. 'This is north, Gisela. And it's the only way. We must follow the track through these marshlands. The boggy ground around here is treacherous.' His eyes flicked over her. 'Once we reach Hoesella we will pick up the pilgrim route towards Beverley. De Pagenal's castle is a little way further north off that path.' He spoke the place-names with certainty.

'Have you been here before?' She tilted her head in question, adjusting the leather strap of her bag across her shoulder.

His quicksilver eyes moved over her. 'Many times,' he said eventually, his gaze drifting over the flat grassland. The wind rippled through the feathery heads of the rushes: a continual swishing sound, blowing the delicate fronds first one way, then the other. Moving in unison, the dark lilac-coloured plumes appeared like the surface of a lake.

'What did you do when you were here?' Gisela asked. The path had widened and she moved to walk beside him.

Raiding, mostly, he thought, glaring at the far horizon. A small frown creased the spot between his eyes. Taking whatever they could find. Women. Land. His Viking peers had a terrible reputation; it was a well-known fact that they wanted the green and fertile lands of England, lands a mere hop across the sea from their own barren homeland. 'Oh, nothing much,' he responded lightly. 'But I travelled enough to know my way around.'

Her eyes flicked up at his evasive answer; she wrinkled her nose at him. 'I don't know why I even asked. Everyone knows what the Vikings did. What they still do, on occasion. Their reputation precedes them.'

'And yet it's a Norman lord that tried to abduct your sister and now holds your brother hostage. And it was a Saxon man who was prepared to leave you to die on the mudflats. All men are capable of great cruelty, Gisela. You cannot say it is only the Danes.'

'You're right,' she murmured, apology clouding her soft voice. 'It wasn't right, what I said to you.'

He nudged her upper arm, a bit too forcefully, and she stumbled, losing her balance. Laughing, he caught her before she fell into the rushes alongside the path. The precious stones set in his brooch glinted in the rising sun. 'Luckily for you, fair maiden, I have a very thick skin. You don't need to apologise, I have had far worse things said to me. And it's true: the Danes have done many bad things.'

Fair maiden. She smiled up at him, grateful for his easy-going manner, grateful for his compliment, even though it wasn't true. His arm was still crooked beneath hers. The powerful flex of his muscle wrapped around her elbow, lay across her forearm. Her skirts lapped against his leather boots. She had no inclination to pull away. 'I don't think it will take too long to walk to Ralph de Pagenal's estates,' she said. 'Not above a couple of days anyway.'

His eyes were like mirrors, a translucent emerald green. His dark eyelashes formed a strong contrast with his bright hair, startling. Her senses lurched.

'But we can reach his castle sooner,' he said, 'if we buy horses in Hoesella.'

'Oh!' Gisela said, startled. 'I didn't realise.'

'I suppose you were planning to walk there with your family, weren't you?' A muscle jumped in the hollow of his cheek. 'But this way will be quicker.'

Her step slowed. 'But, Ragnar, I have not enough coin to buy a horse; you know that.'

'I will pay.' He tugged her along beside him, eager to keep up the pace.

The churned-up mud of the path stretched out before her, leading to a wooden gate in the distance. 'This is wrong,' Gisela said quietly. 'I can't take your money.'

'Consider it a loan, then, or else payment for what you will do for me.' His words made it clear he wanted her to accept, to be helped by him.

'But I would use any extra coin to make up

my brother's ransom money, not waste it on a horse.'

He stuck one hand in his hair, irritation sifting through his expression. 'In the name of Odin, Gisela, why must you argue so? The money means little to me and I refuse to walk when I can easily ride. It's not a waste if it means we can reach our destination more quickly. The only other option is for you to ride pillion, behind me, but that will slow us down considerably. Is that what you want?'

A vivid picture flashed into her mind: of her arms wrapped around that sturdy frame, her cheek pressed against the rough wool of his tunic. Her heart fluttered, a ripple of excitement. The thought of being that close to him, and remaining aloof to him, was pure torture. 'No!' she replied, her voice stinging the air with unusual force. She studied the ground, embarrassed by the violence in her voice, then lifted her chin, attempting to modulate her tone. 'We'll take two horses, then. Have it your own way.'

He laughed, a melodic rumble of humour. 'I had no idea the prospect of riding with me would be so hateful.' He shrugged his shoulders, seemingly unconcerned. 'Two horses it is, then. Truly, Gisela, you are the most obtuse woman I have ever met!'

* * *

They found a horse-dealer easily in Hoesella. The town, being on the main route to the north, was full of supplies for travellers: food, horses, woollen cloaks, even armed men for hire for those who considered the road too dangerous to travel alone. The dealer himself was a short, wiry man with most of his teeth either rotten or missing. As Ragnar and Gisela approached the field of scrubby pasture on the outskirts of town, he eyed them with an air of suspicion, frowning at Ragnar's height and wild hair, the unusual design of his sword.

'Not from around these parts, then?' the man said, his voice rasping with age. The cuffs of his tunic were frayed; greying white threads floated over his scrawny wrists. His eyes were bloodshot.

'You could say that,' Ragnar replied with deliberate vagueness. He leaned on the fence around the field containing horses of varying shapes and sizes, and narrowed his gaze over the animals. Then his eyes switched back to the dealer. 'I need two good horses for travelling.'

'How much money do you have?' the dealer chortled, eyeing the fine embroidery on the edges of Ragnar's cloak. 'I have horses to suit all pockets. That black stallion over there, he'll

cost you forty pounds, and maybe the grey palfrey for the little lady?' He pointed at a small
horse in the corner of the field. 'Five pounds for
her. Saddles and bridles extra.'

'Let me see the black,' Ragnar said.

The man slipped through the gate with a
leather halter and led the black stallion, head
tossing, out from the field. His giant hooves
thudded through the long grass as the dealer
brought him towards Ragnar.

Gisela saw it then. The yellowing of the
whites in the stallion's eye. Despite his healthy
appearance, the high-stepping power of his legs,
Gisela knew that in a few days this horse would
be dead. He carried a sickness that would kill
him. She had spent enough time in the stables
at Carsac, her home in France, to know that.
And the dealer knew it too; his desperation to
be rid of the animal before it died was palpable.
As Ragnar smoothed his hand down the horse's
neck and down its forelocks, Gisela stepped up
to him.

'Not this one, Ragnar,' she said in her halting
Saxon. 'He's no good.'

'Eh? What are you saying?' the horse-dealer
said, hopping from one thin leg to the other.
'There's nothing wrong with this one. Don't lis-

ten to your mistress, lord. She's talking non-sense.'

Ragnar straightened up and stared at her. Then he looked again at the stallion, the long proud nose, nostrils rounding, the shock of black coarse hair fringing down between his ears. 'I see it,' he muttered, evidently spotting the problem with the horse's eyes. 'Not this one,' he said to the dealer.

Grumbling beneath his breath, the man ripped the bridle from Ragnar, turning the horse to lead him back to the field.

Ragnar glanced down at Gisela. 'So, a woman who knows her horseflesh,' he said, admiration tracing his tone. 'I'm impressed. Which horses would you choose?'

'The chestnut just here,' Gisela responded immediately, indicating a thickly muscled horse on the other side of the fence, 'and the grey palfrey for me. The most you should pay for them is twenty pounds.'

Ragnar bent down and whispered in her ear, in French, 'Since when did you become a horse-dealer, Gisela?' His firm mouth brushed the top of her ear; a scythe of giddy warmth vibrated down her spine. 'You never cease to surprise me.'

Her flesh rippled beneath his light touch, a

shudder of anticipation. 'We had a lot of horses…
in France. I practically grew up in the stables.'

'Well, I agree with your choices,' he said,
smiling down at her before turning to the dealer.

'I'm surprised you let him get away with that,'
Gisela said. Pressing her feet down in the stirrups, she adjusted her position in the saddle,
spreading her skirts across the neck and down
the flanks of the horse. 'You paid too much for
them.' Ragnar rode the chestnut at her side as
they inched their way along the busy thoroughfare towards the northern gate of the town. People swarmed alongside the horses, pushing and
jolting them and each other; up ahead an empty
cart drawn by two oxen lumbered slowly.

Eyeing the cart, Ragnar sighed. 'That man
had all the time in the world, but we do not.
I could have wrangled all day, to gain…what?
Maybe an extra pound or two? It wouldn't have
been worth it. But you spotted that sick horse,
which saved us having to buy another animal
further along in our journey.'

'You saw it, too,' she acknowledged, tucking her dangling scarf end beneath her leather
bag strap that crossed her chest. Despite the late
summer sun slanting down between the gable

ends of the houses, the air held the slight chill of morning, a hint of the winter to come.

'Take the praise when it's due, Gisela,' he said. 'You certainly know your horseflesh. Did you learn from your father? Did he trade in them when you were in France?'

'He did,' she confirmed. Her heart vibrated with a pang of nostalgia, a fleeting memory of how her life had been…before, when her father had been lord of his own manor, a string of exquisite animals in his stables. Noblemen had come from far and wide to look at her father's horses; royalty, too. 'He…he was nothing like the man you saw in Bertune. You must understand…his fortunes changed on the day Ralph de Pagenal set eyes on Marie. He went from being a man of importance to a man with nothing. King William has decreed that de Pagenal will have it all, as recompense for not marrying Marie.' Sadness clouded her eyes and she fixed her gaze on the stone carved arch that decorated the gatehouse up ahead.

'You don't have to explain.' He viewed the determined jut of her chin; the slight tremble in her beautiful, rose-plush mouth. The last thing he wanted was to cause her any distress by explaining her circumstances. And yet? He wanted to know; he wanted to find out more about her, the circumstances that had formed this incredible woman.

She rubbed the rough edge of the leather bridle with her thumb. 'I know, but I don't want you to think badly of my father, for what has happened. He…he made a mistake in Bertune.' Hesitation laced her voice. 'He felt bad that I was the one who had found work and thought he would be able to raise the last bit of money by gambling.' She hitched forward in the saddle; the stiff leather squeaked, a stretching sound. 'I just hope that de Pagenal will accept the smaller amount of coin. It's not an insignificant amount.'

'I'm sure he will,' Ragnar murmured, deliberately keeping his voice on the level. And if de Pagenal didn't, then he would make up the difference. 'Especially as he already holds your estates in France. He's done exceptionally well out of demanding your sister's hand.' The wind sifted through the loose strands of hair at the back of his neck, cooling his skin. Anger rose within him, a searing protest at the unfairness of life. Gisela's family had done nothing to deserve this, other than refuse a hand in marriage, and that refusal was wholly justified, in his opinion. And now Gisela was forced to grovel and plead at de Pagenal's feet. He gritted his teeth.

He would not let it happen. He would not allow it to happen.

'It was not a wise decision for my father to go gambling,' Gisela continued, her voice small. 'But I'm sure he knows that now.'

But it brought you closer to me, Ragnar thought, steering his chestnut around a couple of impromptu market stalls set up at the end of the thoroughfare. He ducked his head to one side, avoiding a canvas awning. The striped edge jutted out into the street. *For I might never have seen you again if you hadn't gone out that night to look for the money.*

'He's not been the same since my mother died. He was devastated by her death.' Gisela chewed on her bottom lip, reddening the tender skin.

'How did your mother die?' Ragnar asked bluntly, watching the blood seep slowly back into the curving fullness of her lip. The etched line of her mouth, the velvet indent below her pert nose. She was so close he could see the fine hairs on her skin, lending the surface its dewy softness.

Despite the brusqueness of his question, she welcomed his clarity, the way he refused to sidestep around the nub of a question. It made him

easy to talk to, even about such difficult sub-
jects. A lightness played around her chest, an
easing of clenched muscles. 'My mother...she
hated leaving her beloved France, as we all did.
The sea crossing was long and arduous, and she
became sick then. Because my father had fought
in the Conquest, King William gave us an estate
on the south coast, seized in battle from a Saxon
lord. But even though we had a home, good food
on the table, my mother never recovered from
her illness on the boat.' Her voice trailed away,
her eyes filling with tears.

'I'm sorry,' Ragnar said softly. 'Is that the reason why you travel with your father? Because
there's no one at home to look after you?'

'In a way, I suppose. He doesn't like to leave
us, after what happened to Marie. I think he's
worried that de Pagenal might try again at some
point.'

'And yet he's exposing you both to far more
risk by carting you about the country. I'm surprised he even trusted me to take you.'

'He didn't have a lot of choice.' Her eyes met
his with fierce determination.

He smiled grimly. 'True.'

'But it's good that I can help you in return for
your kindness,' she said hurriedly, trying to take

the harshness out of her last statement. 'And my brother will help, too, of course.'

He nodded grimly, his eyes roaming her gentle face, the way her neat figure sat upright and steady on the grey palfrey, yet moved in harmony with the horse. A natural rider, a woman accustomed to being in the saddle. She was soft-hearted, sweet and delicate, not a bloodthirsty warrior who could cope beneath a shower of raining arrows, who could wield a sword. He doubted she could even lift a sword, let alone wield such a weapon. He had judged Ralph de Pagenal to be a monster, but surely he was just the same, by demanding that Gisela help him to track down Gyda's abductor, forcing her to go with him into a situation of such potential danger?

Chapter Twelve

Heading north, the chalk track rolled away from them across the undulating hills, the landscape rising up from the flat wetlands around the estuary. Cow parsley lined the grassy verges, billowing like white lace. Ripe corn stretched across the sloping fields, a sea of rippling pale gold, basking beneath the thick afternoon heat. A muddy depression at the edge of the field drew swallows, their black angular shapes diving frantically to feast on the insects clustering above the stagnant water. High-pitched shrieks filled the air.

It was time for harvest. Beyond a copse of trees, Gisela could see peasants working, scything the stiff corn into stooks, heads protected from the strong sun with cloth wrappings. Almost in acknowledgement of their hard work, she tugged at her tight headscarf, trying to loosen it slightly, feeling the sweat beneath the fabric gather in the hollow of her throat.

Riding alongside her, the horses plodding in tandem, Ragnar caught her fractious gesture. 'Why not take it off?' he suggested, his voice breaking their companionable silence. 'It's far too hot.'

She rounded her eyes at him, scornful. 'I can't do that!'

'Why not? It will make you feel more comfortable.'

'But... I don't...' Her voice trailed away. What had she been about to say? That because of her scar, she had never taken her headscarf off in daylight before? Most women of her age and status would plait their long hair, as she did, but only cover their heads if the weather were cold, or inclement. She gripped the rough leather of the reins, indecision wrenching her nerves into a constrictive cage.

'Go on,' he urged. 'Your scar does not trouble me, if that's what you're worried about.'

His blunt words stabbed at her; her chin lifted sharply as she narrowed her eyes on him. She remembered his lips on hers in the chamber at Bertune, his growling tones of regret after their kiss. A kiss of pity at the dreadful thing that had been done to her. Desolation rolled over her. Of course her scar did not trouble him; he was not bothered by such a thing, because she, Gisela, meant little to him. Her heart pleated with sadness.

'Fine,' she said, a hint of challenge edging her voice. She laid the reins across the horse's neck, unwinding the cloth from her head, stuffing the material into the leather satchel resting on her hip. She tugged at her borrowed cloak, pulling the coarse, bulky folds away from her throat. The breeze sifted against her heated skin; she resisted the urge to lean her head back, to savour that delicious sensation lapping her neck.

The breeze ruffled the silky curls around Gisela's forehead, tugging out golden-brown strands; they floated in the balmy air. The same colour as the ripe wheat in the field beyond, Ragnar thought. The gleaming rope of her plait curved lovingly around her neck, dropping over her rounded bosom to her waist. The curling end brushed against the point where her dress bunched on to the saddle, the fabric pillowing around her hips. A slow languorous heat rippled through him, building steadily. Had he made a mistake, encouraging her to remove her scarf?

'And you can stop staring at me,' Gisela

snapped, acutely aware of his intense scrutiny. 'You've seen it before. Remember?'

'Seen what?' he asked, bemused, dragging his eyes from the magnificent colour of her hair to her scowling expression.

'Why are you doing this?' She frowned at him in exasperation, touching her plait self-consciously. 'My scar, of course!'

'Oh, that,' Ragnar murmured, distracted. 'I wasn't looking at that.'

His eyes darkened to the deepest green, shimmering pools that spoke of enchanted woodlands, magical places.

The air thickened with incredible speed. All movement slowed: the horses' tails swishing away flies, swallows ducking and diving, the rustle of leaves in the oak trees up ahead; everything took time to push through the air, as if struggling through mud, or a thick, tangible fog.

Gisela flushed, a shuddering breath filtering through her windpipe. He stared at her as if mesmerised, as if she were some sort of beauty. Hunching her shoulders in defensive response, she tried to create some sort of barrier against his admiring appraisal. 'Stop teasing me.' Her fingers plucked in agitation at the scuffed leather saddle.

'You're a beautiful woman, Gisela.'

'Oh, don't be ridiculous!' The dull force of her voice slapped down his words. 'How can I possibly be beautiful with something like this?' Suddenly all the hurt, the fear and anxiety that she had endured since coming to England co-agulated into a massive lump of anger in her chest. His words inflamed her, unlocking the key to this suppressed emotion. Ripping the plait away from her neck, she revealed the silvery line of her scar, stretching her chin to one side so that he couldn't fail to see the line on her neck. 'Look properly, Ragnar. See my scar in daylight. You're making things worse by pre-tending it isn't there, by flattering me. It was all right before…before you came along! Now you make me think about it all the time!'

Ragnar shook his head incredulously. 'Would you prefer it if I were nasty to you?' he asked mildly, raising shaggy, wayward eyebrows, un-moved by her melodramatic behaviour. Half-rising in the saddle, he adjusted his position on the horse, flicking the hem of his cloak out be-hind him. Beneath tight-fitting braies, the firm line of his leg muscle clenched, then relaxed, re-vealing the honed contours of his thigh. Gisela swallowed, her throat tight, focusing her gaze on the plume of her horse's mane, unwilling to acknowledge the tumult of thoughts cascading through her head. *Yes*, she thought. *I would prefer it if you were nasty to me. It would make it easier for me to control my heart around you.*

She twisted her mouth into the semblance of a smile, knowing she had to answer him. 'No, of course not.'

'Good, then at least we are in agreement about that,' he replied. 'Come, let us stop beneath those trees up there and have something to eat.'

As they pulled the horses to a halt beneath the wide-spreading oak, Ragnar jumped down from his destrier and came alongside the flank of her mare. Reaching up, he gripped her firmly beneath the armpits, swinging her down to the ground: a strangely intimate gesture. His large thumbs dug into the soft flesh at the side of her breasts. Heat flooded across her pearly cheeks.

Beside them, the horses stood indolently, tails swishing in the languorous air, mosquitoes dancing above their twitching ears. Ragnar held her for a moment, so she had a chance to regain her balance after the long ride, then turned away to rummage in his saddlebags. She watched in amazement as he produced all the trappings for them to eat: a woollen blanket, which he spread across the wispy grass beneath the tree, cloth-wrapped parcels of food and a leather flagon, no doubt full of mead. The sight of this large Dane involved in such gentle domestic activities seemed incongruous, oddly delightful.

'I'm sorry,' she said, her anger slipping away. 'I have brought nothing.'

Ragnar knelt on the blanket and unwrapped the packages. Amusement lifted the corners of his mouth. 'You have been a bit too busy to go to market, Gisela. This is all from our ship, anyway. Danes always bring provisions.' He glanced up at her. 'Will you come and eat?'

She knelt down slowly on to the rug; the stiff grass made a scrunching noise beneath the colourful wool. Her hips and the back of her legs ached from the long ride. 'You seem oddly domesticated for someone who has devoted his life to battle,' she muttered.

'Even warriors have to eat,' he replied, handing her a substantial slice of dark-brown bread. He laughed at her look of dismay. 'This is rye bread. We eat this with smoked fish.' He indicated the pinkish-grey slices lying on a piece of muslin.

Gisela bit tentatively into the bread. The only time she had seen bread so dark before was when it had burned. The taste was unusual, with a slight sourness, but it was not unpleasant. She chewed hungrily. 'It's good.' Surprise laced her voice.

'My mother makes it,' Ragnar said, laying a slice of fish on top of his bread. 'It keeps for ages before going stale. That's why we take it on our travels.'

'Your mother...?' Her eyes rounded at him in astonishment.

He grinned. 'I do have one, you know. And a father. I'm not the spawn of the Devil, whatever you might think.'

'No, it's not that...' She brushed distractedly at the crumbs that had fallen from the bread on to the lap of her gown. 'You've never mentioned your family before, that's all.'

'Maybe I've had other things on my mind,' he replied. His emerald eyes gleamed over her. 'Much has happened in the past two days.' Since they met. Since he had hauled her, barely conscious, from the swirling brown water.

The sun had shifted position, sneaking beneath the cool shade of the tree, warming Gisela's spine. The stretched tension in her muscles, the strain of the last few hours seemed to dissipate in the shimmering afternoon heat. Swallowing the remainder of the bread, she brought her knees up to her body, hugging her shins. 'Where do they live?' she asked.

'My family, you mean?' He chewed thoughtfully. 'We have an estate to the west of Ribe, in Denmark. Ribe is a port, on the coast: the place where we sailed from, to come to England.'

'Is your father a warrior, too?' Gisela smoothed her palm across the bright colours of the rug, her heart fluttering at the ease of their conversation. If only it could be like this for the rest of the journey, if only they could travel as friends, then… then her heart might survive unscathed.

Ragnar laughed. 'Nay, his raiding days are over. He devotes his life to farming our land now, with the help of a bailiff and my mother, of course. She keeps him in line.' A note of tenderness laced his voice.

'You sound as if you are very close to your parents,' she said. Grief sifted through her as she thought of her own mother, of her wasted journey to England and the fear and sickness that had finally killed her.

In the shadowy light beneath the tree, Gisela's face shone out, revealing her sadness, she was sure. Ragnar shrugged his shoulders. 'I've been lucky,' he replied carefully.

'Your mother sounds formidable,' Gisela said, straightening her spine. Feeling sorry for herself would not help this situation.

'Aye, she is.' Ragnar's eyes twinkled with

memory. 'She's hardly taller than you, yet she rules the household like a battle commander.' He laughed, his gaze drifting across the rippling field, the pale heads of wheat. The sound of rustling grass filled the air, mingling with the occasional shout from the workers in the field beyond. 'You would like her.'

Her heart pounded. What was he saying? That he would take her back to Denmark to meet his mother? A strange longing possessed her: an image of sitting beside a fire, opposite Ragnar, their feet stretched out towards each other, almost touching. Having someone to nurture and to love and to grow old with. That's what he made her think about when he spoke of his family. A widening ache, heavy as a boulder, lodged deep in her belly. It was a dream that she could never hope to have and she would do well to dispel such a notion, unless she was to feel sad for the rest of her days.

'I expect I would,' she replied finally, her voice wooden. Raising herself on her knees, she started to wrap up the open packages, her movements brisk, succinct, trying to cover the hurt surging up within her.

'Hold a moment.' Ragnar's hand shot out, clasping her wrist. 'I haven't finished eating yet.'

'Sorry.' She slumped back on to her heels, her

fingers twisting in her lap. The tight waistband of her gown dug into her side. 'I suppose there's more of you, back in Denmark,' she said, scouting around for something to fill the lengthening silence. 'Have you brothers, or sisters?'

'I have a sister.' The warmth drained from his voice, freezing his low tone.

'And is she as formidable as your mother?' Gisela forced a teasing note into her voice. 'A battle commander in the making?'

'No, she's not.' Ragnar's voice was brusque, harsh. He began to wrap up the packages quickly, rising from the rug to stuff them back into his saddlebags. The easy mood between them was broken, shattered. Her last question had ripped through their easy camaraderie like shears through silk. What in heaven's name had she said to upset him?

'Ragnar...' The tender note in her voice faltered as she twisted around to look up at him. 'I'm sorry if I've said something...that I shouldn't have.'

His fingers stalled on the buckle of his satchel. The horse's rump shimmered before his eyes, glossy and smooth, flies bobbing above the swishing tail. He saw nothing but the white, wretched face of his sister as she was carried off the ship at Ribe. Guilt surged around his heart, pinching cruelly. But his sister's plight was not Gisela's fault. Far from it. She did not deserve to be on the receiving end of his disgruntled shame.

He jabbed his boot into the baked mud at the side of the field, kicked at the crumbling earth. Could he tell Gisela what he had done to his sister? She had a low enough opinion of him already, so maybe such an admission would make no difference. But would it turn her against him for ever? He wondered, for a moment, if he could bear such a thing, to be the recipient of her hate, her disapproval. But what did it matter? Once they had helped each other, they would go their separate ways, back to their families, and they would never see each other again.

'My sister…is not well.' Ragnar's voice, when it finally emerged, cracked with emotion. 'She's the reason I'm here, in this country.' He chewed the inside of his cheek, tasted iron in his mouth. The situation with his sister was one that he scarcely voiced. Shame tingled through him, twisting his gut.

He tugged on the leather strap, forcefully, securing the satchel. His arm rested along the horse's back. 'About a year ago, my sister travelled to England with the man she loved,' he said slowly. 'And a month later, that same man's body was brought back to Denmark. Without my sister. He had been killed and my sister had vanished somewhere in this hell-bound country.' He stuck one hand through his hair, tousling the wind-blown strands. 'No one knew what had happened. I came to England…with a few men, with Eirik, hoping to find her. And luckily, we did. But she is a changed woman.' His voice dropped, a muted whisper. His lean tanned fingers worried at the stitching on his saddle.

He jumped. Gisela was beside him. Her step was so light that he hadn't heard her approach. The heady scent of roses, that poignant smell of summer, filled his nostrils: the perfume of her skin. Her sleeve brushed against his elbow. His torso constricted abruptly in response to her nearness, the faint brush of her body. He drew strength from her, the courage to talk, to confide. 'We took her back to Denmark, but we…my family…don't know how to help her. She weeps continually and will not speak. My mother is afraid that she will take her own life if we don't find out what happened to her in England.'

Her fingers crept along his arm to his hand; she squeezed his hard, warm flesh, rubbing the prominent bump of his wrist bone. 'My God,' she whispered. 'So this man you want us to find...' Her voice trailed off, dismay lacing her tone.

'Whoever he is...he abducted Gyda.' Ragnar's mouth set into a grim, fixed line. 'When I found her, eventually, she was in Hoesella. A travelling merchant had found her wandering alone and had brought her back to live with them. The merchant told me the spot where he had found her, on the road north of Jorvik. But I had no time to go back to that place; I had to take Gyda home.' Pain laced his heart. He did not want to think about what had happened to his sister. Revulsion rose in his gullet. Balling his fist, he thumped it against the flat of the saddle.

'But how will finding this man help your sister?' Gisela asked. She watched the hurt leach through his expression and the urge to reach out and comfort him, to draw him close, surged through her. His pulse jolted powerfully against her fingers.

He shrugged his shoulders. 'We don't know what else to do,' he replied. 'Maybe it will give us some answers, a clue as to how we can help her.' He looked down at her, his mouth terse and rigid. 'I'm prepared to try anything.'

She squeezed his wrist: a gesture of comfort, of reassurance. 'You're a good brother, Ragnar.'

A shudder racked his big body. 'Nay, I am not,' he replied. Rawness stretched his voice, a bitter thinness.

'But you are!' Gisela responded, her voice bright. 'To do all this for her, to try to find out what happened.'

Redness rimmed the startling green of his eyes. A muscle quirked in his jaw. 'It's the least I can do, Gisela.' He sighed. 'You see, I caused the whole situation in the first place.' Above their heads, the arching branches of the oak dipped and swayed, casting a dark stripe of shadow across his body.

'What do you mean?' The heat pressed down in thick layers on the back of her neck, oppressive. Sweat prickled beneath her ear.

'I was the one who encouraged her to travel to England in the first place, with the man she loved.' His voice jolted, forcing the words out. 'My parents were against them marrying, but I could see how much they loved each other. I knew that once they were on board that ship, then my parents could do nothing to prevent them being together.'

'Oh, Ragnar,' she said breathily. 'It was not your fault. You could never have expected such a thing to happen.' Without thinking, she lifted her hands to his face, cupped his jawline, wanting to smooth out the lines of wretchedness that carved his cheeks. Almost instinctively his arms came around her, around her shoulders, then her waist. He winched her close, roughly, as if wanting the comfort of her body against his. Just for a moment.

The lurch of his strong body against hers tipped her off balance. Her hands dropped from his face to clutch his upper arms for support. She was so close to him that the top of her head brushed his chin. She yearned to tuck her face into the hollow of his neck, to breathe in the sweet leathery scent of his flesh, but she held herself rigid, resisting. The muscles in her legs screamed with the effort of holding herself away. What would happen if she threw caution to the winds and cleaved to his body as her heart begged her to do? She would be burned, that's what, and her heart would be destroyed. Better to hold herself aloof, than risk destruction.

Chapter Thirteen

Ragnar closed his eyes, wanting to savour the moment for ever: her delicate scent rising to his nostrils, the satin slip of her sand-coloured hair against his chin. He marvelled at the power in her small body to knit together the ragged threads of his wretched spirit, alleviating the scourging harshness of the guilt that had plagued him ever since his sister had disappeared.

'So now you know what kind of man I am,' he said slowly, tentatively.

She lifted her face, the dancing glow of her cheeks inches from his own. 'It wasn't your fault, Ragnar. You are the same man that I thought you were before you told me.'

'Still a barbarian, then.' He laughed. The sound was harsh, strident, but his attempt at humour eased the tension. Relief coursed through him; he was surprised. He had no idea that her opinion of him mattered so much and yet, he realised that it did.

Gisela pushed back against the muscular brace of his arms, tipping her head to gain a better view of his face. 'Aye, definitely a barbarian,' she agreed. But she was smiling.

A bubble of voices coming along the track floated through the somnolent air, breaking the mood between them. Ragnar's arms dropped from Gisela's waist, reluctantly, and he stepped away, flicking the rug from the ground and bundling the fabric into his saddle bags.

'We should move on,' he said briskly, watching as a group of straggling farm workers made their way along the track, carrying scythes and leather satchels. Their faces were red and sweaty, streaked with grime, and their voices fell silent as they spotted the couple standing beneath the oak. Noticing Ragnar's silver-riveted surcoat, the jewelled helm on his sword, they bowed, one by one, acknowledging his noble status.

The shadows were lengthening, stretching out across the fields of bronze stubble. Ragnar hooked his fingers together; Gisela placed her foot carefully into the cradle of his hands and he boosted her into the saddle. He mounted up, swinging his animal around in a circle.

'Not much further,' he said, nodding towards the track. 'We should reach Ralph de Pagenal's manor before the sunset.'

The untidy sprawl of thatched cottages seemed to float in the middle of the marsh, a haphazard collection of domestic buildings clustered around a timbered hall house. Smoke rose listlessly from individual chimney holes: lazy dribbles of grey against the pale-blue sky. Around the cottages, animals were contained by low fences of split chestnut. All around this raised piece of land, strips of water glinted, bands of silver in the setting sun, evidence of poor drainage. In some places, the ground was completely flooded with not a speck of green grass to be seen.

'Looks like de Pagenal spends more time battling than farming,' Ragnar said grimly, casting a critical eye over the badly maintained ground. 'Although the water provides an excellent defence. Only one way in and out.' They had reined in the horses on the brow of a ridge so they could look down on the Norman lord's estate. The breeze coming in over the flat land from the North Sea ruffled the horses' manes.

Gisela shuddered. Nerves hollowed out her stomach. The prospect of meeting her tormentor again had suddenly become very real, frighteningly close. This was his home, the estate given to him by the Conqueror. But the humble manor that lay below her did not fit with the arrogant knight who had kicked and slashed at her, who had hauled her sister, screaming, against the flank of his horse, until Gisela had pulled her away.

'We should go down,' Ragnar said. 'We will have been seen by now.'

Leaves drifted down from the beech trees behind, rustling close to her ear, scuffing along the tufted grass. Her saddle creaked as her mare sidled beneath her. She knew that if she dismounted now, fear would have driven the strength from her legs; her limbs would not support her. 'What if they attack us?' she asked, her voice cracking with anxiety. 'What if they decide to never let us go?'

Ragnar's clear green eyes swept the pallid disc of her face. 'A couple, travelling alone? It's unlikely. We are worth little to them.'

A couple. His words reverberated in her ear, sending a coil of warmth down through her chest. He made it sound like they were truly together. A husband and wife, journeying on horseback. She flushed, enjoying thinking of that image of herself with him, allowing herself to dream for a moment. Nibbling sharply at her bottom lip, she dragged herself back to reality, to the flooded, barren wasteland below them, to the prospect of meeting Ralph de Pagenal once more.

'I don't trust him,' she said. 'I know what he's capable of.' She kneaded the aching muscles in her right thigh, an absent-minded gesture.

'We will stay only as long as is needed,' Ragnar responded quietly. He read the flare of panic in her eyes and hated it. Hated the man who had done this to her. Who sapped her courage when she needed it the most. 'We will give him the money, claim your brother and leave.'

'You make it sound so easy.' Her slim fingers, agitated, fiddled with the cheap metal pin that held her borrowed cloak together, then she unwound her long scarf from her saddlebag to wind it back around her head.

'That's because it is.' The dull brown fabric obscured the bright sheen of her hair; he mourned the loss of the glistening braid. 'Are you ready?'

'As ready as I'll ever be.' Clenching the reins, her knuckles were white, delicate knobs of bone.

He threw her an encouraging smile. 'Nothing is going to happen to you in there, Gisela. I will make certain of it.'

She took a deep unsteady breath. 'Yes, because you need me to help you.'

'No, because I...' What had he been about to say? *Because I would do anything for you?* How was that even possible for him to think such a thing about her? He had only known the girl for barely two days.

Astounded by his own feelings, he fixed her with his bold emerald stare. 'Gisela, I would protect you whether you were helping me or not!' he replied. 'What sort of man do you take me for? I rescued you from the river when I had no idea who you were. I could have revealed your true identity to the world when I realised you were Norman...'

'All right...all right!' Despite her worries about what lay ahead, she laughed, holding up her palms towards him, appealing for mercy.

'Well, then,' he muttered reproachfully, 'as long as you are fully aware that I'm not about to feed you to the lions.'

Jabbing his heels into his horse's rump, he took off at a fast trot down to the lower ground by the marshes. A series of wooden bridges crossed the boggy land to the farmstead on the island. Gisela followed in his wake, her mare descending the steep ridge more slowly, then stepping up on to the planks. Up ahead, a wooden gatehouse was set into a palisade wall: a wall formed of oak stakes, each one honed to a deadly point. Any man would risk certain death if he attempted to climb them.

There was no guard in sight. A group of labourers gathered in front of the gatehouse watched their approach across the bridges, eyeing the fineness of Ragnar's cloak and sword as he drew closer. Their clothes were dusty, sweat-stained, evidence of hard toil in the fields.

'Good day to you.' Ragnar dismounted, throwing his reins across the horse's neck. He came around to the front of Gisela's mare. 'Stay there,' he ordered her swiftly, as if sensing she was about to dismount. He snagged her reins to stop her animal moving forward.

The men nodded back at him. 'What business do you have here, young man?' asked one. 'If you're after a bed, you'll not be getting one. The lord does not like visitors.'

'Nay, we're not after a bed,' Ragnar said in his oddly accented Saxon. 'But it's your lord that we've come to see.'

The men shifted uneasily. The oldest man, his grey beard grizzled, took a step closer to Ragnar. 'He'll never see you if you go in dressed as you are. You're a Dane, are you not?'

'What if I am?' Ragnar replied.

'We know that you've come to help us Saxons,' the man whispered. 'We had word that the Danish ships had landed. You're going to help us rid our country of these Norman invaders.' He spat derisively on the ground. 'The Conqueror has given this place to de Pagenal, and we must work for him now if we are to survive. God knows where our Saxon chief has gone.'

Gisela shifted uncomfortably in the saddle at the men's revelation. And yet it was unlikely that they would identify her as Norman; she had lived and worked among the Saxons at Bertune for a couple of days and nobody there had questioned her identity.

'Take off your cloak and brooch, and wear this instead.' Lifting the hem of his hooded tunic, the old man yanked the coarse fustian fabric over his head. Removing his cloak, Ragnar bundled the expensive wool into his saddlebag, pulling on the Saxon's tunic over his leather surcoat and red woollen tunic. The hem fell to his knees.

'It's big enough to cover that sword of yours as well. Pull the hood up and hide that Viking hair of yours. That way he'll not be able to tell where you're from.' The men were nodding at each other now, silently congratulating themselves on a job well done.

Swinging her leg forward over the horse's neck, Gisela slid down from the saddle, down in between the two horses, standing at Ragnar's back. He turned, surprised to see her there, eyes widening. 'I was going to lead you in on the horse,' he said. In the shadows of the hood, his sparkling eyes gleamed.

'Ragnar, it's not safe for you,' she whispered, her chest bubbling with fear. 'Stay with these men and I will go in alone.'

'Out of the question.'

She touched his sleeve. 'I am Norman, any guard will let me in. I'm afraid something…' Her voice trailed away. What had she been about to say? *I'm afraid something might happen to you.* Yes, that was it. The terrible image of some Norman soldier driving his sword through Ragnar was almost too much to bear.

He laughed. 'I didn't know you cared.'

Her heart squeezed tight with unshed emotion. *I do*, she thought. *I care more than you think*. A desperate sense of unease flooded through her at the thought of losing him. She smoothed her hand across the napped pelt of her mare, catching the heel of her hand on the saddle. 'I wouldn't want to give de Pagenal the satisfaction,' she said, finally. 'He's caused so much trouble already.'

'You're not going in on your own and that is final,' he said. 'I speak French; they will assume that I am Norman, albeit one that has fallen on hard times.' He plucked at the coarse wool of the cloak, turning down the corners of his mouth ruefully, before looping his arm decisively around hers. The strong muscle in his forearm flexed against her own. 'We're in this together, Gisela.'

Leaving the horses with the Saxons at the gate, they walked through the shifting gloom of the gatehouse, then out again into the brightness of the afternoon. Hens picked their jerky way across the rutted muddy path, searching for grain; geese honked, wild-eyed, as they noticed the presence of strangers, their white-feathered undersides filthy with mud. Fear weighed heavy at the bottom of her stomach, lodged like a boulder.

Ragnar paused for a moment, narrowing his gaze on the scene, gaining his bearings. He watched as a wiry-haired sow, russet-coloured, scratched her backside against a hurdle, making the woven willow bend and creak.

'It's over there,' Gisela said, dipping her head to indicate a large hall house. 'There are Norman soldiers at the door, look.' The guards stood on either side of a wide, oak-planked door, faces concealed by conical metal helmets, armed with swords and shields. She shivered, gripped by doubt. Their presence was arousing curiosity. A woman, sitting on a stool outside her cottage, had been spinning fleece with a drop spindle. Now her hands were stalled, the spindle turning more and more slowly, until it stopped, as she stared at them with bright, beady eyes.

'Come on,' he said. 'We can do this.'

Gisela shifted the bulk of her leather bag more securely on to her hip. She bit her lip, doubt cascading through her slim frame. 'All right,' she agreed. 'But let me do the talking.'

In the end, it was easy. The guards listened carefully as Gisela rattled away in French to them, explaining why it was imperative that she met with Ralph de Pagenal, then nodded and opened the hefty oak latch for them both to pass through into the hall. They barely glanced at Ragnar, his big bulk standing silently at Gisela's side, face shadowed by the voluminous hood.

'They think you're my servant,' Gisela whispered as they plunged into the darkness of an entrance hall. A fusty smell emanated from the packed earth floor. Some of the wooden planks forming the walls were rotten, coated in mould.

'I don't care who or what they think I am,' Ragnar said quietly, 'as long as they let me in with you. Stay close to me.' They passed through a curtain into a smoke-filled, double-height chamber. The hall was sparsely furnished: an elm chest, pitted and scarred with age, butted up against the wall, painted cloths, most faded and in tatters, drooped down in ragged swags over coarsely plastered walls. At the far end was a long trestle table at which a single figure sat: Ralph de Pagenal.

Her heart lurched, nausea roiling in her stomach. Sweat sprung to her palms, making them slip on the leather strap of her bag. Stepping forward, she walked clumsily into the edge of a trestle table, jabbing her thigh; her eyes watered from the impact.

'Careful,' Ragnar said, taking her arm. The taut muscle of his bicep nudged her upper arm.

Slumped back in his high-backed oak chair, de Pagenal watched them approach. His gaze honed in on Gisela, like a fox scenting his prey. 'Well, well,' he said as they skirted around the circular hearth, the fire belching smoke towards the hole in the roof. 'You finally decided to come, my lady. Took your time, didn't you?'

Despite the sun-filled day outside, the room was gloomy, lit by guttering candles. The choking smell of tallow filled the air. Grease spots sparkled down the front of de Pagenal's fustian tunic. Gisela forced herself to look at him, to stare at this man who haunted her dreams and trailed behind her days. It was the same face, and yet...he appeared to be different. Diminished somehow, smaller in stature. Was it the bold Dane at her side who gave her the confidence to see this man for what he truly was?

'I came as soon as I could.' They reached the table, standing in front of de Pagenal. He squinted up at them, scowling, clearly disliking the fact that they towered above them. Pushing his chair back, he stood up, swaying gently. His tunic was too tight; the curve of his belly pushed out over his leather belt.

'Your father is not with you. What happened?' De Pagenal was slurring his words; he lurched forward suddenly, gripping the edge of the table for support.

'He fell ill. So I came alone. I have the money, here...' Gisela patted the leather satchel. 'To pay the ransom for my brother. Where is he, please? I am anxious to see him.'

De Pagenal's bleary eyes moved over to Ragnar, standing silently beside Gisela. 'But you're not alone, are you, Lady Gisela? Will you not introduce your husband?'

'Oh, but he's not my...'

Ragnar jerked sharply on her arm, stopping the words in her throat. 'My name is not important,' he spoke in perfect French. 'But what is important is the whereabouts of this lady's brother. Where is he?'

De Pagenal leaned forward, a slight leer to his expression. 'You...whoever you are—' he jabbed the air with one thick finger '—do not get to dictate terms. My deal was with this lady's father and her family. It is not your affair.'

'Whatever concerns Lady Gisela is my affair,' Ragnar said, pushing back his hood.

De Pagenal's eyes rounded at the sight of his flaming hair, bright strands glowing in the dim light of the hall. He stepped back, banging the back of his legs awkwardly against the chair, confusion crossing his face.

'Do not even think of calling your soldiers.' Ragnar's voice held a menacing streak. 'I would slit your throat in the blink of an eye, before your men have time to race in here and save your skin.'

De Pagenal's gaze flicked warily over Ragnar's stern expression before his eyes whipped back to Gisela's pale face. 'So you've resorted to hiring Danish mercenaries to guard you, my lady. I would be careful if I were you, especially with that ransom money. What would your father say if he knew how low you have stooped?'

Ragnar thumped his fist on the table. The plates rattled and jumped. 'Just give us the boy, de Pagenal, and we will pay the ransom and be on our way.'

The Norman lord collapsed back in his seat, a mocking smile pinned across his face. 'But Richard is not here.'

Gisela moved forward, her feet tangling against the long tablecloth that gathered on the flagstones. 'What do you mean? You took him hostage! He is your prisoner; how can he not be here?'

'You're too late, Lady Gisela.' De Pagenal twisted his mouth to a terse little smirk: a look of gloating triumph. 'I gave up on you and your pathetic little family ever reaching this place. I don't want your ransom. I've sold your brother for three times as much.'

'Nay, you're lying,' Gisela cried out, her voice rising shrilly. Disbelief coursed through her, a shard of ice, driving deep. 'What have you done with him?' Leaning over the narrow table, over the jumble of half-eaten food on dirty pewter dishes, she grabbed two large fistfuls of de Pagenal's tunic, intending to shake the truth from him.

'Get away from me!' De Pagenal slapped at her hands, a heavy chopping motion, instinctive. 'Christ, woman, you were always a feisty piece. Should have sliced my blade a little deeper, shouldn't I? Then I'd be spared all this nonsense!' He flicked a glance at Ragnar. 'You'll not be long in her employ, I'll be bound. How much coin did she have to give you to persuade you to accompany her up here?'

'Stop lying to me!' cried Gisela, her fists digging into the cloth of de Pagenal's tunic. 'Tell me the truth!' Ragnar's arm swooped around her waist, hauling her back, away from de Pagenal, away from the table, wedging her firmly against his chest.

'You've got your hands full there,' muttered de Pagenal. 'Keep her under control, will you?' Beads of sweat rolled across de Pagenal's ridged brow, wobbling orbs of liquid. 'I *am* telling you the truth.' He rolled his shoulders forward, as if contemplating how best to tell his story. 'I sold your brother to the good-for-nothing Saxon chief who owned this miserable castle. He took him away when he left this place; paid good money for him as well.' He turned his palms to the ceiling, shrugging his shoulders, 'I couldn't resist. You can't blame me. I never thought your father would be able to raise the money.'

'You sold him...to a Saxon? My God, he won't survive! The Saxons hate us, hate everything we Normans have done to their country,' Gisela shouted, pushing down Ragnar's arm, an iron band around her waist. His knee was jammed against the back of her thigh.

'Stop fighting me.' His breath was hot, gently caressing the silky lobe of her ear. 'We're in this together, remember?'

'I think he's killed him, Ragnar!' She was openly sobbing now, great gusting tears welling up from deep in her chest. She plucked frantically at Ragnar's sleeve, wriggling in his hold. 'Where is he? Where's Richard?' In desperation she opened the flap of her leather satchel hanging below Ragnar's arm and brought out the pouch containing the gold coins. 'Here! Take this and give me my brother!' Stretching forward, she threw the sack on the table in front of de Pagenal. The loosely gathered neck of the bag opened; coins spilled out over the fat-stained tablecloth.

'I...don't...want...it.' De Pagenal spat the words out, enunciating heavily as he slumped back in his chair. 'You need to leave now, both of you,' he barked at them. 'There's nothing for you here.' He jabbed a finger towards Gisela, with the air of delivering an important lesson. 'You took Marie from me. I loved her and I would have been a good husband to her...'

'No!' Gisela railed at him, waving her arms out in front of her, as if swimming through air. 'How dare you say such a thing! You would have broken her and well you know it!'

De Pagenal's eyes moved slyly to a spot on Gisela's neck. 'Well, at least I made sure no one would have you...' He cackled, drawing one finger diagonally across his neck, a slicing motion. 'We all know what hides beneath that scarf, don't we? Who would bed you now? You will be alone till the end of your days, Lady Gisela.'

As suddenly as he had seized her, Ragnar released Gisela, sending her staggering to one side with the force of his movement. He sprung on to the table, drawing his sword with a sibilant hiss. His booted feet clattered through the plates and goblets, the spill of gold coins; the flagon crashed to the floor. Red wine spilled down the tablecloth. The point of his blade flashed forward, suspended a hair's breadth from de Pagenal's throat. 'You deserve to die for what you did to her,' Ragnar growled.

De Pagenal sprawled back in his chair, his face a pallid grey. 'But you will not kill me,' he managed to spit out through bloodless lips. 'For I am the only one who knows where Richard is.'

'Ragnar, stop!' screamed Gisela, lurching forward. 'Do not!' She pulled at his sleeve, reaching up to tug on his leather waist-belt in an effort to yank him down from the table. 'Come now, come away!' A huge sadness welled in her chest, a wave of grief. 'Come now, come away...' she spluttered out, struggling to find enough breath to speak, gasping and coughing as if all the words she wanted to say became jammed in her throat instead. The room wavered before her eyes, looming large before receding rapidly.

Sheathing his sword, Ragnar jumped down from the table. He caught Gisela as she fell, her knees no longer able to support her wavering frame.

'Get her out of here before I call in the guards,' de Pagenal growled, regaining some of his lost composure. He tore at a hunk of bread and stuffed it into his mouth.

'Don't think I wouldn't do it next time,' growled Ragnar. 'This is not the end, de Pagenal, and well you know it!' He gathered Gisela's coins before hoisting her up against his chest. She lay as if stunned, her head lolling against his shoulder, half-conscious with grief and shock. The Norman guards stood to attention as he passed through the arched doorway and strode across the bailey to the gatehouse, his strides long and purposeful, his gaze raking the high curtain wall for any sign of trouble.

Chapter Fourteen

Gisela's mind hazed, stumbling along, grasping at fragments that made no sense. As she gradually regained consciousness, she realised that Ragnar carried her. His rugged forearm pressed intimately against the back of her thighs, her hip nudged against his chest. For one delicious moment, she allowed herself to luxuriate in the feeling of weightlessness, the feeling that…someone else cared enough to carry her away from trouble. Then slowly, Ragnar turned her upright, letting her slide down to her feet. The hard ground outside the gatehouse jabbed against her heels, sending juddering waves through her shins. Her ankles ached.

'Oh!' she gasped, clutching at Ragnar's borrowed tunic for support.

'Steady,' he said. 'You need to ride now, Gisela.'

'But... Richard?' She peered around in desperation, searching for the brother who was not there: the wooden palisade, the stretch of sparse grass around the stronghold, the watery marshland beyond. The place was deserted. Even the Saxon men who Ragnar had talked to when they first arrived had disappeared; the large wooden gate was firmly shut.

'Richard isn't there, Gisela.'

Reality crashed down around her. She had no wish to remember, to hear de Pagenal's cruel, triumphant words echo around her head like a tolling bell. Her belly hollowed out with grief, as if a great stone had lodged there. Numbly, she allowed Ragnar to boost her up into the saddle; the mare lurched sideways as she settled into the hard, curved leather seat. She swayed forward, reaching out for the reins, holding the worn straps loosely between her fingers, then dropped them, letting them fall across the horse's neck. 'I need to go back in there, Ragnar,' she said slowly, fastening her eyes on the palisade, the roof of the timbered hall peeking above the sharpened posts 'I have to persuade de Pagenal to tell me where Richard is.' She took a deep, shaky breath. 'Even if he's...if he's dead.'

Sighing, Ragnar pulled the borrowed Saxon tunic over his head. Folding the cloth, he laid it by the palisade; the owner would return to collect it at some point. Extracting his own cloak from the saddlebag, he fastened the heavy woollen fabric around his shoulders. The embroidered hem swung down in a half-circle around his slim hips as he gripped both sides of his saddle. 'Not now, Gisela. De Pagenal's too drunk to think straight.' He glanced up at the darkening sky. 'We can come back on the morrow.' He swung himself up on to his horse.

Gisela kicked her foot out from the stirrup and brought her leg over the horse's neck, aiming to dismount. She would go back in there and have a sensible conversation with de Pagenal.

'Don't you dare!' growled Ragnar, budging his horse up against hers, flank to flank, so that her left leg was effectively pinned against the horse's side.

Anger drove through her misery. 'Let me go!' she demanded. 'Why not let me try to speak to him again?' She wriggled violently in the saddle, swinging from side to side, trying to manoeuvre her mare away from Ragnar, but to no avail. She was well and truly stuck.

'I am not going to let you go back in there and make a fool of yourself.' Ragnar's voice was low, but held the thread of steel. 'De Pagenal has nearly killed you once already! Do you want him to try again? He might just succeed if you rile him enough!'

Her eyes traced the carved lines of his tanned face, the generous mouth tilted up at the corners, the semblance of a smile. A deep shuddery breath gripped her lungs, her throat. 'I know you're right, Ragnar—' her voice was wretched '—but I wish you were not. I have to keep trying. I can't bear the thought of going back to my father and sister without Richard. They will be devastated.'

'We will find out what happened to him,' Ragnar replied gently. Leaning across, he touched her cheek.

His warm fingers danced against her skin, the briefest touch, like spider silk. Spirals of desire whipped through her chest, her belly; her face bloomed with heat. She jerked away, staring in desolation at the frothing plume of her horse's mane.

Ragnar glanced at the gathering clouds on the horizon and frowned. 'We need to leave and find a place to sleep tonight.' He tapped his heels into his horse's flank, wheeling the animal around. 'Shall we go?'

Her heart cleaved with wretchedness, but she yanked on the reins, turning her animal to follow Ragnar up the zig-zag path to the copse of oaks at the top of the ridge. The stench of the stronghold clung to her clothes, even now, as she rode away in the strengthening breeze: the sour smell of tallow, the sweat and rancid fat of the food. Her whole journey north had been a waste. She wished she could erase everything, every last bitter detail, and start again, the three of them back with her father in their castle in the south.

And yet, as her horse picked its way carefully up the loose stones of the track and she watched the graceful ease with which Ragnar rode, the sinewy flex of his spine, the breadth of his shoulders blocking out the trail beyond, she realised that she had no wish to forget everything. Certainly not this great Dane, who made her heart dance with treacherous need, whose casual glance drove stabs of desire deep into her loins. Nay, despite everything that had happened, she had no wish to forget him.

Crows, black wings curved like knife blades, flapped wildly in the grey air, trying to control their flight in the savage gusts of wind. The long day was lengthening into evening, a day that had started with her sister on the shore at Bertune and ended with her old enemy, de Pagenal. Yet the day wasn't over. There was still enough light to ride, despite the massive clouds rolling in and obscuring the bright disc of sun that lowered slowly towards the horizon. Leaves whirled down from the towering oaks to their right, littering the air, skipping along the track before them. The line of oaks ended abruptly, the track heading off over open fields. Ragnar pulled on his reins.

'Down there,' he said, pointing towards a small copse of trees in the valley. 'We will be able to shelter there for the night.' He eyed the clouds to the north, bunching ominously into grey florets of blossoming rain.

'How can you be so sure?' she asked, nudging her horse alongside his.

He extracted the leather flagon from his saddlebag and yanked out the stopper, offering it to Gisela. She shook her head. He tipped the bottle up to his mouth, gulping down the refreshing mead. A droplet of liquid shone on his bottom lip and he wiped it away with his sleeve, banging the stopper back into place. 'Instinct,' he said. His mouth twitched.

'I don't believe a word of it,' Gisela shot back at him. 'You have no idea.'

'Correct.' He grinned back at her, stupidly pleased that the colour had returned to her cheeks after what had happened with de Pagenal. The cruel words that Norman lord had flung at her. Her eyes sparkled, a curious sapphire colour in the strange stormy light. If he could make her laugh, then all would be well, he thought.

A large drop of rain hit his head, the water creeping down, cold, against his scalp. Then another. A squall was heading straight for them, a hazy band that stretched from land to sky, sweeping the ground like a curtain. 'Follow me into the forest,' he shouted. Kicking his horse sharply, he took off down the slope. Gisela set her own horse in motion, albeit at a slightly slower speed, galloping down the hill after him.

Breathing heavily from the exertion of the ride, they reached the boundary of the forest, slowing the animals to a walk. The rain had soaked through the layers of Gisela's headscarf and into her hair, rivulets washing over her face. As they picked their way through the trees, the spreading canopy of branches staved off the worst of the deluge, with only a sprinkling of drops working their way down to the forest floor.

They reached a place where the trees grew low and stunted, jagged branches contorted against the monotonous grey sky. Leaves curled inwards, their edges frayed brown; with every squall of wind, a few more detached, spiralling to the spongy forest floor. Squinting through the undergrowth, Gisela pointed to a series of planks, some tilting sideways. 'Is that something?' she asked.

Ragnar jumped down, handing Gisela the reins to his horse, and strode over the sodden ground towards the structure. With every step he took, brown peaty water sloshed over the toes of his boots; a sour, marshy odour filled the air. Reaching the moss-covered planks, he peered into what looked like the remains of a woodsman's hut, then ducked his head, going inside. The ground was dry at least, dusty with old leaves. 'It will do,' he called out to Gisela. 'I can't stand up in it, but it will keep the rain off us for tonight. And we're far away enough from de Pagenal, in case he decides to send his men out after us. They'll never find us here.'

'But what if it belongs to someone else?' she asked. 'They might return for the night.'

Ragnar kicked at the pile of leaves around the entrance, bending to pick up the twigs that had fallen around the front of the hut. 'No one's been here for ages,' he said. He blinked the raindrops out of his eyes, his lashes wet and spiky. The rain had plastered his hair to his scalp, darkening the colour of the strands to burnished copper.

Her heart gripped; she stifled a gasp. She remembered the last time they had shared a room, back at the Saxon lord's castle in Bertune. The heat of the chamber as he had stood behind her as she washed. The water dripping from her bare arms as she had turned to face him.

Straightening up, his arms full of thin, knotted branches, Ragnar caught her look of dismay. He grimaced. 'Look, I know it's hardly a palace, but it's all we have for tonight. It will have to do.'

'It's not that.' Gisela slid down from her horse; her skirts bunching behind her. She flicked down the hem, impatient with the yards of cloth. She would do well to remember what had happened after that moment, after he had seen her scar. His rejection of her. He would think nothing of them sharing this hut, because he was not in the least attracted to her. De Pagenal was correct: she would be alone for the rest of her life.

'What is it, then?' Crouching down, balancing on the balls of his feet, Ragnar struck a spark with his flintstone into a piece of dried moss that he carried for the purpose, then quickly piled small sections of twig around it. The overhanging roof of the hut meant they could start a fire in the dry, without smoking out the interior. 'Gisela?'

Her fingers worked at the stiff buckle at the side of the horse's jaw, her mind searching for something else to say. Why, he would laugh in her face if he knew the course of her true thoughts! 'I suppose… I wanted to say that I'm sorry, sorry for bringing you into this mess. I truly thought I would see Richard again today. I've wasted your time.'

'No, you haven't.' Satisfied that the fire had enough wood to keep it going for a while, Ragnar stood up and came over to her. His thigh muscles, visible beneath his braies, clenched, then released with the upward movement. 'You weren't to know that was going to happen. Besides, you never asked for my help, if you remember. It was I who offered.'

The buckle was too stiff; her fingers ached. Frustrated, she lowered her chin, desperate to rest her forehead against her horse's silky pelt. 'Even so, without me, you would be well on your way to finding your sister's abductor by now.' Her voice was a low mumble, filled with regret.

Ragnar laughed. 'Nay, Gisela, I would probably still be far from finding him. And even if I had, I would be sitting outside his castle, wondering how I would get in.' Pushing aside her fingers, he unstrapped her bridle, hanging it over a tree branch. His green eyes, darkly brilliant, honed in on her pale face. 'I need you, don't you understand? Otherwise I'll never get close to the bastard, whoever he may be!'

She peered closely at him, wanting to believe him, wanting to be needed by him.

'Although you'd be perfectly within your rights to return to your father and sister now.'

'No!' she said. The thought of being away from him was almost too much to bear after the disappointment of her brother. 'I wouldn't do that to you! We had a deal, remember?'

He held up his hands. 'I'm not arguing with you, Gisela. And I'm eternally grateful for you holding up your end of the bargain. Most women would have probably run screaming from me by now.'

'I can't say I'm like most women,' she replied, a gentle smile lifting the corners of her mouth. 'Circumstances have changed me; I wasn't always like this.'

He had gathered a few more sticks and threw a couple on to the fire. 'What were you like, then?'

'Oh, I don't know.' Gisela patted her horse's neck, stroking the pelt. 'I was braver, I suppose, more ready to take on a challenge.'

'You haven't changed, then.' He glanced up at her, fingers stilling above the fire. 'You might look like an angel, Gisela, but you have the heart of a warrior.'

A tremendous heat rose in her face at his compliment. 'Oh, but I...' she began to protest.

He moved across to her, laid a hand on her arm. 'Believe me when I tell you that you are braver than most of my men. You've taken so many risks over the past few days, all for your family, and now you're about to take one huge great risk for me, a man whom you scarcely know at all.'

Oh, but I do know you, she thought. *It's like I've known you all my life.* The muscled dip of his shoulder. The curve of his shadowed cheek like polished wood. The way his eyes seized hers, gripping them, so she was unable to look away. Every small detail of him, burned into her brain so she would remember them for ever. She knew him.

Later that night the rain cleared, the last rags of drifting cloud shifting westwards to reveal the moon, almost full, flooding the sky with a luminous, limpid light. Stars twinkled, pricking the dark velvet of the sky like diamond needle-points. Rolled in a blanket, Gisela turned restlessly, caught in a fitful sleep, beset by shreds of a bad dream. De Pagenal, high above her in the saddle, about to slash down on her neck; her brother, shoving her away, his mouth a contorted circle of rage.

She awoke with a start, heart pounding. Sweat prickled on her neck. Her eyes scratched with exhaustion. A great tide of misery engulfed her; the yearning cavern of not knowing where Richard was squeezed her innards. She chewed fretfully on her bottom lip, her eyes adjusting to the dim half-light, picking out the details of her surroundings. She lay inches away from the wooden boards at the back of the hut; her hands, bunched into tight fists, gripped the two sides of the blanket into the hollow of her throat. The cloth smelled of Ragnar, of leather and horse. The briny tang of the sea.

Ragnar.

She rotated on to her right side, expecting to see the familiar bulk of his body stretched out across the entrance. Earlier, she had listened as his breath slowed gradually to the deep, regular rhythm of sleep, tracing the silhouette of his shoulder in the firelight, the wayward strands of his hair. But now, the space where he should have been was empty. He wasn't there. She thrust herself into a sitting position, head spinning. Panic crowded into her chest, thumping through her blood. Where was he? A tiny voice niggled in her brain. *Maybe you're just too much trouble, Gisela. Maybe he has decided to take off and leave you alone in the darkness of the night.*

Through the looming sense of abandonment, she spotted his cloak, lying in a rumpled pile. The gleam of his jewelled brooch. Leaning across, she tugged at the material, finding his riveted surcoat, and red long-sleeved tunic beneath. Throwing off her blanket, she scrambled awkwardly to her feet, her hips aching from the ride that day, and peered outside the hut. His horse was there, tied to the tree, alongside her own. His sword was missing, but surely he wouldn't have gone far, wearing only his shirt, braies and boots.

Relief coursed through her, a giddy, stupid relief. She folded her arms across her chest, the sense of panic ebbing away. Her reaction had been ridiculous: had it truly come to the point that she couldn't survive without him? She had always been able to fend for herself—indeed, had prided herself upon it. Was his continued presence making her weak, unable to fight her own battles? Her former self would have seized this opportunity to escape, to leap on her horse and gallop back to her family.

But she had changed. He had changed her.

She wanted to stay with him. She clung foolishly to the fact that he needed her to help him; this was the reason she must stay and no other. But there was another reason, one she could not voice. It floated hazily in her mind, nibbling at the edges of truth, taunting her. To admit that truth, though, to voice her innermost feelings, was almost too much for her heart to bear. That this man had come to mean more to her than… than life itself.

Exasperated, Gisela stepped over to the horses. She would be wiser to stamp down hard on those feelings and snuff them out with the stern practicality for which she was well known. For to entertain these ridiculous notions would make their inevitable separation the harder to bear. Better to protect her heart now, than risk running the crashing pain and humiliation later on.

Her hand shook as she patted the horse's soft neck. The mare nickered in recognition. 'Where is he?' Gisela whispered quietly, her ears tuning in to the faint sounds of the woodland, listening intently. Maybe she should just go back to the hut and try to sleep. But the thought of Ragnar out in the forest somewhere niggled at her. He might have hurt himself, or someone might have tried to hurt him. Maybe de Pagenal had sent his knights out after them. She would never sleep. Far better to try to find him and put her mind at rest.

Beyond the rustles and squeakings emanating from the undergrowth, the breeze filtering through the branches above, she could hear water running, then a faint splash. She tilted her head first one way, then the other, trying to work out where it was coming from. There. Over there, behind the hut. Her hand slipped from the horse's neck. Picking up her skirts, Gisela headed towards the noise. Moonlight traced a path along the woodland floor, a gleam of track winding between the ferns and moss-covered rocks. Brambles, muscular arcs of thorn-laden tendrils, snagged her gown, but she wrenched them free with quick, decisive tugs.

And there he was. In a pool, mirrored in moonlight. Beech trees circled the spot, branches swaying gracefully down to touch the water's surface. Pinned by his sword, his remaining clothes were strewn across the bank, as if he had cast them off in feverish abandonment. She staggered to a stop, feet rocking with unused energy, folding herself back behind a large tree trunk. Silent. Her subterfuge astonished her. She should shout to warn him of her presence, announce herself, but she could not, for her heart was in her mouth, stifling all speech.

Ragnar was swimming, bare arms describing wide, lazy circles across the pool, the white shimmer of his naked flesh visible beneath the limpid surface. Her eyes feasted greedily upon the sight, tracing the clench and release of muscle across his back with avid abandonment, before sweeping down the sturdy curve of his spine to his hips, the scoop of defined flesh across his powerful buttocks, the splay of thigh muscle beneath. A slow burning heat gathered in her loins, blossoming dangerously. He drew her like a spell, magical and dangerous, lifting her up and pitching her fast into another world: a world of desire, of dark, secret couplings and love, unspoken. The heaviness of grief lifted from her, leaving her light and tingling.

Ragnar stood. Water sluiced down his honed flesh, bathing his perfect physique in liquid silver. An Adonis beneath the stars. Ecstasy stabbed at her, plucking violently at her self-control. She made a small sound in her throat, swiftly muffled; laid her forehead against the nubbled bark of the tree, admonishing herself for not leaving, for not turning tail and running back to the hut. And yet still she looked.

Raising his arms, he pushed his wet hair back

from his forehead. Strings of pearly water fell from his shoulders, surrounding him in a net of twinkling light. A rippling line of darker hair ran down the centre of his chest, separating the two flat planes of muscle, down across his stomach to the point where his hip bones curved into the patch of dark hair at his groin, partially hidden by the water level.

'I know you're there,' he said quietly.

Chapter Fifteen

Humiliation sliced through her. Clapping her hands to her cheeks, she swivelled around the trunk, jamming her spine against the bark, ripping her gaze from the pool's dark gleam. Her breath punched out, short gasps of pent-up air. How long had he known that she was there, running her eye across him like some prime bull in a cattle market? Her knees sagged as she struggled for composure, fought to rid her mind of all she had seen. Was there time for her to tiptoe away, back along the snaking woodland path, and pretend that nothing had happened, that she hadn't ventured near the pool?

But Ragnar was beside her, his muscular frame materialising in the moonlight. 'How long have you been there?' he asked. Gisela stared resolutely ahead, refusing to look at him. Was he still naked? Surely he hadn't had time to put his clothes on!

'I am dressed, you know.' His mouth twitched at the red patches no doubt staining her cheeks and her tight-lipped, disapproving expression.

She sagged with relief against the trunk, turning to face him. He must have put on his fawn braies at the pool as he was now fastening his sword belt around his hips. His torso was bare, his shirt crumpled beneath his elbow.

'How long have you been there?' he repeated.

He knew she had been spying on him. She explored his carved features for condemnation of her actions. 'Not long.' Her voice was a tentative croak; she cleared her throat. 'I've only just arrived.' Her gaze slid down the powerful cord of muscle in his neck, avoiding his piercing scrutiny; her fingers, hidden in the folds of her skirts, picked nervously at the bark by her hip.

'Liar,' he said, using his shirt to wipe the last droplets of water from his chest. The moonlight slanted sideways across the high ridges of his cheekbones, lending him a devilish look.

Her belly flipped in dismay. Had he truly known she was there all along, or was he taking a wild guess? 'I was worried,' she said, more confidently, jutting her chin into the air. 'I woke up and found you were gone. I thought… I thought something might have happened to you.'

'I'm sorry,' he said ruefully 'I needed to wash. I should have told you, but it seemed such a shame to wake you. You were sleeping so soundly.'

A wave of self-consciousness flooded over her. She hitched one shoulder up, embarrassed at the thought of him looking at her while she slept. But was it any worse than what she had done, ogling him while he swam? 'It's fine,' she replied, attempting to keep her tone light.

'How much did you see?'

'W-what…?' Her eyes rounded in horror at his bold question. 'No! I told you, I didn't see anything! I have only just arrived!'

The shrill protest of her voice told him all he needed to know. 'Everything, then,' he remarked drily. He folded his arms across his chest. 'It makes no matter to me, but I hope I didn't offend your maidenly modesty.'

A droplet of water spun down from his hair to his chest, trailing across the spare, sculptured flesh, like plates of armour, Gisela thought. What would it feel like to savour that warm muscle beneath her fingers? 'You didn't,' she retorted hurriedly. 'You wouldn't offend me, anyway. I've seen it all before.' The plucky lie fell from her lips, unconsidered.

Ragnar grinned, his eyes sparking humour. 'Have you?' His voice held a challenge. 'Who would that have been, then?'

Why, in heaven's name, had she said such a stupid thing? She shifted uncomfortably beneath his questioning, yanking her cloak more tightly around her shoulders, searching frantically for something to say. 'Well…there's my brother…'

'When he was a baby, no doubt.' Ragnar clapped a hand on her shoulder, openly laughing now. 'Caught red-handed, my lady! You couldn't take your eyes off me, admit it!' He smiled down at her.

'Please, Ragnar, stop teasing me. I saw very little, believe me.' Embarrassment sifted across her face. She dropped her head, the simple gesture admitting defeat. 'I've never done anything like this before.' Somewhere above them, an owl hooted, the mournful cry echoing through the shifting branches. A leaf rustled down, brushing past Ragnar's shoulder.

'I should hope not,' he said. His fingers lifted her chin, forcing her to look at him. His skin was cool, damp from the water. She inhaled the fresh scent lifting from him, intoxicating. Her senses reeled, her mind tacking back continually to what she had seen, back there in the pool. His naked flesh, spangled with light. She shivered, trying to drive the image from her brain. She needed to create some distance between them, allow her senses to recover, regain some self-control before she did something really foolish.

'You're cold,' Ragnar stated, misinterpreting her gesture. He stuck his head through the neck-hole of his shirt, tugged the fine linen down over his chest. 'We should go back.'

'Unless...' she said slowly, glancing at the pool. It would give her the opportunity she needed: a place to be alone, a place where she could calm down and regain her composure.

'Do you want to bathe?'

'Can I?' she whispered. Her pearly skin was luminous in the moonlight, lustrous patina gleaming like cream satin.

'You don't need my permission, Gisela,' Ragnar said, 'but the water's very cold.'

'Oh, Ragnar, I don't care about that! I'd do anything to be able to take these gowns off! They're far too tight...' She plucked fretfully at the side-lacings 'And they stink from de Pagenal's castle. My hair stinks, too!'

'I'm not going to stop you,' he murmured. 'Do you...?' He hesitated, clearly knowing that what he was about to suggest was a bad idea. 'Do want me to stay and keep watch?'

'No!' Gisela replied, a little too vehemently. 'I think…it would be better if you go back to the hut.' Springing away from the tree, she hopped from one foot to the other, then stumbled forward in excitement, tripping over Ragnar's toe.

He cupped her elbows, steadying her, his generous mouth curving with humour. 'I can truly say I have never seen anyone quite so thrilled by the prospect of taking a bath.'

'You have no idea,' she said, pulling out of his light hold and stepping towards the pool. The last time she had managed to wash had been when she had shared the chamber with him at Bertune. 'I won't be long.'

'Shout if you need me,' Ragnar said.

'I will,' she promised. But in her heart, she knew that she could not.

Gisela struggled out of the hated clothes, wriggling and contorting until she had managed to yank both gowns over her head, ripping a seam in the process. Face flushed with effort, she dumped the dresses down with her cloak and headscarf on the mossy ground. The dark pool gleamed in the moonlight, a slight breeze scuffing the polished surface. Kicking

off her boots, she rolled down her woollen stockings, trembling slightly in her chemise and linen
drawers. Unlacing the ties at the bottom of her
braids, she wondered whether she should remove
her undergarments. Glancing back into the darkness of the wood, she spotted the faint glow of
the fire at the hut. Could she trust Ragnar not
to reappear? But the thought of that cool liquid
sliding against her naked skin was too much to
bear. Her chemise and drawers floated down on
top of the pile of clothes.

Clutching hold of a branch, she stepped down
into the inky water, gasping at the icy coldness.
Ragnar had not been lying. But she took another step, then another, the mud on the bottom
squelching around her bare toes as she headed
out into the middle. The water level crept over
her hips, up to her waist, and she stood for a moment, shivering, wrapping her arms around her
bare breasts, summoning up the courage to duck
beneath the surface. Then she bobbed down, im-
mersing her body, her unbound hair. The silken
tendrils floated out around her.

The water stung her skin, a thousand freezing needles, numbing at first, but then invigorating. Tipping her head back, the water filled
her ears, blocking out all sound. She floated,
her feet stretched out in front of her, closing her

eyes, the delicious sensation of the water drawing out all the strain and hurt from the past few days. Then she stood, the radiant liquid sluicing down her flesh, as she scrubbed vigorously at her scalp, her hair, washing the dirt away.

Her hands stilled, fell from her hair. Motionless, she listened. Had she heard something? The trees around the pool seemed oddly silent. Her ears strained for sound, hollowing out inside to capture even the slightest squeak. What if de Pagenal had decided to follow them in the forest with his men? Was he lurking in the shadows?

Breath caught in her chest, a knot of panic twisting with her anxious mind. She had to get out of there. Sloshing forward, she staggered clumsily to the edge of the pool, scrabbling through the mud to claw her way out, on her hands and knees. Grabbing her chemise, she clutched it to her chest, then sprinted, fast, darting along the bleached line of the path, back to the hut.

'Ragnar,' she gasped, bursting out of the shadowy trees and into the clearing. He was sitting cross-legged by the fire, the carved lines of his handsome face lit by the flickering flames. 'Ragnar, quick! I think… I think de Pagenal might be out there!'

His leather boots hit the ground with a thump

as he sprung to his feet, drawing his sword with a sibilant hiss. The semi-precious stones set into the hilt winked in the firelight. He turned his head from left to right, his piercing eyes roaming the darkness. In two paces he stood before her, one hand cupping her shoulder. 'Where?' he asked quietly.

'I thought I heard something!' she gulped out, her lungs burning with the effort of running from the pool. 'What if de Pagenal decided to try to find us? He has never forgiven me for taking Marie from him!'

Her bare flesh burned into the palm of his hand. His breath seized, senses unravelling. In the glowing light, the dancing flames enveloped her half-naked outline in a rosy glow, highlighting the dip beneath her clavicle, the enticing slope of her hip. Her pulse beat frantically in the hollow of her throat. The urge to place his finger on the spot and feel the surge of her blood was unbelievable. The chemise held against her stomach scarcely covered her; the top of her breasts were visible: round, creamy globes of perfect flesh. Her wet hair straggled over her shoulder, down, down to the flare of her hips, dark curling ropes against her limpid skin.

His groin tightened, mind hazing with desire. Heat pounded through his chest.

Gisela bit her lip, doubtful now. Had her fear of the Norman made her mind play tricks on her? 'I…might be wrong,' she said quietly. 'I thought I heard something, that's all. In the pool, alone, I felt afraid.'

'Where are your clothes?' Ragnar spluttered out. His tongue moved thickly against the roof of his mouth. Divested of her garments, she appeared smaller, fragile, delicately built. Around her shoulder, his tanned fingers contrasted strongly against her milky-white skin.

'Can you hear anything?' Gisela peered at him.

He forced himself to concentrate, to listen. But all he could hear was the blood hurtling in his ears, his chest; the quick gasp of her breathing. *Step back*, his logical brain told him sternly, *move away from her*. Jerking his gaze up, he focused on the stars above, twinkling in the midnight-blue sky, praying for sanity, desperate to block out the enchanting vision before him, but her image burned on his retina: slender legs indented gracefully at the knee, rounding upwards into soft, creamy thighs. Her womanhood, hidden by the gauzy hem of her chemise. Just.

'Can you?' she repeated, knocking him lightly on the shoulder to gain his attention.

'No.' His voice, gruffly hoarse, tottered out into the night. 'No, I can't.' Lust, the flicking tongue of fire, lapped at his groin, severing his brain from good sense.

'Ragnar...?' She chewed doubtfully on her bottom lip, her panic subsiding as she listened. The chill air brushed her skin, whisking away the water droplets; she trembled. All she could hear were the branches whispering above their heads, the water running into the pool, nothing more. Suddenly she felt very, very stupid.

'I... I have imagined it.' A hot rush of embarrassment flooded her flesh. 'What a fool I am!' Her hands rose to her cheeks in consternation, not thinking. Without the firm trap of her hands, the chemise dipped fractionally, gaped forward. One rosy nipple peeked out.

His lungs emptied of air, breath punching out. 'Thor's teeth, Gisela!' Ragnar seized the chemise, as if intending to yank the material upwards. 'I should never have let you bathe,' he murmured, almost to himself. His knuckles grazed her flesh, knocking the downy side of her breast. His hand flew back, as if her flesh stung him; he jammed his trembling fingers into his sword belt. 'Go now, go and put your clothes back on!' Pivoting away from her, he glared fixedly into the shadowy forest beyond the hut.

Clutching her chemise, Gisela stared miserably at his broad back. Damp tendrils of hair fringed the solid nape of his corded neck. He was annoyed, irritated with her, and rightly so. There was no one in the forest, no one but the two of them. His cold disapproval sloshed over her.

'I am sorry, Ragnar. I did imagine it. But you don't have to be quite so angry with me!'

Air whistled out from his lungs, slowly. He gritted his teeth. 'Nay, I'm not angry with you, Gisela.'

'What then? I made a mistake; I have apologised.'

'It might have escaped your notice, Gisela, but you're wearing almost nothing!'

She shrugged her shoulders. 'Why is that a problem? It matters not one jot to you whether I am fully clothed or stark naked. You've made it perfectly obvious that you think little of me.'

His eyes glittered dangerously as he spun back to face her. 'Have I?' His expression was incredulous. 'Whatever gave you that impression?'

The breeze sifted against her flaming face.

Something was not quite right here; they seemed to be talking at odds with each other. 'Well… that you think of me more like…a sister.' She cleared her throat, wriggling her naked toes against the moss-covered ground.

'Wrong.' The word jabbed out, coiling seductively in her belly. He stepped forward, lifting up her mud-stained fingers, rubbing his thumb across her middle knuckle. 'So when I kissed you in the bedchamber, back in Bertune, I kissed you like a sister, did I?'

Her mind tacked back to the moment with clear, pin-pointing accuracy, knowing the answer. She had no need to speak it aloud.

'Don't you understand?' An edge of desperation hooked his low tone. 'I'm trying to protect you.'

'Protect me? From what?'

His eyes glowed over her. 'From me.'

A single drop of water hung from the lobe of her ear, sparkling like a diamond. He reached out, touched it with the pad of his finger. She gasped as the curve of his thumb grazed her jaw. It was all he needed. The signal. Her simple whispering sigh, heavy with need, with longing. A muscle jumped in his cheek. 'Forgive me,' he said. Restraint loosened, slipped away. He made no attempt to call it back.

His hand slipped down, across her neck, gripping the gauzy fabric of her chemise, tugging decisively, wedging her slight frame against his own hefty muscle. His mouth descended, lips claiming hers, devouring their sweetness. His powerful arms moved around her, roping her tight to him, chest to chest, stomach to stomach. A rolling tide of awareness flooded through him, engulfing, unstoppable.

She collapsed against him. Her mind emptied, shocked by the rapid contact of his mouth, scrabbling for self-control. Why did she not push him away, shout and scream in protest? *Because you don't want to*, a tiny voice niggled her, like a fingernail scraping on wood, mildly condemning. As his lips played along hers, searching, plundering, her limbs melted, suffusing into his brawny outline. Her arms moved upwards, tentatively, arching around his neck, her fingers digging into the bright, flame-coloured strands of his hair. The pulse at the top of his spine bumped erratically against her thumb.

He pulled away, sank his face into the perfumed freshness of her neck. 'Push me away, now!' he commanded, his voice partly muffled by her hair. 'Otherwise I might not be able to stop!' He lifted his eyes to meet hers, silently pleading. 'Do it.'

'No, I will not,' she whispered, her mouth burning from his kiss.

'You know what you are saying?'

'Aye, I do.' She regarded him solemnly, clear-eyed.

'So be it,' he ground out. 'Don't say I didn't warn you.'

She shuddered as he pulled her close to claim her lips once more. His hands moved up the finely built ladder of her spine, exposed to his touch, splaying across the delicate wings of her shoulder blades. His fingers moved to clasp her cheeks, thumbs aligned along her jaw as he deepened the kiss, his tongue darting along the sensitive seam of her mouth, sensual, inquisitive. Fighting for air, she rocked against him, battered by sensation, the sear of his touch like liquid fire. He marched her towards a place unknown: a vague, nebulous destination built only of snippets of information from serving maids, from her own mother. Most of their pronouncements had been dire, full of warning, and yet she trusted him, this big, blond-haired Viking.

Clasped in each other's arms, they sank down to the spongy earth by the fire, Ragnar tearing at his clothes, casting them off into a jumbled heap. Gisela's chemise had slipped down between them, forgotten. Beside them, the flames crackled and spit as they rolled together, flesh against flesh. Breath jagged in her lungs as the lean, naked length of him pressed against her, rigid muscle crushing her velvet curves.

The vivid colour of his eyes deepened, crackling with energy, with need. He plunged his mouth against hers again, the damp ends of his hair tickling her cheek, then his lips moved lower, trailing down her throat, to the sweet hollow between her breasts...

'Ragnar... I...' Sensation buffeted her; she thought she would scream aloud at the intensity of feeling gathering at the base of her belly. Her insides squeezed with delight; a gradual building of sensation, of...something, she knew not what. Her ribcage flexed, quivering with need, tightening with sweet awareness.

He moved with infinite slowness, sliding his brawny limbs across her own, a gentle plundering. Fear gusted through her: a ripple of delight, coupled with the terror of anticipation. His need burned into her, yet he waited, seizing her lips once more, teasing and tantalising as his hand moved up the gossamer length of her thigh.

Logic chased away. Abandoning herself to the fiery seduction of his questing hands, her mind plummeted down to a maelstrom of emotion, a pool of heightened yearning from which she had no hope of escaping. She had no wish to. His scorching touch flayed her, exposing her, yet she wanted to scream out loud at the way he made her feel, her body not her own. Every muscle, every ligament strung taut with anticipation, a rope winched ever tighter, building with a great cavernous hunger towards…what? She did not know.

Little by little, he eased into her, his movements checked by an infinite slowness. She cried out, panting in startled delight at the sliding intimacy, the utter possession. He paused, a question held in the gasp of her name. Had he hurt her? 'Gisela…?'

'Nay, go on!' she pleaded desperately. 'Don't stop!' Her hands flew outwards, clawing for something to hold on to in the battering onslaught of sensation, then clutched at his shoulders, clinging to the possessive glitter in his eyes.

He reminded himself to go slowly, that she was an innocent and did not deserve the full onslaught of his passion, yet he seemed unable to check himself, or hold back, surging into her with a wild abandon that astonished him. The delicate snag of her virginity curbed him momentarily, before he filled her completely, utterly. His quick possession stung her, but he gave her no time to think about it, replacing the swiftness with slow gentle movements.

He shifted within her, deliberately slowing his tempo even more so, before quickening again, moving faster and faster.

She welcomed the increasing rhythm, matching his powerful thrusts with a delighted eagerness of her own. The logical, thinking part of her mind ceased to function; her eyelids fluttered down, her slender frame barely able to contain the deluge of sensation that coursed through her, great gusting waves of pure delight. Her innards tightened, flexed. She moaned, breath ripping from her lungs, a surging wave of release breaking through the constraints of flesh. White-hot needles of light cascaded across the blackness of her vision, a tumult of sparking stars.

She cried out then as unbridled waves of pleasure hurtled through her slender frame, leaving her collapsed and spent. Reaching his own climax, Ragnar threw his head back, shuddering with unstoppable force as ricochets of pleasure drove through him. He sprawled heavily across Gisela's naked body, sated and alive.

Chapter Sixteen

~∞~

For a long, long time, they lay together in silence, limbs entwined, stunned, the aftershocks of their lovemaking pulsating through their bodies. Ragnar sprawled over her, bristled jaw grazing her cheek, the silky fronds of his hair tickling her ear. His heart thudded against her bare flesh, a deep, pulsing rhythm, drumming hard. She relished his nakedness, nay, revelled in it, ordering herself to remember every detail with utmost clarity: the heady scent of his heated flesh, the ridged muscles of his stomach pressing against her belly in delicious intimacy.

'Too heavy,' he muttered vaguely, rolling to one side. A shard of panic scythed through her—surely he was not leaving her, not yet? She had no wish to speak, to voice what they had done, to pick apart their joining with blame and recrimination, for that time would come eventually, of that she was certain. At this very moment, she wanted to savour, to allow her mind to float in a cloud of utter happiness, with Ragnar at her side. Relief coursed through her as he settled close behind her, tucking her against him so her spine rested against his torso, her hips cradled in his. Reaching for his cloak, he tugged it over both of them, shielding their cooling flesh from the night air, his arm slung around her waist.

The fire waned slowly, lazy sparks of burning ash rising into the air above, pinpoints of light. Her cheek pressed into the mossy ground as she watched the bluish kernel of flame dance and waver in the ashy net of half-burned twigs. How could she have known? How could she have known how wonderful such a thing could be? That her body would be suffused with light as they twined together? She had lost all sense of identity, every nerve and muscle fired into ecstatic oblivion. She had never learned this from her own mother, who, with features frozen in grim disapproval, had told her daughter in no uncertain terms what she would have to put up with if she ever wanted to be a wife and mother.

Ragnar moved behind her. 'Gisela…' His breath stirred the drying tendrils of her hair, a warm gust against her scalp.

Her eyelids fluttered down; a flicker of shame stabbed through her. The way she had stepped up to him, willingly, and lifted her lips to his. She could have backed away; why hadn't she? Because…because she had wanted to lie with him. There, she had admitted it. This tall, tousled-headed Dane with his easy laugh had barged into her life, chaotic and disrupting, and had scrubbed out the practical, level-headed woman that she used to be, a woman who scorned men and all they represented. But what had he turned her into? A harlot?

'I suppose you don't think very much of me,' she murmured, her voice low and miserable.

His breath sifted against her hair. 'What do you mean?'

Rolling away from him, she sat up, pulling the blanket up to cover her nakedness. Her hair spilled down over her shoulders, magnificent curling tendrils that touched her hips. Silhouetted in the firelight, she looked like a goddess of old, a fairy Medusa, spellbinding.

'Because…of what we did.' She shook her head and every glorious loop of her hair spun out around her neat head with the movement, the pale brown turned to a flickering molten gold. 'You gave me the chance to step back… but I didn't take it.'

His big hand sprung forward, engulfing her tight little fist at the point where she clutched at his cloak. 'But I knew what lay ahead, Gisela, and you did not. I gave you no time. It...' He sighed, remembering the headlong rush of pleasure, the speed with which he had taken her. 'It should not have happened. What I did was unforgivable.' Regret laced his voice.

The reproach in his tone staggered uncomfortably through her chest. 'There's nothing to forgive, Ragnar.' Her rose-pink lips curved up at the corners. 'Listen to me...you gave me the choice. And I chose...willingly.'

He stared at her, bemused. Her reaction was not what he had expected. Her anger, yes, but not this, this quiet acceptance of what had happened. Why was she not ranting and raving, beating at his chest? 'I had no right, Gisela. What was I thinking, taking your innocence like that?'

She flushed in the darkness at his blunt speech, a heady colour moving chaotically across her cheeks. 'It doesn't matter, Ragnar. I don't care.'

He stood up, a swift rush of movement, the remainder of his cloak falling across her bare shins. His naked limbs glowed in the fire, burnished, the muscle in his strong legs tightly honed, like carved marble. He began to pull on his clothes, his movements abrupt and jerky. Angry.

'You'll care when your wedding night's ruined because your new husband suddenly finds out that you've been with another man!' Winding his sword belt around his leather tunic, he secured it tightly. He looked up, his face lined with wretchedness. 'I'm so sorry, Gisela.'

'Stop this,' she said, biting her lip. Why did he have to ruin something that had been so perfect, so beautiful? 'There's never going to be a wedding night, because I'm never going to marry!'

'Never…?' he replied, incredulous. 'Why not?'

'After what I have learned about the ways of men? After seeing how de Pagenal behaved with my sister? And me?' Unconsciously, her fingers rose to the line of scarring at her neck. *And because no one would have me*, she thought. *I am no fool; I can see the way people look at me when they see my scar, the way they turn away.*

He flinched, thinking how similar his own behaviour had been to that of the Norman knight's. Despite Gisela's words of forgiveness, she couldn't fail to put him on the same level as that bastard. And he deserved her condemnation, rightly so, after what he had done. He had the vaguest sense that he had ruined something that might have been beautiful, ripping it to shreds as he ploughed headlong into possessing her.

'I can see why you would not want to,' he replied, his voice wooden. Hope snuffed out in his chest, smoking blackly like a piece of charred wood. He frowned at the odd sensation. What had he been hoping for? That…that there was the slightest chance that he and Gisela would stay together? The thought stunned him. Up to this point, he had never considered such a thing: to take a wife and settle down, have children. But now, as he looked down at Gisela's neat head, he realised it was because he had never found someone with whom he wished to be for the rest of his life. What had he done? A huge emptiness rolled over him, scouring out his belly: a sense of a future that might have been and now was lost. A future with Gisela, a woman who had given her innocence to him, but wanted nothing in return, the woman who he…? He stopped. What had he been about to say? That he loved her?

'So, it's all right, you see,' Gisela said, trying to decipher his expression in the darkness.

'I decided a long time ago that I would live alone.' Her fingers spread across the cloak over her knees, picking unconsciously at the fine embroidery. She hated to hear the reproach in his voice, the self-recrimination. It destroyed the exquisiteness of what had been and turned it into something sordid, ugly.

Scowling, he turned away, whisking her chemise up from the ground, throwing the limp, gauzy fabric into her lap. 'Stop this, Gisela. I don't want to hear any more. Stop trying to make me feel better for my actions, absolve me of any guilt. I am in the wrong here, not you.'

The white fabric of her chemise shimmered before her eyes. A great surge of tears welled in her chest, clamping tight with misery. So, that was that. He was so consumed with guilt that whatever she tried to tell him would fall on deaf ears. He was furious, she could see that from his terse, precise movements, but furious with himself, or at her, she knew not. She had the sense of a spliced rope pulling apart, fraying ends wrenching adrift, until they finally tore, feathery wisps wavering in the air. The fragile bonds of their relationship had fractured and she was not at all certain whether they could be repaired.

'I will fetch your clothes,' he said tersely, 'and you can sleep in the hut tonight. I will sleep out here.'

The following morning, Gisela awoke early, as the first fingers of grey dawn inched their way into the hut. Last night, she had dragged the tight-fitting gowns back on, the thin cloak, the leather boots and woollen stockings, wrapping herself in the blanket that Ragnar handed silently to her. She had resolutely turned away from him, tucked into a miserable little ball. Beset by a desperate exhaustion, she had slept fitfully, heart swollen with sadness at what she had done, at Ragnar's reaction. What a fool she had been, rushing in, not listening to the warning voices in her head. She told herself sternly she had wanted nothing from him, but her heart crimped sadly at the thought. What had she been expecting? That Ragnar would declare his undying love for her? She almost snorted out loud. The man had barely known her above two days. In the gloom, she hugged herself, trying to find some comfort in the whole sorry mess. At least she had the memory, she thought, the memory of their lovemaking that she clasped close to her heart like a precious jewel. She would always have that and no one could ever take that from her.

Would Ragnar come back with her to question de Pagenal further? She had to find out where Richard had gone. Or had she scuppered any chance of his support by lying with him? Her heart quivered at the thought of facing the Norman knight on her own. She had no one to blame but herself.

The wooded clearing was wreathed in a light mist, floating above the damp hillocks of dew-soaked grass. Sunlight struck through the trees, highlighting the swirling haze, parting the veiled air as if it were constructed of thin layers. Ragnar hunkered down next to the fire, laying thin twigs in criss-cross fashion above the flames. The worn leather of his calf-length boots bent forward, creased at the ankles. Beneath his braies, his big thigh muscles bunched heavily. The cloak that had wound around their naked bodies was now slung around his shoulders.

Her breath caught, eyes sliding away. Over by the trees, the horses were already saddled, girth straps tightened around their bellies, bridles attached. Rolling on to her knees, bundling the blanket between her hands, Gisela walked out from the hut into the open towards him. Dew darkened the hem of her blue underdress as she walked through the long grass.

Hesitating, she stood before him, wadding the blanket between her hands. 'I… I understand if you don't want to come back with me…to de Pagenal.' Her voice echoed out with a stilted weakness.

Balancing on the balls of his feet, unusually graceful for such a large man, Ragnar flicked his gaze over her face. 'What do you mean?'

The piercing intensity of his emerald eyes unnerved her. Surely this was what he wanted? To be rid of her? 'I thought… I thought it would be for the best,' Gisela said quietly.

'So you think that facing the man who nearly killed you, on your own, is for the best.' Breaking another stick in two, he chucked it on to the fire, narrowing his eyes against the smoke.

She angled her head, puzzled. Was this some sort of trick? 'I don't want you to think…well, that you have to do it.'

'You cannot go back alone,' Ragnar said, poking a stick into the innards of the fire, stirring the glowing embers. Sparks snapped up into the air.

'Oh, but…'

'No, Gisela,' he repeated, his tone stern. 'Look, I quite understand that you hate every bone in my body right now, but I am not about to let you do that. You will have to put up with me for a bit longer, I'm afraid.'

I don't hate you, she thought. Her heart leapt with joy at his words, but she fought to keep her expression bland, neutral. 'You…will come with me, then?' she asked carefully. Hope inched through her, a flutter of expectation. Maybe it would be all right.

He rose to his feet, a sudden, dynamic movement that unnerved her. The light striking through the mist fired the gemstones in his brooch, radiating streaks of blue fire. 'Yes,' he said quietly. 'Because I need you to help me gain access to my sister's abductor. When I finally track him down.'

She hunched her shoulders, frowning, trying to subdue the bubble of excitement that played around her heart. Could she do this? Could she stay with him, but keep her distance? If it was her only chance to try to rebuild their fledgling relationship, then she would seize it, gladly, with open arms.

'Thank you, Ragnar,' she said slowly, as if testing her words. 'I will still help you.' She eyed him warily. 'It's just that…' Could she speak about last night? Or would it be forever buried, never to be spoken of again?

He cleared his throat. 'And…about…last night,' he murmured. 'It will never happen again, I promise you.'

Through the shifting layers of mist, they retraced their route of the previous evening. The track was too narrow for the two horses to walk side by side, so Gisela dropped back, glad of a moment to collect her scattered wits. A sweet ache beset her body after the previous night; Ragnar had taken her to a place to which she had never been and now she had returned, a wholly different person. The practical, reliable Gisela, whom people turned away from, whispering about 'the girl who fell foul of de Pagenal's sword', as they pointed at their own necks to demonstrate what had happened, that girl had completely disappeared and turned into…what?

Under Ragnar's questing hands and mouth she had become like a woman possessed, someone she failed to recognise: a responsive, sensual woman, who revelled in the touch of his masculine body spread across hers. A wave of self-consciousness pulsed through her; she flushed. What must she have looked like, sprawled naked beneath him, begging him shamefully not to stop. It must have taken every ounce of his self-will to stop himself bursting out with laughter.

Hunching forward in the saddle, she stared miserably at his broad back, tracing the powerful sculpt of his shoulders beneath his cloak.

At the edge of the forest, Ragnar reined in his horse, a small crease appearing between his eyebrows. The wide valley that spread below them was wreathed in smoke, billowing up in dark grey plumes to cover the bright blue sky. Flames flicked, orange and gold, from the upper windows in one of the castle towers.

'I don't like the look of this,' Ragnar muttered. Beneath him, his horse hitched nervously, pawing the ground, and he leaned down, patting the animal's neck.

'What do you think is happening?' Gisela moved her mare alongside his, trying to keep the note of panic from her voice.

'I think the dispossessed Saxons have decided to object to de Pagenal's lordship and the stealing of their lands. Look, down there.'

Gisela peered more closely. Men were everywhere, some on horses, some running, armed with swords and axes. They swarmed along the stone walls of the castle, their powerful, long-legged strides taking them in and out of the gate. Blades glinted in the early morning sun, as the air filled with war-like cries.

Ragnar nodded, confirming his own suspicions. 'Definitely Saxons.'

'Dear God, Ragnar.' Gisela turned to him, catching at the sleeve of his surcoat. 'Then we must go down there before they kill de Pagenal. I must find out where Richard is!'

'I agree.' Ragnar's gaze traced the exquisite detail of her face: the fine skin like pouring cream, beset with a rosy blush from the exertion of riding; the intelligent assessment of her bright blue eyes. His heart snared with memory from the night before, those sweet limbs wrapped around his own.

'Ragnar…?' Her clear voice broke into the growing silence. 'What are you waiting for? Let's go!'

He rubbed at a rough spot on the reins, his expression terse. The smoke billowed up to obscure the watery disc of the sun, hazing the light. A wave of doubt crawled in his chest. 'I think you should stay here. Let me go down alone; the Saxons are no danger to me, but…'

'I prefer to come with you,' she said. 'I hate the thought of waiting around, not knowing… what if something happened to you?'

'What if it did?' he said bluntly. 'Would it matter to you?'

She hitched one shoulder up, considering her response. 'If we don't…find my brother, then I'll need an escort back to Bertune,' Her expression was bland. 'I can't ride back alone.'

'Yes, of course,' he replied, a great hollow opening up in his chest. His heart sank. He had wanted her to say the words, anything, any hint or clue that she cared for him. So for all her protestations to the contrary, she was not going to forgive him for what he'd done to her, after all.

'Hail there, Viking!' A burly Saxon stepped forward from the gatehouse, sheathing his sword as they walked their horses forward, coughing in the acrid stench of the smoke. 'Now is not the time to be visiting this place.' His eyes flicked briefly to Gisela. 'Take your woman and leave quickly.'

Kicking his feet clear from the stirrups, Ragnar jumped to the ground, ignoring the man's request. 'What is happening here?' he demanded.

The man scowled. 'Waltheof, our chief, has decided to reclaim what is rightfully his. When that bastard threw him out, he went north, gathering support. It hasn't taken him long to find some willing fighters. And now he's returned, taking back what belongs to him.'

'And what has happened to that Norman, de

Pagenal?' Gisela interrupted, leaning forward in the saddle. Her English vowels were slow and measured. 'Where is he?'

The Saxon regarded her curiously. 'Waltheof will know. You can ask him yourself, he's through there, in the bailey.'

Squinting through the haze that filled the arch of the gatehouse, Gisela stared at the men gathered in the bailey. Dust covered their faces; some wiped their blades, others talked in low, muted voices. Her eye roamed across the huddled group, trying to spot an obvious leader. Her gaze snagged on the back of a tall, athletic man, with hair of smooth sable. Close-cropped, in the Norman style.

All thoughts of finding de Pagenal drained from her mind, like water coiling down a culvert. Her breath snared in her throat. The man was dressed like the Saxons around him: a plain buff tunic with little decoration; coarse woollen leggings, mud-coloured, bound with narrow leather straps from ankle to knee. Was it him? Or was she just seeing who she wanted to see? A tremor ran through her wrists, a trembling of excitement tingling along her forearms. Throwing her leg forward over the horse's neck, she dismounted clumsily, hips bumping against the saddle, the reins slipping from her hands. She started walking, her strides at first unsure, then lengthening as she gathered pace, blue skirts flicking around her ankles.

'Gisela…?' She barely registered the thump of Ragnar's feet as he jumped off his horse behind her, catching at her elbow as they entered the dank shadows of the gatehouse. 'Wait…' he cautioned, nudging the length of his body against hers as he fell into step beside her. 'Not so fast. Let me talk to Waltheof, not you.'

Emerging out into the bailey, Gisela paused, her eyes lifting to Ragnar. His white-blond hair shone in the sunlight, gilt-edged, the vigorous strands riffling across his forehead in the breeze. 'It's not Waltheof I want to talk to. It's him.' She pointed, indicating the group of men. 'That is my brother Richard. I am sure of it.'

At the sound of their voices, the dark-headed man turned.

A rush of emotion gripped Gisela's heart, memories flooding through her. He hitched one shoulder as he turned, an old habit, head setting into its customary tilt. It was him.

'Richard!' she cried, stumbling forward, laughter bubbling up from her chest. Oblivious to the curious stares of the other men, she reached for her brother, arms outstretched. 'My God, I thought I would never see you again!'

'Gisela, what on earth…?' Richard seized her upper arms, his gaze scouring her fine, delicate features, as if he couldn't quite believe who he was seeing. 'What are you doing here?' His eyes flicked warily over Ragnar, standing silently behind her, massive arms folded across his chest. 'With a Dane?' he added in a fierce whisper.

'Father was taken ill in Bertune,' she explained Ragnar's presence in a rush. 'And Ragnar was kind enough to escort me here in his stead to pay your ransom. But when we met de Pagenal yestereve, he said he'd sold you…'

'He did sell me, Gisela, to Waltheof.' Richard nodded at a short, thick-set Saxon who watched their exchange with interest. 'And I have been fortunate for Waltheof has turned out to be a better man than de Pagenal. He treats me the same as his other men and has promised to give me my freedom by the end of the year.'

'But I can pay off your service to him with the money that we brought,' Gisela said excitedly. 'You will be able to come away with us now.'

'It's possible, I suppose…' A wave of doubt crossed Richard's face, 'but now is not a good time to talk to him.' He jerked his head up as the wide-shouldered Saxon chief strode over to them.

'Greetings,' Waltheof addressed Ragnar first, seizing the Dane's hand in his bear-like grip and pumping it vigorously. 'You and your lady are welcome here...' he swept one arm derisively around the burning castle '...such as it is. And at any other time, I would be glad to sit and share a meal with you.' He drew his great, bristly eyebrows together. 'I need to find de Pagenal before this place burns to the ground. He set the place alight as we approached, no doubt just to spite me. He's hiding somewhere. I will slit his throat before this day is out and that is a promise.'

A shout went up from outside the gatehouse, then a Saxon appeared, beckoning to Waltheof. 'They've found him, lord, crawling through the wheat fields!'

'Then let's get the bastard!' Waltheof roared, raising his sword high into the sunlight, the sibilant hiss cutting through the still air. 'Come on, Richard, you can catch up with the maid later.' He clapped one hand on Ragnar's broad shoulder. 'Want to join in the fun, Viking?'

Ragnar glanced at Gisela. 'Do you want to see this? He is the man who nearly killed you, after all.'

She shuddered. 'Nay, Ragnar, I have no wish to witness any man's slaughter, even such a man like de Pagenal. I have never sought revenge for what he did to me.' She followed Richard's lithe step as he strode off to join the Saxons. A joy suffused her heart; her brother was here and he was safe. All her days of worrying about him, the nights of fretful anxiety, lifted away from her slender frame, as if a boulder rolled away down a steep mountainside.

'Then you are a better person than me,' Ragnar growled, a muscle clenching beneath the taut skin of his jaw. 'Because I cannot wait to exact revenge on whoever abducted my sister.'

She lifted one hand, intending to touch his face, then tucked her fingers away, embarrassed, remembering the night before. His mouth on hers. Their bodies locked in tight embrace. 'I haven't forgotten, Ragnar. I will still help you, even though I've found Richard. I will still help you to find the man who took your sister. And Richard will help, too.'

'You don't have to, Gisela.' His voice was quiet, subdued. 'Now you have found your brother, you have someone to take you back to Bertune, back to your family. You don't need me any more.'

Yes, yes, I do! she wanted to scream at him. *I need your love.* Her heart plunged low, gripped with an unbelievable sense of loss.

'Gisela…?'

'Nay, I made a deal with you,' she said, her mind scrabbling desperately for reasons to stay with him. 'And you have given up valuable time to help me find my—' Gisela jumped forward suddenly, digging her fingers into Ragnar's arm as something fell in one of the towers behind her, a hideous cracking sound.

'The wooden floors are collapsing.' Ragnar raised his gaze to the west tower, the leaping flames reflecting in his shimmering green eyes.

'Listen! Can you hear that?' Gisela twisted her head, trying to locate the source of the sound. The bailey was deserted now, emptied of men as they funnelled out of the gatehouse to watch the final demise of the Norman knight. 'Ragnar, there's someone in that tower.' She jabbed her hand towards the flames. Her skin held the sheen of a limpid pearl as her midnight eyes rounded in horror. 'I can hear them!' A reedy wail, rising above the crackling sound of the flames. Her heart plummeted, swooping with fear. It sounded like a child.

Chapter Seventeen

For a fraction of a moment fear made them both hesitate, before instinct took over, driving energy into Gisela's feet and limbs. She took off, sprinting across the cobbles, her step light and fast. Her blue skirts chased around her ankles as she charged towards the burning building.

'Gisela!' Ragnar bellowed. 'Come back here!'

But she was either ignoring him, or had simply failed to hear above the ominous roar of the fire. She had reached the narrow arched doorway; he caught the glimpse of a spiral staircase inside. Surely now she would stop, he told himself. Fear pleated his heart as she slipped into the shadows of the stairwell, disappearing into a wall of smoke. Had she completely lost her senses?

Her utter recklessness drove him to action. Covering the bailey in long, decisive strides,

Ragnar plunged into the stairwell, chest constricted with terror. He had to stop her! He had to reach her, haul her to safety before a spark took hold of her gown or her hair, or worse, before she plunged to her death through burning floorboards. He ran up the steps, leaping three at a time until he spotted her ahead, her slight figure climbing with a steady determination, white hand trailing along the knotted rope that served as a handrail. His breath gusted out with relief.

'Got you!' he said triumphantly, lifting his arms to snare her waist, deliberately pulling her back against him so that she lost her balance, her hips and spine thumping heavily against his torso.

'No!' Gisela cried, struggling wildly, her fingers pushing down on the fierce clamp of his arm around her belly. Smoke caught in her chest, tightening her diaphragm, making it difficult to breathe. 'Ragnar, let me go!' she spluttered out. 'There's a child up there! Can't you hear?'

He could. A frantic screaming, almost hysterical, coming from behind a door on the first floor of the tower.

Releasing Gisela as abruptly as he had caught her, he barged past her, climbing the last few steps to the door. Trickles of smoke leaked out from between the thick planks. He kicked it open with one large booted foot. The door swung inwards, half-falling from its iron hinges.

Gisela was at his side. 'Oh God,' she said, peering round his shoulder into the hazy gloom of the circular chamber. Over on the far side, a woman sat huddled beneath a window, holding a small child close to her chest. The child was screaming, sobbing helplessly, tears streaking its puffy, terrified face. Smoke rose up through the floorboards, a shimmering orange glow streaking the cracks between the wooden planks. The fire was about to break through. The heat was extreme.

'We have to get them out of here!' Gisela said, shoving past Ragnar into the chamber.

'Nay, *I* will get them out of there,' Ragnar yelled, hauling her back into the stairwell, 'and you will stay here!' Avoiding the smoke that billowed out into the centre of the room, Ragnar trod carefully around the edge, his fingers running along the stone wall as a guide to reach the woman.

Gisela saw him take the child and drag the woman to her feet, nudging her before him until she reached the doorway.

Gisela reached for the woman's hand, intending to lead her down the steps. Her skin was clammy. 'We need to go. Come with me now.'

The woman stared at her blankly, not understanding. Gisela had spoken in French. She repeated the words as best she could in the Saxon tongue.

'The child...?' The woman's lined face was streaked with smoke and sweat. Tears glistened in her eyes.

Ragnar was one step above them, holding the baby in his arms. The terrified screaming had subsided, reduced to a series of shuddering hiccoughs; the child's hand curled tightly into Ragnar's cloak. 'Go, Gisela, go quickly,' he urged her. Behind him, the floor of the chamber fell inwards with a prolonged cracking sound, sending a fountain of sparks gusting through the open doorway.

'We have the child,' Gisela reassured the woman. She led her down the steps, Ragnar following close on her heels, the baby in his arms. They burst out into the noonday light, eyes watering, coughing and spluttering as the fresher air entered their lungs. The woman sank to her knees, her rough gown spreading over the dank cobbles, weeping copiously. She raised her knotted fingers skywards, thanking God.

'Oh, my lady,' she spluttered out in her thick

Saxon burr, 'I thank you from the bottom of my heart. I thought we were going to die.' Lifting the hem of her gown, she wiped her face, smearing her tears into the soot on her cheeks. 'How did you know we were there?'

'I heard the baby crying,' Gisela said, glancing at Ragnar. Amazingly, the child was quiet in his arms now, his small head nestling in the crook of his powerful neck, one fist resting against Ragnar's tanned throat.

Her heart twisted with unbelievable longing. A need. She looked away, peering fiercely at the woman, seeing nothing. What was she thinking? That she would love to have a child and for Ragnar to be the father of that child? To see him cradle that baby with such tenderness made her chest swell with delight and pleasure.

'Don't you ever do that to me again,' Ragnar said quietly. His voice held a flinty edge.

Gisela raised her eyebrows. 'What do you mean?'

'Sprinting away from me like that, when I had no idea what you were doing,' he ground out savagely. 'Risking your life!' He stepped towards her. Caught between them, the child stared at her with enormous green eyes. 'Gisela, you could have died in there!'

'*They* would have died,' she replied. 'If I had

heard the screaming and done nothing, with only a regard for my own safety, then it would have been on my conscience for ever.'

'You could have explained…before you rushed off like that!' He pushed one hand through his tousled hair, flecked with grey ash.

'There was no time, Ragnar,' she replied softly. 'You saw how the fire took hold; if I hadn't gone when I did, well…'

'I know, I know,' he bit out. 'It's the…the thought of what might have happened.' *To you*, he added silently. His heart pinched tightly in his chest, squeezing the air into a tiny space beneath his ribs. The thought of physically losing her loomed up before him like a monster, lodging like a gigantic weight in the bottom of his chest. The enormity of such a thing. And yet, with her brother just outside, they would soon have to go their separate ways. What would he do then?

The child in his arms jiggled suddenly, bouncing up and down on his massive forearm, playing with his brooch. The semi-precious stones winked and flashed under the small chubby fingers. Ragnar peered down at the bright tousled hair, the long fair eyelashes, as if noticing the boy for the first time. He couldn't be beyond his first year.

'Why did you stay in the tower?' he asked the woman in English as Gisela tucked an arm beneath the woman's elbow and helped her to her feet. 'Why did you not try to escape when the fire started?'

'I was frightened,' the woman said. 'I saw my people come, with the Saxon chief. But they would have killed me, for taking care of this child.' Her voice shook.

'Is he not yours?' Ragnar rapped out. His voice echoed harshly around the empty bailey, contrasting oddly with the baying shouts of the Saxons outside the castle gates.

'No, I was brought here to look after him by the Norman lord. I had no choice.'

'Where is his mother? Did the Saxons kill her?' Gisela asked. The baby was making gurgling noises beside her, a stream of half-formed words, incomprehensible. Suddenly his hand shot out, touching her glistening hair, an escaping strand floating out from her headscarf. Despite everything, she laughed.

The nursemaid tugged her woollen shawl around her shoulders, crossing the frayed ends across her ample bosom. 'No, his mother left a long time ago. It was a bad business. Once Lord de Pagenal had the boy and he was weaned, he sent the mother away. Sent her back to her people.'

'Mama,' burbled the child, happily. '*Mor... mor...*'

Ragnar froze. An icy chill radiated through his spare, rangy frame. Shoving the child abruptly into Gisela's arms, he brought his face down close to the woman's, glowering at her, eyes flashing diamond knives. 'What was her name?' he asked roughly. 'What was the mother's name? Tell me!' Grabbing the nursemaid's shoulders, he shook her slightly, as if that would bring the information out more speedily. The woman's head knocked back with the violent force of the movement.

'Ragnar! Stop this, what are you doing?' Gisela cried at him.

Lines of wretchedness scoured his face as he half-turned towards her, his hands dropping from the woman's shoulders. 'I know who that child's mother is,' he said jerkily, 'but I want to hear it from this woman's lips. I want to hear her say it.'

Gisela frowned, shifting the boy's rounded weight more securely against her chest. 'But who is it?'

'The child speaks Danish. He is Gyda's child.'

'Gyda,' the woman nodded. 'Aye, that was her name. Do you know her?'

'She is my sister.' Anguish whitened Ragnar's face. 'Odin's teeth! So that bastard de Pagenal is the father!' He shook his head violently, drawing his sword. 'How could I not have known? How did I not guess when that bastard was sitting there, grinning at me from behind the table, last night?'

'Ragnar…how could you have…?' Gisela said. But Ragnar was already running towards the gatehouse. 'Stay here!' he flung back at her, gold hair flying in the breeze, strands whipping back over his forehead. 'Stay here until I return!'

Watching Ragnar's tall lean figure disappear through the gatehouse, the nursemaid turned to Gisela. 'So this child is…?'

'Ragnar's nephew,' Gisela explained. 'He came here to find his sister's abductor, to find out what had happened to her.' She chewed her bottom lip, recalling his raw expression, the lines of wretchedness scouring his face before he had vanished into the shadows. The pain of his sister's plight must be unbearable.

'So he wants to talk to de Pagenal,' the nursemaid said.

'He does,' Gisela confirmed. Against her

neck, the child had begun to fret and grizzle, jerking his chubby legs up and down in a frenetic movement. She hugged him closer, trying to calm him, but he only cried more loudly.

'Here, my lady, give the little mite to me,' the nursemaid said. 'It was a bad business. Gyda was with Lord de Pagenal when he attacked this castle and threw everyone out. And when the baby was born, I became his wet nurse.' Her voice lowered. 'I had lost my own child a few days earlier.'

Gisela placed her hand on the nursemaid's shoulder. 'I am so sorry.'

The woman shrugged. 'It happens,' she replied sadly. 'But it helped, having young Torven to look after. And Gyda was a lovely young woman, so full of life, despite her situation. De Pagenal kept her a virtual prisoner in that chamber where you found us, unless...'

'Unless...?'

'Unless he needed her in his chamber.' The woman's mouth formed a despairing line. 'She didn't fight him, so she was spared the worst of his anger.'

'I can't even begin to imagine what she must have gone through,' Gisela murmured.

'It will be hard for her brother to hear what

happened to her. I can't believe how much he looks like his sister. Same hair, same eyes.'

'The baby is the same, also.' Gisela smiled down at the gilt-haired boy in the nursemaid's arms. Green eyes, identical to Ragnar's, stared back at her.

'Aye, luckily he takes after his mother and not his pig of a Norman father.' The woman paused, adjusting the boy's position so that he lay more firmly against her. She smiled at Gisela. 'You can call me Bertha, my lady, if you wish.'

'I do wish it. Thank you, Bertha.'

'Will you and your husband take the child?'

'Oh, but he's not my husband!' Gisela blurted out in surprise, laughing.

Bertha's eyes widened. 'You do surprise me, my lady, for you both behave as such. As if you are married,' she added.

'We are travelling together, that is all,' Gisela replied, lowering her voice, glaring down at her mud-encrusted hem. Had last night changed the way she behaved around Ragnar? Was the evidence of her sin plastered across her face and body, like a brand upon an animal? 'We scarcely know each other.'

'If you say so.' The nursemaid threw her a sly smile. 'Don't worry, mistress, your secret's safe with me.'

'There's no secret!' Gisela protested.

The nursemaid shrugged her shoulders, a gesture of obvious disbelief, then abruptly changed the subject. 'Do you think he will take the child?'

'I cannot speak for him.' Gisela chewed fretfully on a nail. 'But I think he should. It's the right thing to do, to take a child back to his real mother.'

'I agree,' said Bertha. 'But I would look after the boy if he does not.'

'I hope it won't come to that,' said Gisela, doubt trickling through her belly. If Ragnar was reluctant, then she would have to persuade him, but how on earth was she going to do that?

When the noise died down outside, the two women emerged tentatively from the gatehouse, the baby jiggling fretfully in Bertha's arms. Behind them, the castle smouldered, the fire in the tower having died down of its own accord. On a flattish field to the west, the Saxons were setting up a makeshift camp and the smell of roasting meat rose into the air.

Ragnar stood at the other end of the drawbridge, deep in conversation with Richard. Her heart plummeted at the sight of the tall Dane, his face besmirched with soot, lending him a devilish cast. He looked up at Gisela's approach, his expression terse, unsmiling, then scowled as he caught sight of the child in Bertha's arms.

'I was too late,' he said. Despair clawed at his voice. 'The Saxons had already killed de Pagenal before I got to him.' He wrapped his arms over his broad chest.

Gisela touched his sleeve, a fleeting gesture. 'I am so sorry, Ragnar. I know this is not how... you would have wanted it.'

He angled his head away, mouth compressed into a stricken line. 'He's dead and that's all that matters, I suppose.'

'But you have the child, your nephew. Surely that is some recompense for Gyda's ordeal?'

His face went white. 'You think so?' he croaked. 'How can that be?'

Shock rattled through her; she ducked her gaze, studying the ground intently, as tears clouded her gaze. So that was how it was going to be, she thought. He would reject the child. The silence lengthened between them, awkward, uncomfortable.

Richard stepped forward, clearing his throat. 'Gisela, Ragnar has agreed to take you back to our father and Marie. I am needed here, with Waltheof.'

'Oh!' She jerked her head up, glad of a distraction from Ragnar's brooding stare. 'But I thought you were coming with us! What about giving Waltheof the coin intended for de Pagenal?'

'No need!' Richard replied. Excitement threaded his voice. He seized Gisela's hands. 'Waltheof has already granted me my freedom, and, more than that, he has given me this castle and the lands as a reward for what I have done for him. Imagine that, Gisela!'

'So…so you will stay here, then?' She smiled at the happiness in his voice.

'Yes,' he said slowly, laying a hand on Gisela's shoulder. 'But I promised to go with Waltheof now, to fight with him, as a freeman. After that, Gisela, you can stay here and live with me. Father and Marie, too.' He glanced at Ragnar, lowering his voice. 'You'll be all right with the Dane, Gisela. You can trust him.' Planting a kiss on his sister's cheek, and shaking Ragnar's hand, Richard bid farewell, walking off towards the Saxons.

Gisela stared after her brother, a muted sadness wrapping her heart, then switched her gaze back to Ragnar's piercing green eyes, his brooding expression. *Aye, I can trust him*, Gisela thought. *But can I trust myself?*

As Gisela watched her brother depart, Bertha

stepped forward, the child grizzling in her arms. 'I need to feed the baby, mistress. There's hot food and milk for him, at my brother's house.' Her speech faltered slightly. 'You'd be welcome, my lady, and the lord, too, if you don't mind the state of our cottage. You could eat and take some mead with my family. Stay the night if you wish. You saved my life, both of you, and I thank God for bringing you to me in my hour of need.'

'It would be good to eat something,' Gisela said, narrowing her eyes at Ragnar in challenge, knowing that he would disagree.

He glanced up, studying the white puffs of cloud shifting across the clear blue afternoon sky. 'We'll eat and then we'll leave,' he said. 'It's light enough for us to keep riding,' he said. 'We can at least start the journey back to Hoesella.' His green eyes raked over her soot-stained cheeks.

The cottage was small: a ground-floor chamber, with an open sleeping platform up above, accessed by a makeshift wooden ladder. Straw covered the earth-packed floor, a loose layer. As Ragnar followed Bertha and Gisela inside, stooping beneath the lintel, a cluster of children inside eyed him with curiosity, entranced by the impressive flash of his sword hilt, his muscled

shoulders. The silver rivets on his leather surcoat sparkled in the gloom. Hopping nervously
from one foot to the other, Bertha introduced
her brother and his wife, a petite dark-haired
beauty, who wiped her hands down her apron
and pushed the children out of the door. 'Go and
feed the animals,' she ordered. 'It's not time for
you to eat yet.'

'You are most welcome.' The man stepped
forward in greeting, clasping Ragnar's hand.
'Please, sit and rest a while. Will you take a bowl
of stew? Your lady…here.' He indicated a three-
legged stool for Gisela. She sat down, smiling at
him, and took the earthenware bowl of steaming meat that was handed to her. Knowing how
unwelcome the Normans were, she decided it
would be better to keep her mouth shut while
she was among the Saxons.

As the baby chewed on a piece of bread
in Bertha's arms, the nursemaid explained in
rapid English who Ragnar was and her brother
clapped him on the back in sympathy, bowing
his head. As Gisela spooned the hot stew into
her mouth, she lost the thread of Bertha's explanation to Ragnar about what had happened to
Gyda, but she watched as his face grew pinched
with tension, whitening about the edges of his
mouth. When Bertha had finished, he handed

the bowl back to the brother's wife, half-eaten, and stood up abruptly. From the leather bag slung over his shoulder, he drew out a bag of coin and handed it to the nursemaid. 'That is for the baby. I will make sure you receive payment every year for looking after the child. I hope it is enough.'

'I will look after him as if he were my own, my lord,' replied Bertha, stealing a glance at Gisela's strained expression.

'We're going now,' Ragnar barked at Gisela, in English.

She glared at him in frustration, then nodded silently towards the child, chuckling happily in Bertha's arms. Ragnar glared at her, shaking his head. 'Come on!' He held out his hand, waggling his fingers impatiently.

Refusing his help, fists bunched in fury, Gisela rose to her feet. She couldn't talk to him here, held in a captive silence by her own identity. She had to move him away from these Saxons, so that she could talk to him in her own language, persuade him to take the child. Dipping her head in thanks towards Bertha, her gaze sliding over the bright-haired child, she followed Ragnar out into the sunlight. He had tied the horses up to a wooden fence-post outside.

'Ragnar…' She touched his arm, her voice

so quiet that he was forced to bend his head towards her. Her soft breath brushed his ear as she whispered in French, 'I must talk to you.'

'There's no point,' he replied stonily, cupping his hands so she could place her foot within them so he could boost her into the saddle.

She kept her feet firmly on the ground, refusing to do his bidding. 'There's every point!' she hissed fiercely, winding her arms across her breasts, constructing an additional barrier between them.

His eyes narrowed, glinting emeralds that pierced her soul. 'Climb on the horse, Gisela, before I throw you up there!' he demanded.

'You wouldn't…' Her mouth clamped shut mid-sentence as Bertha's brother came out of the cottage, smiling amiably.

'Do you need anything more for your journey?' he asked, oblivious to the argument between them. He had wrapped a threadbare woollen cloak around his rangy frame, securing the two sides with a rusty metal pin.

'No, thank you,' said Ragnar tersely, unlinking his hands and straightening up. He studied the mutinous line of Gisela's mouth and knew full well that she would make a scene if he forced her on to the horse. 'I think we will walk for a while and stretch our legs.'

'Where are you headed?'

'South. Towards Hoesella.'

The man nodded. 'You need to take the track through the forest. Over there.' He pointed across a shallow stream towards a dense pine forest, trees clustering heavily on the skyline. 'If you keep a good pace, you should make Skelton Moor, about halfway, by nightfall.'

'Thank you,' Ragnar said. 'And thank you once again for your hospitality.' Seizing Gisela's elbow in a pincer-like grip, he propelled her forward, holding the horses' bridles in his other hand. She had no choice, she would have to stumble along beside him, otherwise he would drag or carry her, of that she was certain. The brute strength in his grip radiated up her arm as he yanked her across the low bridge over the glistening stream, then up the gentle slope towards the edge of the pine forest.

'Let go of me!' Shaking off his hold, Gisela sprang away from him, panting slightly from having to keep up with Ragnar's accelerated pace. Despite the sun, a chill breeze nipped around her ankles as she moved into the shadow of the tall pines. A chaotic cross-hatching of brown pine needles littered the ground, soft and springy beneath her feet. They were far away from the village now, out of earshot. Eyes sparking anger, she braced her legs in combative stance.

'Go on, then,' Ragnar said. 'You may as well say your piece, for I know we'll go nowhere until you've told me what you think of me.'

'Do you truly mean to leave that baby there?' She swept her hand over the village spread below them, the blue wool of her overgown contrasting starkly with the creased brown trunk at her back.

'Yes.'

'Ragnar, what's the matter with you?' Her voice trembled with emotion. 'You have to take the child back to your sister!'

He flicked the end of the reins across his hand, slapping his palm in irritation. 'And have her reminded every single day of what she had to endure in this place? Hell's teeth, Gisela, did you hear what happened to her? Day after day?'

'The child will heal her.' Gisela spoke slowly, trying to control her rapid breathing, trying to subdue the haphazard rush of emotion climbing in her chest. 'I am certain of it.'

He jabbed his toe deliberately against a raised tree root. 'Or push her over the edge, Gisela. She is so fragile at the moment…her mind is frail. How do you know what will happen?' Tension rippled through his velvet tones.

'Your sister has lost everything, Ragnar,' Gisela continued, desperation lacing her voice, 'but she still has this baby. He's part of her. She gave birth to him, fed him, cuddled him…he will mean something to her when she sees him again.'

Ragnar lifted his eyes up to the sky, as if searching for the answer amidst the skeleton pattern of the branches. Tears glinted in the corner of his eyes. The silence stretched between them, broken only by the repetitive strike of an axe against wood rising from the village. Her heart turned over, a strange twisting sensation, as she read the desolation in his face, but she resisted the urge to reach out and take his hand. To comfort him. *Please*, she prayed. *Please do this thing for your sister.* Her fingers knotted tightly against her belly.

'No, Gisela, I cannot take the risk,' he said finally, shaking his bright head. 'The shock of seeing him again might kill her.'

Renewed anger rose within her, flaring chaotically. 'Nay, you must!' she cried, thumping him squarely in the chest. Instantly, he snagged her fingers, crushing them against his ribcage. 'And if you don't take him, then I will!' she blurted rashly, words spilling out before she even had time to consider their meaning. 'I will carry him to Denmark on a ship and my father and sister will come with me! That poor little mite is the innocent in all of this and he needs to be with his mother! If you don't do this, then I will!' She stopped suddenly, breathing heavily, rocking back on her heels. Only his grip on her fingers held her steady, keeping her upright.

Astounded by her impassioned words, by the energy that flowed from her in waves, all Ragnar could do was stare at her. A rapid pulse in her wrists beat hard against his thumb. A rose colour suffused her cheeks, ragged and wild, daubing her luminous skin, snow-drop white in the shadows. 'You're angry with me,' he croaked out eventually. 'You don't know what you are saying.'

'I do,' she countered vehemently, thrusting her chin up to meet his eyes. 'And I have enough money to do this, now that my brother is staying with Waltheof.'

His hands fell away. 'But why…why would you do such a thing? My family…my sister… you don't know them.' A plan was beginning to form in his mind, radical, outrageous. His heart leaped with possibility.

'No,' she replied, rubbing her wrists tentatively, 'but I know it's the right thing to do. I think you will regret not taking him.'

The dense pine trunks seemed to close in, a huddle of shadow around their figures. Somewhere, high up above, an owl hooted, the hollow sound echoing eerily around the tree tops.

Ragnar crossed his arms over his thick chest, tracing the downy curve of Gisela's cheek. He should be taking her back to her family in Bertune and bidding her farewell. But he had no wish to bid her farewell.

'I will take the child on one condition,' he said.

Stunned by his sudden change of heart, her eyes widened in astonishment. 'Ragnar, truly?' she whispered. 'Do you mean what you say?'

'Yes, I do,' he said carefully. 'But you haven't asked on what condition I will take him.'

'What is it?' She eyed him airily. 'Whatever it is, it won't matter. All that matters is that the baby is returned to his mother.'

'My condition is that you come with us. With me.'

Chapter Eighteen

Disbelief burst through her, a sudden flood of dislocation. Why did he continue to do this? Pushing her off balance so that her whole world twisted out of kilter. Staggering back, bereft of speech, she felt her spine hit the gridded bark, hips bumping painfully against the iron-hard wood.

'What…what are you saying?' Had she misunderstood his words?

'If I take the baby to Denmark, then you must come as well.' He stood below her, legs astride on the needle-covered ground, the bulky contours of his shoulders almost blocking out the village spread out on the valley floor. The gemstones set into his silver brooch winked and glimmered in the shadows cast by the towering pines.

'But…you can't do this!' she cried, levering herself away from the tree. 'It's not fair!'

His emerald eyes gleamed. 'No, it's not fair, Gisela. But it's the only way that child will reach Denmark.'

After what had happened last night, their naked limbs tumbling together, she suspected he was counting the hours until he would be rid of her, free of her company, but she never wanted that moment to arrive. But now, because of her stubbornness in wanting the child to be returned to Gyda, he had given her the perfect opportunity.

'What about my family? They are waiting for me in Bertune…waiting for news of Richard. I have to explain to them…'

'And you will,' Ragnar countered. 'I am meeting Eirik and the rest of the ships in Hoesella. We can take the ferry across to see your family. There will be time before we set sail.'

'Why are you doing this?' she whispered, tracing the firm, determined line of his top lip with her gaze. 'Why are you forcing me to go with you?'

He was behaving like an oaf, heavy-handed and belligerent, living up to his true Viking reputation. For a moment he wanted to relent and take his demands away. To take this baby back to Gyda was a bad idea, of that he was certain, but he would do it for Gisela, to see her eyes light up with pleasure, with approval at his actions. His fingers tingled. And he had seized the chance to bully her into coming with him. But he had to be careful. If she suspected his true feelings, he would scare her away and make her fear him, without a doubt. *Tread softly*, he told himself.

'I am not forcing you,' he replied. 'You have a choice.'

'Hardly.' She raised her finely etched eyebrows. Her scathing glance was laden with disapproval. 'There's no choice at all. The only way Gyda will have her baby boy again is if I go with you.'

'Precisely.' Was it his imagination or did he sense the slightest weakening in her demeanour? His heart swelled with hope, with the anticipation that she would agree to his demands.

She wrinkled her nose. 'But I don't understand why you want me to come? Surely I've caused you enough trouble already? The baby is used to Bertha, she has been with him since your sister left, so why not ask her to accompany you?'

Because I don't want her to come. I want you.

His mind cast about frantically for an explanation as to why the nursemaid could not come. 'She has her own family to look after, Gisela. It wouldn't be right to take her away from her own children, or her husband.' The slenderness of his excuse was obvious and he wasn't even sure that Bertha even had a husband and children. He hoped Gisela wouldn't probe too deeply, searching for the weak spot in his answer, a chance for her to wriggle out of all this. But luck was on his side. He read the acquiescence in her slender frame, the softening of her tense shoulders, and knew she would come. His heart leapt with sudden pleasure, delight suffusing through his chest.

The breeze tugged at the trailing ends of her scarf and she wound the loose fabric decisively around her neck, fixing him with eyes of limpid sapphire. 'Well… I suppose you know what I am like to journey with.' Her chin jerked up, slightly angled: a belligerent, feisty gesture to show that she had relented, but would not make the process easy. She was not happy with him, he could see that, not happy at the underhand methods he had engaged to persuade her to come with him. But he cared not. She would be at his side and that was all that mattered.

'I do,' Ragnar agreed. His brilliant gaze

roamed over her pallid expression, the defeated stance of her slim frame. Oh, how she must have been hoping to be rid of him! In two days she could have been bidding him farewell and riding on south with her father and sister. Only it was not to be. He was behaving like an ogre, but he had to fight for this, for her, by whatever means possible. He had to make good the wrong he had done her last night, even if it meant forcing her gentle spirit into things that she had no wish to do. Because this woman, this infuriating woman, with her hair of glossy sable and eyes of midnight blue, had invaded his heart, driving out the guilt he had experienced over his sister's plight and replacing it with...was it love? He was not about to give that up without a fight.

Bertha's round face cracked into a wide smile as she opened the door. 'I knew she would persuade you!' she cried, stepping back to allow Ragnar and Gisela into the cottage. She raised her eyebrows at Gisela in silent congratulation. 'He's ready for a journey. He's been fed and I've put clean linens on him. I've packed a bag with all the things that he will need.'

'I see.' Ragnar glanced at Gisela. 'So you women had this planned all along. How did you think you would make me agree to this?'

Gisela peered around the cottage, thinking she could not speak for fear of being overheard, but the space was deserted apart from Bertha and the little boy, kicking his legs up happily from a small wicker basket. 'I had no plan, Ragnar, other than that it was the right thing to do. You know that. I didn't think you would resort to blackmail.'

Her words jabbed hard into his solar plexus. Stung. A muscle contracted sharply in his jaw. He shrugged his shoulders, rolling away the jibe. 'It's the only way, Gisela. You know how I feel about this child.'

She held his emerald gaze for a moment, acknowledged the determined thrust of his chin. He was right: this was the only way, for neither of them would retreat from their opinion. 'You take the bag, then,' Gisela said, briskly. 'And I'll carry the baby.' For one single terrifying moment, she wondered how she was going to do this. She hadn't even considered the practical side of caring for a child and suddenly the thought of taking him on such a long journey seemed wholly daunting. She looked at Bertha, who was smiling broadly as her gaze swung from Ragnar, back to Gisela, then back to Ragnar again.

'Bertha? What do you call him?'

'When Gyda was on her own with him, she called him "Torven".'

'What does he need? I have no idea of such things.' There, she had said it. Let Ragnar laugh at her inadequacy if he wanted. She had no intention of letting this little boy down.

'He will eat what you eat, mushed up with a little milk or weak ale if you can find it. Change his linens once or twice a day, keep them swaddled tightly for the rest of the time. He's wearing warm clothes, so he should be fine in the open air.'

'I hope...' Doubt tangled in her voice.

'You'll be fine, my lady. He's an easy baby. Bind him to your chest when you ride and feed him when you eat. Change him before he goes to sleep at night and when he wakes up. That's all there is to it.'

'Let's go, then,' Ragnar said, swinging up the leather satchel that Bertha had packed for the baby.

Bertha darted to the corner, returning with a small leather pouch. 'Here, my lord,' she said, holding the bag out to Ragnar. 'It's yours. We have no need of the coin, now you're taking the child.'

'Keep it,' Ragnar replied curtly, 'I'm sure you will put it to good use.'

Bertha nodded. 'Thank you. And thank you to both of you, for saving my life.'

The burning tower at the castle; the baby's frantic screaming—what a long time ago that seemed, thought Gisela, as Bertha hoisted Torven up against her, binding him tightly to her chest with a deft criss-crossing of linen bands, knotted firmly into the small of her back. The baby's head tucked up beneath her chin, the downy fuzz of hair tickling her skin like feathers. She followed Ragnar out into the balmy afternoon air, towards the waiting horses. A few hens pecked the ground in a pen alongside the cottage, but otherwise, no one was about, apart from Bertha, who stood in the doorway, waiting for them to leave.

She frowned, wondering how she was going to climb into the saddle with the baby strapped to her. Ragnar stepped forward, a slight twinkle in his eye. 'How do you want to do this?'

'I don't know!' she replied, a rough despair fringing her voice. 'I've never done this before, have I?'

'Can you use my foot to mount?' he asked. His heart hollowed out with a peculiar craving, a sudden hankering for the picture of domesticity created by Gisela and the baby, an image of what might be. The baby rounding out her belly made her look like she was with child and, after what had happened between them, that was a possibility. His ribcage constricted, a rush of sweet pressure.

'I can try.'

But it was useless. The bulk of the child prevented her from lifting her foot more than a few inches off the ground; her toes failed to reach the cradle of Ragnar's fingers.

'Oh!' she cried out in frustration. 'How do other ladies with children do this? I've seen them riding horses!' They heard Bertha's cackle from the doorway; spots of colour rose in Gisela's cheeks.

Ragnar laughed. 'Have you? I thought noble ladies usually travelled in litters, carried by servants. And the peasants walk with their babies. Let me help you.' Gripping Gisela's waist, he lifted both her and the baby up into the saddle. She swung her leg over immediately to balance herself. His hand grasped the toes on her boot, feeding her foot into the stirrup; moving around to the left flank, he performed the same operation, pulling her cloak out from where it was bunching at the back of the saddle, and flicking the coarse fabric across the horse's glossy rump.

'Why didn't you do that in the first place!' she muttered in irritation.

He vaulted into his own saddle, swinging his horse around. 'Because you are so determined to do everything for yourself, I thought I would give you the choice,' he said.

She frowned, drawing the fine arch of her brows together. Her pert little nose wrinkled with annoyance. Fear was making her grumpy.

Ragnar caught the flicker of concern in her eyes, the slight constriction of her rose-coloured lips. 'It will be all right, Gisela,' he said suddenly, wanting to comfort her.

She sent him a sharp look, tense and worried. 'There's no point in saying such things to me.' Bitterness creased her soft voice. 'I know you don't mean it. You don't want this to happen.' She cast her eyes down meaningfully to the bronze fluff on the baby's head.

'Yes, but despite what I think, this should not be an ordeal for you. He is my sister's baby, after all.'

She jabbed her heels into her horse's rump, following him towards the bridge, retracing their path up to the pine forests. The baby bumped comfortably against her belly, his cheek pressed against her bosom. She should have been angry, annoyed at the way he had forced her into travelling back to Denmark with him, but in reality she was glad. Glad that she had a chance to be with him for longer, to relish that big muscled body close to her own. Aye, she knew that he held no real affection for her; that much was obvious in his cobbled-together apologies after they had slept together, his avowal that such a thing would never happen again, but she didn't care. It was enough to have him close, to catch the quick flash of his diamond eyes, the amused tilt of his ready smile. She would take any small crumb of attention that he threw her way and be happy with it. She only hoped that her heart would remain intact.

At the sight of the imposing Dane filling his doorway, a wilting wife and baby at his side, the innkeeper immediately ushered them to a private chamber, promising that hot food would be sent as soon as it was prepared. Ragnar and Gisela followed him along a narrow passageway, the only light emanating from a guttering torch held high by the innkeeper, and passed open windows where men and women drank and laughed in a clatter of loud merriment. The thick smell of mead and woodsmoke filled the air.

'Here,' said the innkeeper, the flickering torch highlighting the fleshy lines of his face. 'There are clean linens on the mattress.' His voice contained a faint pride at the room he was offering.

The baby began to snuffle, agitated, against Gisela's chest, tiny hands kneading against her neck, clutching and releasing. The muscles in the small of her back ached from carrying him; placing her palms against her spine, she kneaded the sore spot above her hips. She longed to stretch out and ease her cramped limbs; to lie on that bed and sleep. Exhaustion scoured her eyeballs, shadowing the wells beneath her eyes, deepening them to a purplish-blue colour.

'I'll leave the light with you,' the man said, thrusting the torch into Ragnar's hand. 'Ask the servants if you need anything.'

Ragnar shoved the door shut after the man's retreating figure, kicking the bottom of the wooden planks as they jammed against the ground. He slung the torch into an iron ring set at head height by the window. 'Hardly a palace.' His mouth twisted grimly as he surveyed the vague rectangle of straw on the floor that served as a mattress, the cracked earthenware bowl and jug of water on a low stool in the corner. A rotten smell pervaded the damp air. 'In fact, hardly a chamber.'

'It will be fine,' Gisela said, her elbows bent out to the sides as she rubbed her back. The baby whimpered, his little body jerking back in the makeshift sling around her body. 'But I think little Torven might need some food.'

'Which bag did Bertha put it in? Yours?' Ragnar dumped the bags at the foot of the bed.

'Could you take him off me first, please? Before you find the food?' Gisela asked, wriggling her painful shoulders.

He moved behind her. She stiffened as his knuckles grazed her spine; he undid the knot with deft fingers. 'Hold on to him,' he ordered, releasing the two ends of the linen band. Tilting forward, Gisela tipped the baby away from her chest, and laid him in the middle of the bed. Released from the sling, Torven kicked his arms and legs into the air, gurgling with pleasure.

'Ah, that is good,' breathed Gisela, hunching her shoulders up and down, easing out her stiff muscles. She removed her cloak and unwound her headscarf, her plait falling across her breast, glistening in the torchlight.

Crouching down by the leather satchels, rummaging among the contents, Ragnar threw her a look of admiration. 'You've ridden a long way with him,' he said. 'Why didn't you say that he'd become too heavy? I could have taken him for you.'

Gisela took the earthenware pot that he held

out to her. Sitting on the bed, she lifted Torven on to her lap, holding him steady with one arm while she spooned the thick milky gruel into his mouth. He bounced on her knee, dribbles of the liquid spilling down his chin, dripping on to her lap. 'Because I didn't want to give you any excuse not to take him,' she replied honestly. 'Back to Denmark, I mean,' she clarified.

'Do you truly think I am that much of an ogre?' he said, rising to his feet. There was a knock at the door and he opened it, taking a tray of food from the servant who was standing there. He placed the tray on the table set hard against the planked wall, drawing up the two stools so that they could eat.

'Yes,' she said. 'When it comes to this child, I think you might be.' The baby's pot of gruel was empty and she placed him back down on the bed, where he sat upright, eyeing her curiously for a moment, before playing with the wavering threads on the blanket.

'The decision was made, Gisela. You agreed to come and I won't go back on my word now, however doubtful I am about the outcome.'

'So you don't intend to throw both of us in the sea on the way to Denmark.' She moved across to the table, sliding her frame neatly on to one of the rickety stools.

Her hair was the colour of golden ash, he thought, sitting down opposite her. His big knees hit the underside of the table, lifting it slightly, rattling the pewter dishes above. Gisela had removed her scarf without thinking and his heart gave a small leap of happiness that she was starting to relax in his company. He grinned at her. 'Now you're being ridiculous,' he said. 'Please tell me you've not been thinking of that.' He stabbed his knife into the slices of cold chicken on the platter, dividing it between their two plates. Bread rolls and mashed swedes, barely warm, completed the frugal fare.

'It did cross my mind,' she admitted truthfully.

He snorted with laughter, loading her plate with food until she held up her hand in protest. 'Then I think you might have a pleasant surprise when you reach Denmark,' he said. 'For we are not quite the heathen race that you obviously believe us to be.'

'Oh, I don't…' She picked at a bread roll, her fingers slender, white.

'Come on, Gisela, there's no point in trying to hide your feelings. I know what you think of the Danes, of me. We have shared enough over the past few days for you not to be honest with me.' He stopped, suddenly, realising the full import of his words.

Her cheeks flared with colour, her face burning with the memory of everything they had shared. Delight, a jagged rip of excitement, knifed through her belly.

'I mean…'

She held up her hand. 'Nay, please don't speak of it.'

Tipping back on his chair, Ragnar chucked his bread roll on to his plate. 'I'm sorry, Gisela, I spoke without thinking.'

She hunched her shoulders forward, immediately self-conscious in his presence. Her hand, placed flat on the table, began to shake; she tucked her fingers quickly into her lap before he noticed the effect he had upon her. 'It doesn't matter, Ragnar. I told you that.' She had no wish to hear how sorry he was, for that was to belittle the experience, to take away the joy and wonder.

'It does matter, Gisela. If I could live that night again, I would make sure that I behaved very differently.'

I wouldn't, she thought. *I would behave in exactly the same way.*

A faint grizzling cry arose from the bed. Torven. Gisela stood up so abruptly that her stool knocked over behind her, hitting the packed earth floor with a thud. 'I know you regret what you did and that is enough. Please, let's not talk about it.'

But I don't regret it, he thought. Not deep down. He was saying all these things to her, but he didn't mean them, not really. Not even the guilt he felt at taking her innocence could erase the delicious leap of desire that he experienced every time he thought about the previous night. His body and soul revelled in the sensual memory of her silken flesh laced tightly with his own. He watched her pick up the fretful child, bringing him close to her chest, rocking him gently as she walked around the tiny chamber, pointedly ignoring him. To any outsider peering in, they would be a family: a husband, wife and child, travelling south. Was it such an impossible dream for him to have?

In the grey light of dawn, Gisela sprang awake. Panic rushed through her, a searing burst of energy jolting along her veins. Fully clothed, she lay on her back beneath a blanket of rough, itchy wool, gradually easing back to full consciousness. Her eyes roamed the ceiling. Thatch poked through the gaps in the rafters, the chamber walls were coarsely plastered; a narrow table held empty plates, stacked, smeared with grease. She remembered: Ragnar…and Torven. Where were they?

Abruptly, she sat up, forcing herself to think, to drive the sluggish process of her brain to full alertness. What had happened last night? After the awkward ending to their meal, she had rocked the baby, then changed his linens. Desperate to be away from her, Ragnar had gone in search of the inn's midden pit to dispose of the baby's soiled wrappings, while she had curled on to the mattress with the sleepy baby tucked in to her side. She must have been asleep when he returned. But where was he now? And where had he taken Torven?

Disquiet stirred her chest, a fleeting thread of vague anxiety. Flinging back the cover, she yanked her boots over her woollen stockings, winding her cloak around her shoulders. She flicked her scarf around her head and went outside. The air was much colder this morning, chill droplets of moisture adhering to her skin as she walked down the narrow passageway into the yard. The stables sat opposite the inn in a series of low-arched barns. A voice emerged, low and lilting. Ragnar, talking to someone in the stables.

Darting across the straw-strewn cobbles, between the piles of horse manure, her leather-soled boots made little noise. Reaching the stone curve of the arch, she peeped around. Ragnar stood in front of his horse, Torven held in the crook of his arm. Both were stroking the horse's nose, Torven chattering away, his eyes wide-eyed with curiosity. Gisela's mouth gaped open in surprise and she clutched at the wall in disbelief. 'W-what are you doing?' she gasped.

Ragnar smiled over at her. 'He woke very early this morning,' he explained. 'I brought him out here so he wouldn't wake you.' He thought of the stoical way she had matched his fast pace yesterday, managing to keep her horse level with his despite the extra weight of the baby, never complaining.

A vague blush tinged her cheeks. 'There was no need. I have had enough sleep.'

'It was *very* early,' he reassured her. When the baby's fretting and snuffling had woken him, Gisela's slim frame sprawled on the mattress beside him had immediately drawn his gaze. Her lips had been slightly parted, her head flung back so that the soft, creamy skin of her neck and throat were revealed. Then his eyes had prowled downwards, across the tempting curve of her bosom, the flare of her hips. Scooping up the whimpering baby, he had bolted from the door, gulping in the chill morning air, glad of the cold to douse his desire.

The boy had distracted him. He had spoken some words to him in Norse and found, to his delight, that Torven understood him. They had walked over to the stables, the boy pulling at his chin, tugging the lobe of his ear, in such an easy-going manner that Ragnar couldn't fail to respond. His sister's baby, he thought, aware that his initial reaction to the child's existence was changing. If it hadn't been for Gisela, he thought, Torven would still be in that Saxon village, being raised as a Saxon.

'Give him to me,' said Gisela hurriedly, assuming that Ragnar would not want to hold Torven any longer. 'Thank you for taking him out, but there was really no need.'

'I've been speaking to him in my language,' Ragnar ignored her terse protestation, glancing down at Torven's fluffy head. 'And he understands me.'

Gisela moved over to the pair of them, her hem catching at wisps of straw. Two identical sets of emerald eyes fixed on her face. 'So...' she ventured tentatively, 'are you thinking that taking Torven to Denmark is a good idea then, after all?'

The firm contours of his mouth tightened. 'Gisela, I have no idea. But the little chap is sweet, I have to admit. He looks like a Svendson and he has the Svendson manner about him, no doubt about that. Despite his father, I cannot find any space in my heart to hate him.'

'Why not take him on your own then, if you like him so much?' Gisela replied, her tone acerbic, recalling the awkwardness with which they had finished their meal last night. Leaving him now, before he broke her heart, was surely the sensible thing to do.

'Oh, no…' His jewelled eyes roamed her face. 'I can't do that. There's no way I'm taking him on my own. You still have to come with me.'

Chapter Nineteen

The foreshore of the river glittered in the afternoon light. A low tide revealed a vast expanse of stones: white and dry above the water mark, green and thick with algae nearer the river. Below the shingle, below a thin, undulating strip of damp sand, slack water flowed out to sea at a lazy, languorous pace. Seagulls wheeled in the air, grey-white wings outstretched, screeching hoarsely, orange-rimmed eyes swivelling, searching for food. Following the path through the stiff, tall grasses, Ragnar and Gisela headed towards the Danes on the shore. They had traded the horses in the town and walked back out along the raised banks to the place where they had left Ragnar's men and the Danish longships.

What a difference a matter of days could make, thought Gisela, hitching Torven around on her hip, so that his chubby legs settled comfortably either side of her. Was it only a couple of nights ago that she had travelled with Ragnar, a stranger at her side, along this muddy path and away from here? And now, she glanced at him covertly, it was as if she had known him for ever. A lifetime. He had turned her world upside-down, ransacking every corner, forcing her to confront the reality of her numb, curtailed existence in a rush of vivid sensuality. Of desire. She was not the same person who had left this place. Without Ragnar's help, she would never have faced up to de Pagenal, or come to terms with the damaging legacy of her scar; without him, she might never have known how to love a man.

Her heart stalled at the realization, a great swoop of unbridled excitement. Aye, she loved him, the stupid, witless woman that she was. He had coerced her into accompanying him back to Denmark, an act of outrageous blackmail, and she still had agreed to go. Any woman with an ounce of sense would have taken that chance to run from him, to take her leave and bid farewell. But it was as if Ragnar, with his polished eyes and quick smile, had bewitched her, bound her tightly with some spell, so she was powerless to do anything except follow him blindly, without question. Her heart would surely be broken. Yet it was a risk she was willing to take.

Trapped in her thoughts, Gisela's toe stubbed a big stone and she staggered forward, trying to prevent Torven from crashing to the ground in her arms. Ragnar snagged her elbow, preventing her fall. 'Give me the child,' he said briskly, lifting the boy from her arms and settling him against his chest.

Her eyes roamed his face, the lean, carved features so familiar to her now. The dip in the bridge of his nose, the firm line of his generous top lip. If she closed her eyes she would be able to recreate in her mind's eye every last detail of the man who stood beside her. It was laughable, pathetic really. If only he knew the thoughts that churned around her head: how she felt about him, how she loved him. The vulnerability of her spirit in his presence. Fragile. Exposed.

'What is it?' he murmured, aware of her intense scrutiny, the enigmatic look in her huge blue eyes. 'What's the matter?'

She looked away, across the glimmering expanse of water, tugging irritably at her dress, which had rucked up uncomfortably around her waist. 'Nothing. I was wondering what your fellow men will make of…us…of the fact that I'm still with you, I mean. If things had gone according to plan, then I would have returned with my brother. I shouldn't even be here.' It was a lie, but one that sounded feasible in the circumstances. He could never know the true path of her thoughts. She nodded towards the men on the shore, one tall figure detaching from the group around a fire, and striding up the beach towards them, an arm raised in greeting. The prince.

His chest squeezed against his ribs at the flicker of sadness in her eyes. 'Life rarely goes according to plan,' he murmured. 'The men will think nothing—'

His speech stalled as Eirik clapped him heavily on the shoulder. 'Ragnar! At last!' The thick fronds of his hair shone in the sunlight like a raven's wing, black and glossy. 'Am I glad to see you! I knew you wouldn't let me down.' Eyeing Torven with intense curiosity, he bent down to the child's level, squinting more closely at the bronze hair, the deep green eyes. He straightened in surprise, a puzzled question crossing his hard features.

'Aye, you have it right,' confirmed Ragnar, seeing the same recognition Gisela saw in the other man's eyes. 'This is Torven... Gyda's child. The result of her abduction.'

'I am sorry,' said Eirik. His liquid brown eyes

moved to Gisela, standing quietly next to Ragnar, roamed across the pearly exquisiteness of her complexion. 'I thought the babe was yours at first, mistress,' he addressed her in very bad French. 'But that would have been quick work!' His eyes darted significantly from Ragnar back to her, a knowing grin stretching his chin wide. A great gust of laughter rolled up from his lungs.

Despite his garbled vowels, Gisela understood him. A wild, vivid colour chased across her cheeks, a flag of embarrassment. She threw the Danish prince a fierce glare of outrage, before turning her attention to the child in Ragnar's arms, fussing with his shawl, tucking it more closely around him.

'In Odin's name, what have you done?' Eirik muttered to Ragnar, switching back to Danish.

'Exactly what you are thinking,' Ragnar replied, scowling darkly. 'I have done her a great wrong, Eirik, but I hope to right it, in time.'

'And how do you propose to do that when her father waits for her in Bertune? You have no time.' Eirik shifted his big boots against the shingle, crossing his massive arms across his chest. A couple of pebbles skittered down the slope, rolling out on to the dark sand. '*For hel-*

vede, Ragnar, what were you thinking? She is a noblewoman, a Norman!'

'She's coming back to Denmark with us,' Ragnar supplied. His mouth tightened. 'I gave her no choice; I wanted to leave the baby with the Saxons, but she insisted that Gyda should have the chance to see him. So...' he hesitated, unwilling to reiterate how he had persuaded her. Remorse flooded through him.

'Not only did you sleep with her, you also blackmailed her,' said Eirik sternly. 'Hell's teeth, Ragnar, you can't do such things! You should be ashamed of yourself.'

'I know. I am,' Ragnar replied, bleakly. 'But I could think of no other way to bring her with me. The child was a godsend in a way, a reason why she had to come with me.'

'But why? Why not let her go back to her family? Why do you want her to—?' Eirik broke off, peering closely at Ragnar. He whistled through his white, even teeth. 'I knew it!' He placed one hand on his friend's shoulder, chuckling. 'You have fallen in love with her. You love her.'

Not understanding one word of their complex language, Gisela stood patiently at Ragnar's side, twining her slender fingers with Torven's, jogging his rounded arm up and down as she waited for them to finish talking. The boy laughed, a delicious gurgle of happiness. Ragnar's gaze drifted across the luminous oval of her face, the generous curve of the mouth that he had kissed, then down across her slim, lithe body. Conscious of his intense scrutiny, her eyes snapped to his; he caught the full force of her shimmering blue gaze, reading the hint of question in her expression. Yanking his gaze away, he turned his attention back to Eirik. 'Yes,' he said, his voice hitching on the simple admission. 'I do.' Anguish swirled through him, a slow realisation of what he must do. His nerve-endings tingled, a rippling wave of disquiet. The anticipation of losing her. He loved her, yet he was behaving like a bully. He scowled, drawing his shaggy, brindled brows together. Grief coursed through him, leaden weights dragging on the bottom of his chest. He had to give Gisela the choice, the choice to come back to him of her own free will and love him in return. But after what he had done to her? He would surely lose her.

'Tell me what's happening,' Gisela said as they walked down the shingle towards the river. Eirik had insisted on taking Torven from Ragnar, carrying him over to the men sitting cross-legged around a large fire. The men fussed over him, some pulling funny faces to make him laugh. Satisfied that they weren't terrifying the child, her gaze drifted along the shore, to the two vessels hauled up on the beach. 'Where are the rest of the longships? Surely there were more here when we left?'

'Eirik has sent them home,' replied Ragnar, trying to keep his voice on an even keel. His conscience spun in his head, chastising him, urging him to do the right thing, to speak. And yet, he could not. Not yet, at least. For that would be the end. The end of her radiant figure walking at his side, the comforting nudge of her elbow, the pale flare of her braid. Her warm scent, sliding over him, catching him unawares. Her slim body against his own, snared in the heat of their desire. His chest ached with solid pain at the prospect of losing her, splitting in two, as if someone had taken an axe to his heart.

He sighed, winding his arms around the muscled planes of his chest, tucking his fingers beneath his armpits. 'A message came from Edgar Aethling to say that the Danes were not needed after all. Apparently King William and his barons struck a deal with him, an agreement to negotiate for peace. So, no marching, no fighting.' He inclined his head to the Danes on the beach. 'The men are fed up. They want to go home, back to their wives and children, before the weather turns bad for winter.'

'Ah, I see now. You were gabbling away so fast, I hadn't a hope of understanding.'

He watched the slight grimace travel over her face, the splash of colour, and thanked Odin that she couldn't speak Danish. She had no idea of what Eirik and he had been speaking about. No idea that they had been talking about her, about how he felt for her. Loved her. Air trembled beneath his diaphragm, a fluttering leaf of torment. For the first time, in a very long while, he felt genuinely afraid. He couldn't lose her. How would he ever survive?

'I told Eirik that you and the child are coming to Denmark,' he said.

'And what was his response?' she asked, a dull colour stealing across her cheeks. 'I know that he guessed that…' Her voice trailed away dismally. 'He must think very little of me,' she finished lamely, hunching her shoulders, a wary, defensive gesture.

Ragnar angled his head, the gilt strands of his hair dishevelled by the breeze. 'On the contrary. It was me he was displeased with, not you.'

'Because of the way you blackmailed me to come to Denmark?'

'Yes,' he said, 'he knows that I gave you no choice in the matter. And also…because I slept with you, Gisela. Because of that,' he croaked out. 'Because of the way I treated you.' A muscle shifted in his jaw, a defined, stiff movement. 'Eirik is married, with three children. He is a man of honour, of principle.' He paused. 'Which I am not. Unfortunately for you.'

Or fortunately, she thought. In her whole life, there would surely be no other occasion like the one she had shared with Ragnar. It was her responsibility now to remember every single perfect detail and preserve it, like a shimmering crystal, in the dark recesses of her mind. And not just that, she thought. It was everything about him: the touch of his hand, the way he scooped her up before she stumbled; his ready laugh, the quick easy smile. It was everything about him.

She shivered in the chill breeze rising from the water, hauling her cloak more securely around her shoulders. 'You know I don't blame you, Ragnar,' she said softly. 'You need to stop blaming yourself.' The freshening wind tugged a tendril of hair out from beneath her scarf; she snagged it, coiling the glistening strand around one finger.

A drift of birds landed elegantly on the surface of the river, ruffling the silver skin of water. 'We will never agree on that,' he replied thickly, watching her wind the hair around her finger. 'Your forgiveness will never absolve what I did. Gisela… I…' he managed to croak out. 'I want to say that…'

She tilted her head to one side, eyeing him keenly. What was the matter with him? Ragnar had the strangest look in his eyes: savage, possessive, and yet beset with such a sad melancholy that she had never seen before. 'Ragnar…?' She touched his sleeve. The flexed rope of his muscled forearm rubbed against her fingers. 'Are you…? What ails you?'

He cleared his throat. 'I will take Torven to Denmark on my own.' His words emerged in a rush. 'You don't have to come, Gisela. I can take you back to your family this afternoon.'

His blunt words echoed tonelessly against her ear. Shock engulfed her; she staggered back, clapping one hand to her mouth to stop the screech of sound emerging. This could not be happening! Desolation crashed over her, a great rolling tide of loss, abandonment. Why was he saying such things? He was dismissing her, pushing her away. The base of her belly quivered with unhappiness. Confidence wilted, curling in on itself, a papery leaf shrivelled in flames.

'I... I don't understand!' she said, a shrill note gripping her voice. Her mind struggled to comprehend, to make sense of his damning words. 'I thought you... I thought you said you wouldn't take the child without me!' Hope whipped away, a snapping flag breaking loose, chased away by despair.

'That was before...' He paused, looking at her strangely, as if her reaction to his words was not as he expected.

'Before what...?' she cried out on a half-sob. 'What has happened to change your mind?' *It's me*, she thought. *I've done something foolish, said something untoward.* She'd certainly caused him enough trouble over the past few days. Or was it simply the prospect of travelling further with her that he could not endure? He had had his fill of her and was now sending her away. 'Is it Eirik who has told you to do this?' Her eyes slid past the rounded bulk of Ragnar's shoulder, searching the group of Danish men for their tall leader, the head of jet-black hair. 'Let me speak to him! He will understand if I talk to him.'

Stunned, Ragnar gazed down at her. 'What

are you saying?' he said slowly, his voice lifting almost in wonder.

Gisela frowned at him as if he were dim-witted. 'If I could just speak to Eirik,' she repeated briskly, 'then he will understand why I have to come.'

'But—' He broke off, puzzled, tilting his head to one side in question. He placed a hand on her shoulder, cupping the soft muscle in the palm of his hand. The coarse skin on his fingertips rustled against the wool of her gown. 'But… I've told you, you don't have to come. Gisela, I am giving you your freedom! Why are you not seizing it with both hands and running away as fast as you can?'

Her heart teetered. As if she stood on the edge of an abyss, peering down into a bottomless black pit. The unknown. She could step back now, place her feet on a firm footing and return to her father, never having risked her heart to tell Ragnar how she truly felt about him. Or she could jump, skirts flying out about her, into the unknown. Her fingers linked with his on her shoulder, grazing his big knuckles. His big frame tensed, stiffening beneath her touch.

'Because I have no wish to do that,' she said, jerking her chin in the air, as if willing him to contradict her. There, she had said it. Let him laugh if he wanted.

His pupils widened, the brilliant darkness engulfing the emerald of his eyes. 'Why not?' A hoarseness scraped his throat.

Her confidence wavered. 'This is going to sound so foolish…' she muttered.

'Try me.'

'Well… it seems like…like I have fallen in love with you.' She looked away, across the muddy waters of the river, at the shingle, the longships. 'How foolish is that?' Winding her arms about her torso, she hugged herself tightly, bracing herself to hear his condemnation.

Ragnar held his breath. 'Nay, Gisela, not foolish at all.' His voice was low, thready with emotion.

She stared resolutely at her boots, unable to meet his eyes. 'When you pulled me out of the mud on the first day you met me, I had been living a life of fear. I jumped at the slightest shadow. I kept thinking that de Pagenal would appear around the nearest corner and take another swipe at my neck. I was so frightened… that I didn't know… I didn't know…'

'…how to love,' he concluded for her, his great arms swooping around her, gathering her to his torso.

She nodded, her eyes shining with happiness as she finally tipped her chin to look up at him. 'I love you, Ragnar. I think I might have loved you from the first moment that I saw you.'

Emotion crushed his chest at her solemn tone, delight suffusing his limbs. A light, powerful feeling. Strong. 'What, when you came around on the beach and saw me grinning down at you? I'm surprised you weren't scared out of your wits!'

Her knees bumped against his. 'Even then. Your kindness towards me, your care…your love…' Her pupils dilated, dark pools against sparkling sapphire. 'Your love has forced the fear from my soul and mended my spirit.'

'Gisela.' He breathed out slowly. He could scarce believe what she was saying. 'I never thought…' He buried his face in her neck. 'I thought I would lose you,' he mumbled against her perfumed skin, the heated flesh. 'I thought after what I had done…how I treated you, you would want nothing to do with me.'

Her fingers twisted in the silky hair at the back of his neck. 'That's where you were wrong, Ragnar. I want everything to do with you. I never want to be parted from you again.'

He lifted his head. 'You have my word on

it,' he promised. His hands gripped the sides of her face. His mouth moved over hers, seizing her lips in a kiss that would last for a lifetime, for ever.

Epilogue

Outside the great hall on the Svendson estate, it had started to snow. Grey, lumbering clouds had rolled in from the east, pressing heavily on the land. Great fat flakes spun down, drifting white like feathers, down on to the cobbled bailey, some melting quickly, some settling. Soon, the snow would settle for good, as winter extended its icy breath across these northern lands.

Inside the hall, the wedding feast was in full swing. A great fire blazed out from the centre of the hall, smoke rising lazily to a hole in the timbered roof, rows of flaming torches lighting the vast chamber with a warm, golden glow. Trestle tables ranked across the flagstone floor, laden with food and mead to satisfy the appetites of the guests who had travelled from far and wide to witness the wedding of Olaf Svendson's only son, Ragnar. Squeezed on to the narrow benches, the chattering guests ate and drank, casting interested glances towards the Svendson family sitting along the top table and towards Ragnar's new bride. A Norman lady, no less. The stories of how such a marriage had come into being knocked back and forth among the guests: how Ragnar had rescued the maid, half-dead from the mud, although some said it was the other way around and that she had pulled him out, although that seemed impossible, given the bride's diminutive size.

'Look,' whispered Gisela, pointing at the flakes brushing the diamond-shaped window panes. She turned in delight to her husband, her heart brimming with love for the tall Viking at her side. She wore his mother's wedding gown, a heavy cream silk, encrusted with tiny seed pearls that winked and glimmered in the flickering torchlight. Following the Viking tradition, she wore no veil, only a simple silver crown, studded with rock crystals. Her glossy sable hair flowed down over her shoulders, the curling ends pooling in her lap.

'I hope you like snow.' His brilliant eyes roamed over her, hot, possessive. 'There's a lot more of that to come. It was the right decision to bring your father and sister with us when we left that day. They would never have been able to travel otherwise.'

'And we have my brother's blessing,' she added, 'even though he cannot be here in person.' She turned to look at Marie, who sat further along the table, talking animatedly to Eirik's wife. And on her sister's other side sat her father, smiling happily. 'This snow means they can stay here with me until the spring,' she added brightly, turning back to Ragnar.

'They have no choice.' Ragnar grinned. 'For the weather will be too horrible for them to even attempt such a journey. The snow piles up in great drifts and the harbour often freezes over.

'Well, then I love snow,' she said, enthusiastically. She splayed her fingers flat on to the pristine white tablecloth, watching her new wedding ring gleam in the light. 'Torven will love it, certainly.' She glanced at the bronze-haired maid sitting next to Ragnar's parents. Torven was sitting on her lap, one chubby hand lurching out across the table to grab at food, a plate, a goblet. Laughing, Gyda seized his little fingers, lifting them to her lips. 'I'm so happy that...' She paused. 'I'm pleased that Gyda seems better.'

'She is,' Ragnar agreed. It was a month since the two longships had arrived back in Ribe, a month since Gyda, frail and mute, her hair in tangled disarray, had glanced up and spotted her child in Ragnar's arms as he walked into the great hall. In recognition, she had screamed out loud, rushing forward to wrench her little son from her brother's hold. From then on, Gyda had come alive again, growing back into the woman she had once been, talking and laughing; animated. In quieter moments, she had confided in Gisela and the two women had become close friends.

Reaching for his pewter goblet, Ragnar rubbed the stem with his thumb. 'You were right, Gisela.' His eyes darkened. 'If you hadn't been there to persuade me, then…then she would never have healed.'

'You mustn't think like that, Ragnar. I was there, and I did persuade you.'

'And I thank Thor that you did.' He glanced along the table, at Gyda's happy face looking down at her child, at his father's wide smile as he raised his goblet in silent congratulation towards his son, at all the Viking warriors and their ladies who had gathered here to celebrate their wedding and his heart swelled with happiness, with a great gust of love for the woman at his side. Gisela, his darling love, his *elskede*, whom he would cherish for a lifetime.

* * * * *

COMING SOON!

We really hope you enjoyed reading this book. If you're looking for more romance, be sure to head to the shops when new books are available on

Thursday 21st February

To see which titles are coming soon, please visit

millsandboon.co.uk/nextmonth

MILLS & BOON

Coming next month

THE CINDERELLA COUNTESS
Sophia James

Lytton chose the second and took her hand in his, a small hand with two broken nails and the turquoise bracelet above it on her wrist.

He did not speak. He merely looked at Annabelle and she looked back. It was not surprise on her face he saw, but something much more intense. An ordained purpose, perhaps, or simply acceptance. Her tongue licked the dryness of her lips and she tipped her head back against the cushioned leather of the seat.

In invitation and in knowledge.

Carefully he ran one finger across her cheekbone, high and delicate, before lowering it on to her lips, tracing the outline and knowing the shape. He needed to be careful, to slow down, to not frighten her.

'Can I kiss you, Annabelle?'

Question sat in her sapphire eyes.

'I will not hurt you, I promise.'

A foot became six inches and then there was nothing between them save warmth. She still had her eyes open, the blue in them threaded with caution.

'This is just for us,' he whispered, claiming her mouth under his own and as soft as he could make it.

He had meant to barely kiss her, to see what she would allow, to settle nerves and find the boundaries.

But he couldn't. One touch had released a desperation for he wanted things he'd never had before, things like honesty and trust. Grace was there, too, and decency and charm, unfamiliar and strange.

He adjusted his angle and came in deeper, the quiet kiss becoming more fierce. And then she kissed him back, leaning closer, volatile, mercurial and surprising.

She was not the timid and restrained woman he might have expected. No, she was brave, her hand entwining around his arm and holding him there. The breath she took was shaky, but her eyes were bold, slashed in blue directness. The slam of connection intensified, his body hardening under promise.

God, he was in a carriage careening through the busy streets of London and none of the curtains were drawn. He broke off the kiss and pulled back, panic building as he realised how close he had come to losing control.

Continue reading
THE CINDERELLA COUNTESS
Sophia James

Available next month
www.millsandboon.co.uk

Want even more
ROMANCE?

Join our bookclub today!

'Mills & Boon books, the perfect way to escape for an hour or so.'

Miss W. Dyer

'Excellent service, promptly delivered and very good subscription choices.'

Miss A. Pearson

'You get fantastic special offers and the chance to get books before they hit the shops'

Mrs V. Hall

Visit millsandbook.co.uk/Bookclub
and save on brand new books.

MILLS & BOON

LET'S TALK
Romance

For exclusive extracts, competitions and special offers, find us online:

- facebook.com/millsandboon
- @MillsandBoon
- @MillsandBoonUK

Get in touch on 01413 063232

For all the latest titles coming soon, visit
millsandboon.co.uk/nextmonth